Northern Exposure

All roads lead home when that's where you've left your heart.

Silas Compton always had his eye on Lucy, the veterinarian's daughter. He was even content to wait for the girl of his dreams to grow up before getting anywhere near her with his family's double-edged legacy.

Waiting around led to fooling around with his best friend—and an impulsive eruption of desire that Lucy's innocent eyes weren't meant to see. Figuring Compton Pass wasn't big enough for either the three of them or the pain he'd caused, Silas let loose his tightly reined wanderlust and headed for Alaska.

Ten years later, when an oil rig accident sends him home, he braces himself for the reopening of old wounds. Instead he finds himself in the care—and welcoming arms—of Lucy and Colby, whose marriage has plenty of room for the man they both still love. And forgive with all their hearts.

As things start to unravel at Compass Ranch, Silas must dig deep for the strength to assume his rightful place in the Compton family...and lay the foundation for a future with his lovers. If he can forgive himself.

Warning: This book is overflowing with sexy cowboys who like to saddle up and ride each other as well as the woman of their dreams. The likelihood of becoming addicted to their ranch family is high. With three more stories yet to come, beware. You won't be able to read just one!

Southern Comfort

Caught between desire and a promise...

Seth Compton knew from the first that his boss's daughter was all wrong for him. She was too feisty, too damned independent and, at seven years his junior, too damned young. When she comes home with a college diploma and fiancé on her arm, though, he can't quite remember all the reasons he held her at arm's length.

It's not just his jeans-tightening reaction to her all-grown-up curves. Something doesn't feel right about her impending marriage, and he won't rest until he's stopped her from making the biggest mistake of her life.

The morning after her wild bachelorette party, Jody expected a hangover. The surprise? Waking up tied to a bed with sexy-as-sin Seth. He's got some wild idea about proving they belong together, but she's not buying it. Besides, she has a promise to keep that's too close to her heart to risk, especially not with a man who, until now, made his disinterest plain.

No one ever said Seth backed down from a challenge. She's going to make him work for it? No problem. Luckily for him, he has plenty of rope...

Warning: This story contains a bondage lovin' cowboy who kidnaps and hogties a cowgirl to his bed and does all sorts of naughty things to her. Fun, right?

Look for these titles

Now Available from Mari Carr

Because of You

Because You Love Me

Black & White

Erotic Research

Tequila Truth

Rough Cut

Happy Hour

Power Play

Slam Dunk

Print Anthologies

Learning Curves

Dangerous Curves

Now Available from Jayne Rylon

Nice and Naughty

Men In Blue

Night is Darkest

Razor's Edge

Mistress's Master

Powertools

Kate's Crew

Morgan's Surprise

Kayla's Gifts

Devon's Pair

Nailed to the Wall

Hammer It Home

Play Doctor

Dream Machine

Print Anthologies

Three's Company

Powertools

Look for these titles

Now Available from Mari Carr & Jayne Rylon

Compass Brothers
Northern Exposure
Southern Comfort
Eastern Ambitions
Western Ties

Love's Compass

Mari Carr and Jayne Rylon

Samhain Publishing, Ltd.
11821 Mason Montgomery Rd., 4B
Cincinnati, OH 45249
www.samhainpublishing.com

Love's Compass
Print ISBN: 978-1-60928-971-3

Cover by Valerie TIbbs

Northern Exposure, ISBN 978-1-60928-382-7
First Samhain Publishing, Ltd. electronic publication: March 2011
Southern Comfort, ISBN 978-1-60928-497-8
First Samhain Publishing, Ltd. electronic publication: July 2011
First Samhain Publishing, Ltd. print publication: September 2012

Contents

Northern Exposure
~13~

Southern Comfort
~153~

Northern Exposure

Dedication

This book is dedicated to all the people at Samhain Publishing who help make our dreams reality.

To Crissy Brashear for creating a home for our books, her outstanding business acumen and her belief in us.

To our fabulous editors, Bethany Morgan and Lindsey Faber, for making our writing the best it can be.

To Marty Matthews for answering questions at all hours of the day and always being there with a smile and a hug when we need it.

To Jacob Hammer for making sure our books are pretty and sending them to places where readers can get their hands on them.

To Jimmy Barnett, Amanda Brashear and the rest of the team who send us our absolute favorite emails of the month.

To the Samhain Reader Cafe mods for keeping the party going.

To all the other authors who inspire us with their stories.

To the rest of the team; we're sure we don't realize all you do behind the scenes, but we appreciate it regardless.

Prologue

Dry brush crackled under the hooves of Silas Compton's roan gelding. It hadn't rained in a while. He could tell it would be a long summer by the clouds of terra cotta dust rising in the wake of his brothers' galloping horses as they raced across the mountain ridge.

Not that he'd know it where he was headed. Alaska would provide a total change of scenery. Exactly what he needed. Pain lanced his chest, causing him to tense in his heirloom saddle. Rainey's ears flicked up. Silas patted the loyal animal's neck, settling into the rhythm of their canter, and wondered how he would survive so far from the land that had been a part of him since he'd been born.

Somehow he would have to make it work.

He sure as hell couldn't stay.

Like the three-legged dog they'd had as kids, he would learn to cope without an integral part of himself. If only he and his puppy had reined in their curiosity and avoided those damn traps...

But they hadn't.

Lucy Silver, the veterinarian's sweet daughter—who'd been dancing through his dirty dreams since he'd been old enough to have them—had spotted Silas making out with her boyfriend in the barn. It'd been like the day he'd watched his puppy scramble toward the razor-sharp jaws lying concealed under a pile of straw all over again.

Removing himself from the equation seemed like the only way he could halt imminent disaster and protect the two people he cared about most outside of his family. He'd already destroyed enough of Lucy's innocence.

Christ, he couldn't explain what had driven him to kiss Colby in the first place.

Impulsive. Rash. Reckless.

Qualities Silas didn't value. The one time he gave in to the dark urges he wrestled, he paid a horrible price. But he'd caught Colby checking out his sweaty muscles as they'd worked together in the heat of the day. Desire had arced between them.

Irresistible. Delicious. Forbidden.

Until the agony on Lucy's face had slammed him back to reality. Silas vowed to leave the couple to mend their fences and live in peace, without the threat of his interference ripping them apart. Lucy and Colby devoured each other with desperate gazes when they thought no one paid attention. It didn't take a genius to figure out their love was the real deal.

He'd go, even if it meant giving up everything familiar and cherished, including his brothers and his two best friends. Because he sure as shit couldn't stay and keep his hands to himself. Not with a double helping of temptation running wild.

Amber rays from the setting sun ignited the prairie below. The glowing grasslands seared into his memory. He'd never lose track of his roots. He'd never forget his heritage, Compass Ranch, even if he couldn't accept his destiny as its head.

His brothers would pick up his slack.

Seth, a year younger than him, whooped then grinned over his shoulder as he spurred his mare faster. Wild as a mustang, he flew over the landscape to the spot they'd claimed as their own. The twins, Sam and Sawyer, followed suit.

They hadn't discussed their plans for the evening. As soon as Silas had made his announcement to the family, the boys had glanced around the dining table—where all important family business was conducted—and nodded. They hadn't objected to his desertion, but strain lined their faces, sorrow dimmed their eyes and the betrayal he feared flashed in the air a split second before they began planning how they'd support him.

Christ, their generosity had made him feel lower than the shit on the bottom of his muck boots because he hadn't had the guts to admit why he really planned to leave. None of *them* would have been dumb enough to mess with something that wasn't theirs. And if they had, they wouldn't have lied about it on top. Such strong souls would thrive with or without him. But could he cut out something so essential to his being and live so wounded? So lost?

Cut adrift, he might not make it.

Silas gripped the reins too tight. He forced himself to relax his fingers.

One night. He'd give himself these final hours with his brothers to say goodbye to all he treasured. Tomorrow, he'd ride out. Forever.

The driving hoof beats slowed as they approached their destination. By the time they ducked beneath the shelter of the mountain cypresses, the rocky terrain forced them to walk their mounts. None of the teenagers would jeopardize the safety of their animals or their brothers.

He squeezed his eyes shut, trying to contain the agony lassoing his heart as he realized he'd never be close to the men they'd grow into, their families or the children who'd take their places in the tight-knit community like so many generations before them.

The last damn thing he wanted was to bawl like a sissy.

If his family caught on to his pain, they might not let him go. Luckily, he'd learned from the toughest sons of bitches in the west how to be a real cowboy. If that was the only way he could honor his legacy, he'd man up and do it. Somehow.

They dismounted, reverting to familiar patterns. Seth and Sawyer tied the horses as Sam gathered kindling for their bonfire. Silas patched the pit left from prior visits then dug some supplies from his pack, including hot dogs despite the fact they'd eaten dinner before they left. These days, the four of them could shovel in enough to feed an army.

Or so their mom said.

"Si, you're bleeding." Count on Sawyer to notice.

"It's nothing." Silas faced the youngest, by twenty-two minutes, of his brothers. The kid's twin had already picked up on the vibe. Damn their weird-ass mental connection.

"It's something." Sam sidled up behind him to take a peek. "It's too uniform to be a cut."

"Did you do it?" Damn if Seth didn't tip his hat and glare from beneath his dark brows. When Silas didn't answer, Seth stomped over. "Holy shit. You did. You got a freaking tattoo. Without me? Without us? You asshole!"

Silas dodged his brother's half-hearted punch toward the sore spot between his shoulder blades. The disappointment radiating from the guy in waves did more damage than his fist would have. After Silas's sudden declaration of independence, this looked bad, but he couldn't come clean and admit the craving he'd had to brand himself with some symbol of home before he took off. Not if he had any hope of escaping.

"I had a hard enough time convincing Snake to ink me. If I'd brought you guys with me, he never would have caved. He only did it because I'm eighteen now."

If Silas had told Seth, they wouldn't have been able to stop Sam and Sawyer from tagging along too.

"Well, I suppose that's true. Plus he's probably afraid JD will kill him if he finds out." Sawyer let Silas off easy, as usual.

"Yeah, that's why I took the bandages off. Didn't want him to notice."

Pride for their badass father glowed from the kid. Silas agreed. As head of Compass Ranch—the center of Compton Pass, Wyoming—JD Compton wielded vast financial clout but his personality made him larger than life and, most important, earned him respect by the acre.

"But you gotta let us see it at least," Sawyer insisted.

"Sure." Silas dropped a wedge of firewood on the crackling flame Sam had started, and then stood. All three of his brothers lined up behind him—Seth in the middle, the twins on either side—when he tugged his gray T-shirt over his head, wincing a little at the sting of his sweat in the open wound. The three usually raucous kids didn't make a single peep when he revealed the artwork. "It's swollen and stuff—"

"Whoa." Seth broke the silence.

"It's awesome." Sam laid his palm to the right of the emblem, careful not to touch the raw skin.

"Sweet," Sawyer agreed then added his hand on the left side of Silas's back.

"Does it hurt?" Seth completed their connection, touching the area below the design.

"So bad," Silas gasped, struggling not to drop to his knees.

"I'm still doing it. Next year. The minute I turn eighteen," Seth whispered into the gathering twilight. "Exactly like this."

"Me too," Sam chimed in. "The compass design is fucking great. And the ranch brand is perfect. It matches the one we use."

"I didn't know Snake had this kind of shit in him. The shading is so cool. It looks 3-D." Sawyer's hand shook on Silas's back. "I want one now. Like yours. But without the fancy N."

"You're only fifteen," Silas barked. "Wait a while and make sure it's what you really want."

"I know what I want."

"Things don't always happen like you expect, Sawyer." Silas felt the pressure of his brothers' hands bracing him as he heaved a giant sigh.

"Is that why you're leaving?" The high pitch of Sam's question reminded Silas that even though his youngest brothers had started fooling around with girls in their class, and he'd busted them splitting a six pack they'd swiped from the bunkhouse, they still had more boy than man in them.

"Yeah." He couldn't give them more of the truth than that. It embarrassed him. Angered him. And threatened to drown him in despair.

"Well, some people might flip flop around. Not me. Not going to change *my* mind." Sawyer stuck to his guns. He'd always been the most determined to prove himself despite being the baby of the group. Maybe because of it. "I'm joining the Coast Guard. Gonna see the world."

"What?" Silas pivoted to stare at the kid, severing the connection with his brothers. He regretted it instantly, but he had to search Sawyer's eyes for the truth. "You've been watching too many freaking commercials. Your place is here, on the ranch."

"No, it isn't," the teenager whispered.

When the other two nodded in agreement, Silas staggered backward.

"You're not planning to stay?" His forehead crumpled as he tried to understand. "None of you?"

"Don't look at us like that." Seth waved his hands in front of his chest. "I figured you'd understand. I need to get the hell out of here. Find my own place. Same as you. Not Alaska though, I hate winter. You're crazy to take on all that snow. Somewhere warm. Maybe I'll head down south. Yeah, that's what I'll do. A fancy S instead of an N on my compass, bro."

"What? No!" Silas couldn't explain. "It's not like that. I mean—"

"We understand, Si." Sam smiled then nodded. "I'd like to go to college. Earn a degree, find a real job. Something where I don't have to dirty my hands to rake in cash. I'll have fancy clothes, a slick apartment and a kickass car. I'll party every night with the hottest girls in the city."

The relief washing over his brothers filled Silas with anxiety and left him reeling. Who would help their father with the ranch? Who would continue their family traditions? Who if not him? Or Seth? Or Sam?

"Oh, no." Sawyer shook his head as he kicked a rock. "Don't give me that look. I told you, I'm *not* getting stuck here. Fuck that. You think someone should hang around, then stay put. It ain't too late to cancel your plane ticket."

"I-I can't."

"And neither can we." Seth slugged his shoulder. "Come on, start the dogs. I'm starving. Jake slipped me a couple Playboys for doing his chores last weekend so he could bang Misty Trelane."

"Nice! Me first." Sam managed a head start for their brother's backpack as Sawyer launched himself after his twin.

Silas watched them wrestle, laugh and call each other names as though his entire world hadn't been ripped apart. Then he pivoted and stared out to the horizon as the sun set on his childhood.

Chapter One

Ten years later

Silas frowned into a cracked, empty glass as the burn of whiskey permeated his chest, faking a warmth he hadn't experienced in a decade. He slammed the tumbler on the shitty plank bar then motioned for another. A few more and he might actually believe he languished in the middle of a perfect Wyoming summer.

But what would be the point?

He'd wake tomorrow morning, miserable and lonely as usual.

He studied the fresh picture hanging, a little crooked, on the Wall of Death. Macabre? Maybe. But the lifers who came to Alaska to seek out her dangerous jobs formed a kind of brotherhood where each member understood that, for some, a tragic early ending came as a welcome relief. They all ran from something—war wounds, screwed up childhoods, a life of monotony—God only knew what.

In addition to the misfits, a few others rounded out the mix. Foolish men and women, who didn't comprehend the risks, attempted to make a quick buck. Adrenaline junkies on a permanent high soared from hazard to hazard. Still, for the most part, broken men littered the gorgeous, frozen landscape.

Silas saluted the deceased captain of the crabbing boat with his refilled glass then downed the next dose of poison too. Despite his tarnished past, Captain Robert had saved Silas's ass a time or two during the tours Silas had served harvesting on the vessel before he moved on to long haul driving along treacherous routes. He remembered the screams he'd heard on occasion when the captain had a particularly bad night and the times they'd drunk themselves into oblivion to avoid the darkness a little longer.

Hopefully the man had found peace at last.

He started a mental list of all the comrades he'd lost in the extreme positions he'd mastered—expedition guide, crabber, big rig driver and pilot on top of his current gig as an oil rig motorhand. After several dozen, their faces blurred in his mind.

Could have something to do with all the alcohol he'd consumed in those ten years. Or the numbness infecting his soul as he wandered so far from the place and people he loved.

Silas glowered in an attempt to scare off the woman headed straight for his permanent spot at the dive. In this mood, he'd make no kind of company for a lady.

"Knock it off, Compass." Red, nicknamed for the bright jacket he wore on the job, elbowed Silas's ribs. "I'll take her off your hands if you're not hungry. It's been a long time since I had a meal that fine."

Silas squinted, trying to focus despite the solid drunk he'd been heading toward. Red had a point. A sweet thing like her didn't wander into their territory often. In fact, women in general were in short supply here, at the end of the world.

The deficit made him long for the squandered plenty of his youth. And provided the perfect opportunity for him to slake his lust for men.

Rough, raw craving would build inside him for months until he surrendered to gnawing need. Companionship came at a high price around here for most men, but once rumors of Silas's edge had spread, he'd had a line of willing partners a pointed look and a nod away.

For the past six months or so, he'd spent the majority of his off time with Red. The man made it easy on him, never asking for more than Silas could give. After the first time they'd hooked up—when Silas had allowed the man to suck him off in the bar's grimy bathroom—Red had made it clear he'd welcome a quick fuck in the back of a truck, a shared night with some woman they happened across or whatever else suited Silas's violent mood swings.

Silas never allowed himself to take advantage of the more generous offers lurking in Red's eyes, though. Shit. Those emotions grew day by day. He dropped his head in his hands, spearing his fingers through his unkempt hair as he realized he'd have to distance himself from his roommate before the man got hurt. He'd move out after their double shift this weekend.

Two people and two people alone inspired more than carnal savagery in him. It wouldn't be fair to give Red hope that Silas's longing for Lucy and Colby would change in this lifetime. If ten years hadn't killed his dedication, nothing would.

Hell, Silas couldn't bear companionship some days. He didn't remember how to be a friend. It'd been too many years. Pride in a hard day's work and the reassuring discomfort of a solid hangover, which insured he'd passed out for at least a few hours before heading to the job to do it all over again, propelled him forward through week after week.

"Your friend looks like he could use some cheering up."

Why in the hell did his surly temper attract women like bees to honey? It seemed the more he growled and tried to warn them off, the more they wanted in his pants. Insane. Every one of them. Just like him.

"And what about me?" Red turned to the woman with his best imitation of Silas's genuine misery. "Maybe *I* need some of your healing touch."

"Don't worry, handsome. I'm the kind of woman who can handle two strapping men at once."

The sassy introduction made the corner of Silas's mouth curve up despite his resolve. Tough Alaskan women reminded him of Wyoming cowgirls in a hell of a lot of ways.

Sexy ways.

Here, like home, the imbalance in the population of men and women made folks open to some interesting possibilities. He glanced at the brazen woman out the corner of his eye. Through vision blurred by windburn and too many fingers of Jack, she bore a slight resemblance to Lucy.

At least, how Silas imagined the woman of his dreams might look today. A riot of red-gold curls and bright blue eyes had his cock hard in an instant.

How had he gone so long without seeing her? His parents? His brothers?

His stagnant life disgusted him. Working toward someone else's dream. No land to show for it. Nothing like his great-great-grandfather had built and no one to pass it on to anyway. Just fistfuls of cash and far too many meaningless fucks. That might not have seemed so bad in his early twenties, but he'd be thirty soon for Christ's sake.

"Lucky for you, Silas and I like to play hard too."

"Not tonight, Red." Silas shook his head then shoved from the bar. He staggered two steps toward the door before his bunkmate and the cute barfly chased after him. "Count me out."

His friend's jaw went slack.

"Shush, Si." The woman's soft entreaty teased the side of his neck.

Shit, no one had called him that in ages. He didn't give a shit how she'd found out his name. He had a reputation around these parts.

It sounded…nice. Right.

"Let me make you feel good then tuck you in." The woman ducked beneath his arm and plastered herself against his side. Her soft breasts covered in a fuzzy sweater cushioned his ribs. Without thought, his hand dropped to her ass.

Maybe she had a decent idea. Some of his desperation morphed into desire, relieving the pressure on his heart. Still, as the front door banged open and they piled into Red's all-wheel drive truck, he cautioned the minx.

"I'm in one hell of a mood tonight, sugar." He couldn't be sure she'd heard since she didn't pause her exploration of his jaw on her path to his lips. He stopped her before she attempted to indulge in mouth to mouth. Ever since Colby he hadn't permitted the intimacy.

She straddled him, grinding against his erection through his jeans.

He took her delicate shoulders in his hands and shook a bit until her gaze met his. "Do you understand?"

She paused and a slow smile spread across her plump lips when she noticed the beast straining to slip its chains. He couldn't hide the feral desire in his eyes. Not that close.

"I won't be gentle," Silas growled.

"Promise?" She bit her lip. "Is it so difficult to believe I *like* it rough, Compton? I heard you could give me what I need."

Gravel pinged off the exterior of the truck as Red departed in a lurch for the seedy dorms a bunch of the oil workers shared. Not having a place of his own to take a woman had never bothered Silas before. Tonight it did.

He wanted to make her scream.

He was too old for this clandestine nonsense.

"Amuse yourselves for a bit. I'll have us there in twenty minutes." Red careened along the treacherous roadway, dodging snowdrifts and frozen road kill. He peeked over at them groping each other every couple seconds.

Silas decided to give the man a show. He flipped the truck's heater to the max then unzipped the woman's down vest. He shoved the puffy, ice blue garment from her shoulders before burrowing his hands beneath her sweater. Her satiny skin seared his work-roughened fingers. She didn't squeak or flinch when the calloused surface of his palms scraped her nipples.

Instead, she moaned then arched closer. Her hips rocked, searching for some contact on her pussy. Even through the layers she wore, he could smell her arousal.

"Mmm, you're a dirty girl, aren't you?" He pinched the puckered tips of her breasts.

Hard.

"The sweetest looking ones always are." She tilted her head then purred, "Haven't you figured that out by now?"

If only her theory were true then Lucy wouldn't have fled when she'd caught him and Colby messing around. One moment had changed the course of his life forever. If Lucy had stayed, or come closer—curious—he and Colby could have taken turns gifting her with pleasure after pleasure.

Silas had already brought the hungry woman on his lap to multiple orgasms, wishing she truly was the girl he longed for, by the time they reached their quarters. He refused to call the shithole home. Only one place deserved that honor, and it sure as hell wasn't some cinderblock dormitory in the middle of frozen-fucking-nowhere.

He threw her over his shoulder and strode for the back of the building. Red ran ahead to their window, hopping through the pane they left unlocked most nights they went out. No matter how rough their fuckmate liked things, flaunting an eager woman to an entire crew of isolated, horny men suffering eternal boredom couldn't be forgiven.

Silas wrapped his hands around her dainty waist then handed her to Red. After he pulled himself up and through, he shut the window tight, covering it with thermal protectors. Hands on hips, he took stock of the situation. The ride had sobered him some, enough to assess his two willing partners, who ripped each other's clothes off on the bare mattress in front of him.

He crossed the ten meager steps to their door, which opened into the dorm's hallway. After a quick check through the peephole, he wedged a chair beneath the knob. Things could get loud. He wouldn't chance anyone coming to investigate, hoping to bust in on the action. In the past decade, he'd had to fight off more than a few overzealous brutes.

Despite his less than sterling track record, he wouldn't stand for a woman to be hurt. Unless he inflicted controlled pain that detonated an explosion of rapture.

From the steady slaps and moans behind him, he figured Red had a head start in that department. Silas let the man have his fun because once he joined the game, the tables would turn and Red would beg to please him. It happened without fail.

Memories of the man bending over for Silas had precome dribbling from the head of his cock. He padded toward the couple wrestling on the sagging bed. In the glow from the bare bulb over the can—the sole light in the room—his mind played cruel tricks. Red and their hookup resembled Colby and Lucy.

Why had he never noticed that about Red before? Maybe his subconscious obscured the real reason he'd allowed the man to worm closer than anyone in years. Silas stroked his stiffening shaft and permitted his imagination to run wild.

"Get on your hands and knees, baby." Red directed the woman to present herself to Silas. "He loves to fuck from behind."

His roommate spread the woman's legs until her pussy lips separated, the moist tissue glistening in the diffuse light. Silas didn't lose concentration as he reached to the table beside the bed for a condom, ripped it open with his teeth then rolled the latex over his throbbing cock.

"She's had enough teasing, Compass." The other man dipped his fingers in the drenched slit awaiting him. When its owner cried out, Red painted her arousal over her clit, playing with the sensitive nerves there. "Take her."

How could he resist a gift like that? Silas pretended the wanton beckoning him was Lucy. *His* Lucy. The girl he'd grown up with, shared his aspirations with, known from the first instant could handle the rough Wyoming lifestyle. The woman he'd lost before he'd had a chance to make her his own.

He shucked his shirt then nudged the waistband of his jeans.

"Jesus, that never gets old. Wait 'til you see him, honey. He's gorgeous."

Silas's pants dropped to the floor.

"A bonus, for sure. But I'm more concerned with how he fucks. I need it. Bad."

Silas practically ran to the bed then leaped upon it. If he had it to do over, he'd make sure she never went without again. He'd stake a claim so primal she'd never dare to date another man. No, he'd establish a bond so essential she'd thrive in the aftermath of his attention and that of the man he'd come to realize he craved equally.

Silas wrapped the fingers of one hand in the hair of the woman. With the other, he shackled Red's wrist and guided the fervent man to surround his cock. His partner understood what he demanded.

Red caressed the thick hard-on in his grasp, aligning the purple tip with the entrance of the woman's pussy. The first touch of Silas's cock on the woman's hot flesh threatened to scald him through the thin barrier protecting them both. They all moaned their approval. Red fed Silas's erection to the woman, using her ample arousal to lubricate the thick, veined shaft.

When all of Silas's length tucked into the humid channel, he shifted his hips so his balls rested on Red's hand. The man cupped him. Red peered up at Silas, his head tilted, awaiting orders.

"Get down there," Silas barked. "Lay on your back between our legs. Suck my balls. Lick her. Make it good. I'm going to ride her hard. She better come before I do or your ass will be too sore to sit tomorrow."

He saw the momentary debate waging in Red. The man must have considered disobeying him on purpose. He relished a tinge of pain with his pleasure. In the end, he complied as though he could tell Silas wasn't in the mood for games tonight.

No, Silas needed the real thing. If he didn't find an outlet for the rage and frustration building inside, he'd shatter. Thank God his bedmates required the same.

The woman writhed on Silas's impaling cock, trying to shove him deeper as she ground herself on Red's face. When his roommate's tongue lapped along the center seam of his sac, Silas pulled out of the woman's pussy, drawing his cock across the eager muscle licking juice from his full-blown erection.

He changed direction, sinking inside the woman once more, loving the pressure that built on his plump head before it squeezed past the clenched ring of muscle guarding her entrance. She shrieked as he bottomed out with one fierce push.

Silas set a rhythm none of them could withstand for long. He blanketed the woman's back, biting her shoulder when he realized she smelled like Lucy too. Strawberry shampoo always propelled him to the brink of madness. He pounded her pussy, gauging her excitement from her pants, which edged toward screams. The talented manipulation of Red's tongue over her clit and Silas's balls enhanced his assault.

Silas ran one hand along her waist, up her center then filled his palm with her breast. He squeezed hard, concentrating on driving through her tightening grasp.

"You like that. Don't you, Lu?" He growled in her ear and redoubled his strokes.

"Damn straight. Except my name isn't—"

Colby must have nipped her to cut her off so quick. He whispered, "Don't ruin Compass's fantasy."

Lucy nodded then shuddered beneath Silas as Colby resumed his treatment. When Silas sensed her hovering on the verge of orgasm, he knelt upright, never altering his course inside her clinging sheath.

"Harder?" he roared then jammed his hand beneath her.

Colby sucked the finger Silas extended, coating it with saliva and the excess from their partner's soaked pussy.

"Yes!" Lucy surrendered. Her whole body went lax in his hold, allowing his cock to plunder a fraction of an inch deeper. "Make me come. Oh, God. Please. Make me come."

Silas yanked his finger from Colby, allowing the man to return to his exploration of Lucy's clit. He spread her cheeks wide with one hand then notched the tip of his spit-soaked finger in her ass. She rocked toward him at the same time he inserted his digit in her tight, hot hole.

Then she spasmed, choking his cock and his finger, threatening to drown Colby between their legs. She wailed. Her tremors continued for long minutes as he fucked her with slower, steady passes, massaging her clenching passage. When at last she sighed, he pulled free. A viscous strand of her fluids stretched between them, decorating Colby's cheek.

The man swiped the evidence of their debauchery from his face then ingested her pleasure. He never blinked, never took his stare from Silas's raging hard-on. "My turn? Please, Compass?"

"Damn straight, Colby."

The man prepared Silas, stripping the condom from his cock and replacing it with a fresh one in a matter of seconds. When he flipped onto his knees at the speed of light, Silas chuckled. "So eager. Is that cock of yours nice and hard? Let me see."

Colby whimpered and rolled to his side next to their recovering mate. Sure enough, his cock stuck straight out—red and defined by his lust.

"Very nice." Silas smiled as he inspected the man's tool. "It'd be a shame to waste a quality boner like that. Lu, you want more?"

Lucy cracked her heavy eyelids and grinned. She rotated to her back then spread her arms and legs in welcome.

"You want me to fuck her?" Colby verified, unwilling to risk misbehaving.

"Get in there. Put that cock in her pussy so I can fuck you both at the same time." A rush of pure adrenaline more potent than ten bottles of whiskey made him drunk on pleasure as he watched Colby suit up then slide home.

The motion of his partner's hips as he screwed deeper on every pass was jerky—not as refined as Silas's expert fucking—but that didn't keep Lucy from whimpering as Colby's hard-on stimulated the swollen walls of her ultra-sensitive pussy.

"There you go." Silas petted Colby's flank as he pressed tight to their woman, his cock embedded as far as he could reach. "That's the way."

Without warning, Silas dropped a resounding spank on Colby's ass. The slap of his palm reverberated throughout the room. Colby lunged forward, forcing a cry from Lucy beneath him. Silas grinned then did it again, and again, until the man's ass glowed red in the artificial twilight of the room and Lucy's restless heels drumming on the bed proclaimed her ready for another round.

Silas leaned over and snagged a half-empty bottle of lube from the table beside the bed. The cool gel soothed his flaming palm as he slathered it over the length of his cock.

"Hurry." Colby grunted as Silas fucked in tiny strokes, trying to hang on. "I'm not going to last much longer."

He didn't have to ask twice.

Silas pressed his hard-on into Colby's crack then clenched Colby's ass as he tipped his hips forward. He kept the bulbous head of his cock from popping out of the tight ring of muscle with two fingers on the top of his shaft while he overcame the man's last resistance. Once the ridge of his fat head penetrated the tissue strangling it, he sank several inches deep in one thrust.

Colby shouted then drove forward into Lucy. Silas watched her nails dig into the exposed skin over his partner's shoulders, leaving half-moon indentations as proof of her approval. That she enjoyed her men fucking did more to arouse him than any of the delicious friction they generated together.

Silas pumped his cock into the depths of Colby's ass, massaging the man's gland repeatedly. The powerful body beneath him began to tremble. Lucy soothed Colby, urging him to come in her pussy, accepting the dark desires that ensnared them all.

She shouted her satisfaction at the same time Colby milked Silas's cock with his ass as his orgasm struck. Assured he'd pleased his partners, Silas allowed his restraint to evaporate. He flooded the condom nestled in the man's back passage with spurt after spurt of his seed and still his climax continued.

He closed his eyes and floated, nearly weeping with the joy he found in sharing himself with his lovers.

For a few seconds he embraced the heat, thawing his heart. Until he crashed to earth and realized the pair in his bed weren't his lovers at all but merely his roommate and some willing woman they'd carted home from a bar.

"Son of a bitch." He ripped himself from Red's still shuddering body and dropped to his knees on the floor beside the bed. A wave of nausea assaulted him, but he swallowed the bile burning his throat.

In the background he heard Red whispering to the drowsy woman in his arms. It added another weight to Silas's conscience to inconvenience her when she'd been so generous, but he couldn't stand to return and pretend the couple in his bed was comprised of the people he craved.

Even after all this time.

Some things *never* changed.

"Get dressed, honey. I'll take you home." Red gathered the thong dangling from their gear stacked in the corner before helping her arrange the rest of her clothes. "If you want to snuggle up there, I'm game."

"But Compass..."

"He always sleeps alone."

Chapter Two

Red lights swirled across the steel structure, casting eerie shadows as the whine of sirens scared sane men toward the exit. Silas grabbed a helmet, a fire jacket and a hatchet from the supply station then fought against the current, deeper into the rig. The incessant scream of the emergency warning and the *clomp* of work boots on the riveted grate walkway made it impossible to hear anything above the racket but he caught a glimpse of Red in his peripheral vision.

No mistaking that jacket.

He grimaced as he considered the conversation he'd have to have with the man tonight. Investigating a dozen rig fires sounded more appealing than undertaking that task. Christ!

As a motorhand, he could have left this duty to the roustabouts but he always volunteered. Other than a couple minor sparks, which he'd extinguished easily, there'd never been an issue.

Red, on the other hand, could be a problem. Silas didn't do emotions. Not anymore.

Together, the pair wove between the thinning crowds, picking up speed as they burrowed into the belly of the station. Machinery lined the walls of the control room they burst into. Silas shook his head to clear the ringing in his ears when Red slammed the thick door shut behind them, cutting off the roar of the evacuation and dimming the squeal of the alert.

They worked through their checklist, finding no signs of

trouble in any of the monitored rooms on camera. Another faulty sensor probably caused the ruckus. They'd had a handful go sour lately. Now they'd have to work two hours longer on a standard eighteen-hour shift to recover the lost time. Not that Silas had anything better to do but some of the guys tired faster than he did and a bunch more couldn't withstand the frigid cold that long.

Mistakes occurred in bad conditions.

"Hey, Compass..."

"You got something?"

"Nah. My side's good to go." Red cleared his throat then continued. "You don't have to explain."

"What?" Silas took his eyes from the instrumentation to glance over his shoulder.

"I can tell you're ready to move on. What I'm sayin' is I know you're done. With me. With us."

"There never was an *us*, Red." Son of a bitch, this was not the time. A bitter taste filled his mouth when his bunkmate flinched. The guy didn't deserve his asshole treatment. "I mean—"

"Don't."

When Silas's eyebrows drew together, the other man explained.

"Don't lie now. You've always been clear you were about no strings and all that shit. It's good. Anyway, I booked a ticket out of here. Ah, you kinda reminded me of what things used to be like. What it could still be like if I quit hiding in deep freeze. I'm going home, Compass. Leaving tonight."

Silas found he couldn't speak around the shock clogging his throat. When he didn't respond, Red swiveled, focusing his attention on the task at hand. Silas did the same as his mind whirled. Red was heading home.

Respect, admiration and envy warred for top billing.

The drill shaft and seven chambers remained to clear.

When only two were left, Silas asked, "You think you can go back? To normal stuff? Your old life?"

"I'm gonna try."

"Son of a bitch!" Silas's eyes bulged.

"It ain't *that* crazy—"

"Fire! Sector A. Engine room." He smashed the button used to engage the chemical suppressant system. Nothing happened. "Oh, fuck. It's busted. I'm going in."

"Silas! No!"

If the man tried to persuade him further, the entreaty disappeared beneath the blast of the alarm, which crescendoed when Silas ripped open the door and skidded around the corner toward the site of the trouble.

He leapt over the handrail to the level below rather than take time scrambling down the treacherous incline on the access ladder. Adrenaline made his hefty axe light as a feather in his grasp. He kept running, ignoring the fact that every step put him closer to danger. If he didn't stop the fire from spreading, it would ignite the gas vent in the chamber three doors down.

The men who'd evacuated wouldn't be guaranteed safety. Red and the other crewmembers troubleshooting the alarm from inside would stand no chance. Not to mention the ecological disaster that would follow on the heels of such a catastrophe.

He dropped his shoulders and sprinted, thanking God for each second that passed without an epic kaboom. At least he wouldn't have time to suffer if things ended in the crapper. They'd be obliterated before they had a chance to register their demise.

A Zen-like surrealism cocooned him as he charged along the corridor, thankful he'd kept his affairs in order. If something happened to him, everything important—his parents, his brothers, the ranch, Lucy and Colby—would benefit from the odds he'd beaten for ten years.

He slowed as he neared the pod containing the fire, trailing his fingers along the metal walls to test for conducted heat. Nothing yet. Maybe one of the other guys had coerced the suppression system to kick on.

Or not.

A bang sounded from his left like a rifle shot, spurring him to jump a solid six inches off the ground. Not the mother of all detonations. More like a water pipe bursting as steam built inside it.

Silas tapped his fingers on the door to the engine room. Warm, but not impossible to touch. He had to try to stop the chain of events while he could. He kicked the long steel door handle with the heel of his boot, popping the entrance open even as he ducked to the side.

No flames shot out of the exposed portal. A nervous laugh tumbled from his chest as he figured he'd watched too many movies during the long, dark Alaskan winters.

"You're a crazy bastard, Compass." Red caught up, his breath sawing in ragged gasps that reminded Silas of the time he'd made the man come hard enough he claimed to have seen stars. "Gonna get us both killed and cracking up about it."

"Head out, Red. Tell the rest of the guys what's up. Move them as far away as you can. A bunch of them have families."

"*You* have a family, Compass. You go."

"Don't argue—"

"Not this time. I'm not your bitch anymore." Before Silas could do more than gawk, his bunkmate slapped Silas's ass then darted through the gaping doorway where he disappeared in the thickening haze of smoke.

Silas tugged his shirt over his nose and mouth then dove after Red, his bright jacket blurred by the shimmer of heat waves in the charged air. The clang of metal on metal reverberated through the hiss and pop of flames, which seemed to grow with every slam of Silas's heart against his ribs.

Sparks flew from the junction of Red's axe blade and the

pipe running from the fire suppression system, but several mighty blows didn't make enough progress in denting the surface for Silas's liking. He checked over his shoulder. Flames billowed higher and higher—obscuring his vision—in a semi-circle that would soon cut off their exit route.

A fit of coughs threatened to keel him over.

Fuck this. They didn't have time. He shoved Red toward the door, knocking the man farther from the worst of the danger. With a roar, Silas laid all his energy into swinging his axe at the black valve capping the end of the pipe.

A plume of chemicals formed a beautiful rooster tail as they sprayed over the blaze, dampening the worst of the flames. The angle of saturation didn't quite match the intended zone due to his improvised delivery method. Within seconds, a couple of spots smoldered but the troubling line of fire headed for the main vent had extinguished.

He turned to Red in time to catch the man's grin and fist pump. Backup would be here in no time. They'd clean up the rest. Silas's knees went weak.

How had they ended up so lucky? Insanity would rule the bar tonight for sure.

Still, the toxic chemicals wreaked havoc on his lungs so he'd wait for later to celebrate. He neared Red, about to pound the man's outstretched fist when his partner's eyes widened.

Silas flew across the room and slammed into something unforgiving before the blast deafened him. His ears rang as he tried to figure out where he was and what had happened. When he struggled to climb to his feet, his left leg gave out, sending a wave of pain crashing over him. He wished he hadn't looked at his thigh when he caught sight of something white poking through his ripped jeans. Blood slicked his hands as he dragged himself along the floor grate, shouting for Red.

The door should be to his right. That's where he thought he'd last seen the man. He snaked across the mangled surface, debris ripping his hide to shreds, but the drive to aid his friend eradicated every other thought.

“Red!” he screamed, but he couldn’t hear himself, never mind an answer.

A moment later, a scrap of tattered crimson cloth waved ten feet or so away, beyond the enlarged exit. Somehow, Silas crossed the space in a flash.

Red sat in the hallway, his legs at a funny angle in front of him. A serene smile crossed his face when he spotted Silas dragging himself near.

Thank God.

Then Silas noticed specks of blood dotting the man’s face. More and more splatters gathered like obscene freckles. A segment of the railing emerged from Red’s chest, where it had impaled him. His jacket, neck and face grew brighter by the second.

“No!” Silas crumpled with his head on his friend’s thigh. He couldn’t say if blood or tears made the heated tracks down his cheeks.

Red’s fingers closed on Silas’s elbow, encouraging Silas to use the last of his dazed momentum to roll onto his back and meet the dying man’s gaze.

“Go home, Compass.”

Silas still couldn’t hear. He read the man’s trembling, soot-covered lips.

Light faded from Red’s eyes. The man refused to quit, fighting to the end. “Before it’s too...late.”

Silas gasped like a fish out of water, trying to breathe as his friend went limp in his arms. Bright blood seeped from the corner of lips he’d never allowed himself to kiss.

The man’s favorite color.

Iron tang overpowered smoke when Silas levered himself up the railing to press his mouth to the man he held. Who had he been trying to kid?

Red hadn’t been some meaningless fuck. He’d been a

friend.

A damn good one at that. Yet, he'd never have the chance to tell the guy so.

What more had he pretended to be oblivious to?

Silas's life flashed before his eyes, stripping off the illusions he'd crafted. Denial had caused him to forsake all he valued. How much had his family suffered when he severed ties with them despite the infinite love and opportunity they'd lavished on their prodigal firstborn? What had seemed noble for ten years looked selfish as anguish—both physical and mental—seared away his flimsy excuses.

Unforgivable.

The idea of returning home, begging absolution, took root as sparks showered around him and acrid smoke scorched his lungs. Too bad he couldn't move, would never make it out.

Silas collapsed, recalling the faces of each of his brothers then Lucy and Colby to keep him company in his final moments. A secondary explosion shook the room. He still couldn't make his body react to his demands.

Move! Run! Crawl!

Anything.

Oh God, anything.

Instead, he lay helpless except for the jarring shockwaves from a chain of miniature bangs. The reserve gas tanks, under pressure in the engine room, must have been giving way—one by one.

Flaming bits and metal shrapnel pelted his back as he curled into a ball, refusing to relinquish his connection to Red. When the main tank went, it'd all be over.

At least the fire seemed contained. It hadn't penetrated the chemical barrier they'd laid down or he'd already be toast. Red's sacrifice would not be in vain.

Through moisture not entirely caused by the acrid clouds smothering him, he spotted an open doorway on the level below their landing. His survival instinct stretched, yearning to fly toward the ultra-slim chance, but his muscles had quit taking orders from his brain as his body shut down.

"Go home, Compass."

Silas knew his friend had already departed, but Red's demand echoed in the silent realm of chaos surrounding him, driving him to regroup.

"Your place was always on the ranch." The twins peered over Seth's shoulder as his brothers tried to grant him the strength to move.

"Yes, come back to us, Si."

"Lucy?" What was she doing here? On the rig? He had to get her out. Silas scrambled on awkward elbows and his working knee, ignoring the slices he gouged into his joints as he slithered toward the ghost of her in that gauzy sundress he'd been enchanted by as a kid.

"I've missed you, Silas." Colby had one arm around Lucy's waist and the other extended to him in invitation. Why weren't they running?

Silas tumbled down the stairs then made one final lunge, trying to shield his loved ones. His arms flailed through the mirage.

Alluring ghosts.

A fantasy.

Grateful for their safety, he recoiled at losing them again.

He attempted a half-hearted pounce for the platform he'd somehow reached. A tertiary explosion had projectiles pinging off surfaces all around him. It took him a few seconds to realize the pain lancing his body meant he'd stopped at least some of the macabre confetti with his flesh.

He started to cover his mouth—the gasses entering when he gulped stung his lungs—but a chunk of metal stuck in his palm. Odd, he couldn't feel it anymore.

One final reverberation, larger than the ones before, tossed him into the corner like a rag doll. The sick crunch of his ribs guaranteed he'd broken one or two at least.

The fringes of his vision dimmed.

As darkness claimed him, he saw his parents, his brothers, Lucy, Colby and even Buddy—his childhood dog—waiting on Compass Ranch. When they welcomed him with open arms, he accepted that he'd died and gone to heaven.

All he could think was that he didn't deserve such an honor.

Chapter Three

"Colby! JD!"

Lucy didn't give a damn if she spooked every animal on the ranch. The screen door to the main house slammed behind her. She screamed for her husband again as she tore along the porch and crossed the yard, past the freshly painted barn.

Ranch hands stared at the unusual display, several jogging after her to offer assistance. None of them would do.

In the distance, she caught a glimpse of the two men she sought astride gorgeous mounts. When she waved her arms but kept running, they spurred the horses to a gallop. It was silly. She couldn't reach them faster than they could ride back. Still, she didn't bother to stop herself from ducking between the rails of the fence to intercept them a millisecond sooner.

Thank God they hadn't left for the outer pastures yet.

On any other day she might have taken an instant to admire the two powerful men racing side by side—the owner of Compass Ranch and his foreman—as they barreled down on her. Right now, she needed the arms of her husband as she delivered terrible news.

The stuff of a parent's nightmares.

Colby started dismounting before his horse had come to a complete stop. He dropped beside her, cupping her shoulders in his broad hands to peer at her tear-stained face.

"What's the matter, Luce?" His sun-kissed cheeks appeared pale, an impressive feat. "What is it?"

He shook her a bit when the truth strangled her.

JD pried Colby's fingers from her arm then snuggled her into a paternal embrace. In the six years since her dad had suffered a massive heart attack and died while treating a foal in the middle of the night, JD had taken over as her honorary father. After raising four sons and countless ranchers, he got a mite protective over his little girl.

He smoothed her hair, shooting a glare at Colby after inspecting the red marks lingering on the skin bared by her tank top.

"Shit! Sorry." Her husband whipped his hat from his head and slapped it on his thigh. "You're killing me, baby. What's wrong?"

Lucy gulped, reaching for his hand. He cradled it this time, begging her with those sky blue eyes not to say their worst fear aloud. She couldn't give him what he hoped for.

"It's bad." She smothered another sob. "It's Si."

"Oh, Jesus."

"Is he..." Even tough-as-nails JD Compton couldn't finish the thought.

"He's alive, but seriously injured. There was some kind of explosion. He's been in the hospital for three weeks." Regret knotted her guts, making it almost impossible to continue. She drew one ragged breath, then another and another. "Twenty-three days. Suffering. Alone. With no one by his side when the doctors weren't sure he'd pull through."

Relief chased terror across the faces hovering over her. She could relate. Her heart hadn't stopped stuttering since she'd taken the call from a concerned nurse who had the good sense to ignore Silas's idiotic request not to notify his family.

From one caregiver to another, Lucy could understand. Sometimes the patient couldn't determine the best course of treatment. She owed the woman big time.

"The fool broke his femur, three ribs, sustained countless lacerations, contusions and burns. Plus, he had one hell of a concussion. Internal bleeding and the damage to his lungs caused the most concern, though. He's had seven surgeries and they say he'll probably always walk with a limp."

Anger had replaced the initial horror swamping her as the woman in the Anchorage hospital relayed the extensive list of Silas's injuries. How dare he keep his family ignorant when he needed them? She'd had enough of his arrogance. What gave him the right to steal other people's choices?

The girl she'd been might have bowed beneath his heavy-handed ruling.

The woman she'd grown into certainly would not.

"The oil company is recognizing him as a hero. They say he saved hundreds of lives when their safety equipment failed." She glanced between JD and Colby.

She'd shared the brief phone conversation she'd had with Silas's roommate a couple months ago. She hadn't been able to stand the silence when he'd stopped emailing his brothers for two weeks, cutting off her information pipeline. The guys had tried to reach out to Silas when she pestered them. None of the three had gotten a response.

So she'd broken down and dialed, expecting to hang up on Silas's terse greeting like usual. Instead, the unfamiliar man on the other end of the line had startled her into making a betraying gasp. She'd begged him not to tell Silas she'd called. After he'd agreed, she couldn't help prying, just a little.

Silas had picked up extra shifts. No biggie there. She'd wondered if he had finally moved on when the sweet man on the other end of the line appreciated her genuine concern and expressed curiosity about Silas's history. Lucy had given him enough to help him understand the situation. It had hurt, but she'd hoped Silas could find some measure of happiness. In fact, she hadn't worried when he dropped off the grid this time because she assumed his obvious lover had kept him too busy for correspondence.

The poor man. "Red Covington died in the blast."

JD made the sign of the cross.

Colby swept her into his arms, surrounding her with his gentle warmth and reliable shelter. God, how she loved this man. So much, she accepted that she could lose him when Silas came home.

Tomorrow.

After a decade of exile, Prince Silas would return to his kingdom. Colby might still be under his spell. Denying her own infatuation would be pointless, though she wasn't the one in danger of being captured.

The passionate exchange she'd interrupted between Colby and Silas had fueled her best dreams and worst night terrors for ten long years. Never far from her mind, she remembered it often. How it had boiled her blood and frozen her heart.

The two men she craved wanted each other.

Not her.

Despite her naïve attempts at seduction, both men had kept her at arm's length. Colby had held her hand, kissed her sweetly and melted her heart. Neither had shared the raw lust she'd discovered they were capable of. At least not then. After Silas left, Colby had gradually warmed. She had no complaints about their love life but neither had he shown her that abandonment to raw obsession again.

Only one person had inspired that in him.

"They're sending Silas home. I arranged the flight with the hospital. Judy agreed to take over three of my homecare patients to clear time in my daily schedule. They're releasing him into my care." She cupped Colby's jaw with her trembling fingers. Could he read her understanding? His enduring desire for the other man didn't make her prize him less. No, even more, because he'd remained faithful to her all this time when she couldn't give him everything he needed, no matter how badly she wished she could. "Our care."

"Silas is coming home?" Colby sounded like she felt. Dazed. Excited. Terrified.

"Silas is coming home." JD whooped then hugged them both, a solid arm around each of them. "Things are gonna work out. The way they always should have been. You'll see."

Colby watched his wife jog to the house. She'd left Silas's mom, Victoria, inside. The woman had probably already rung half the state to arrange all they'd need to bring her eldest son home.

Colby distracted himself from worrying about the man he'd called his best friend once by studying Lucy's fine ass in those snug jeans, the curves highlighted by her soft pink shirt and the wild mass of her untamed hair. He adored those fiery curls, especially when they fanned over his chest each night as they fell asleep together.

She issued a watery smile over her shoulder before ducking inside. The quiet desperation thinning her lips made his stomach do flip-flops.

"What the hell are you going to do now, boy?"

"Don't have a fucking clue. Go on as usual, I suppose." Like anything could be normal with Silas at Compass Ranch again.

"Your wife is in love with my son. Has been since she was no higher than my knee."

"You think that's news to me, JD?"

"And what about you? Gonna admit you want Silas too?"

Colby spun on the heel of his boot, forcing himself to close his gaping mouth with a snap. He couldn't say what surprised him more, that JD knew or that he didn't seem too upset by the idea. No point in pretending things might have changed. What he carried for Silas couldn't be obliterated by time or distance.

"It don't matter. I'm married. Happily. I won't fuck around on Lucy. Si never wanted me anyway. Not with the fire he'd get in his eyes every time he saw Lu."

"No man's a good judge of shit that close to his heart. What seems obvious to others gets distorted, like the horizon on a hot day, when you're twisted up with need and devotion."

"Then why—?"

"I don't have all the answers, Colby. And I'm not trying to bust your balls either, just talking. This next bit will be rough for us all. More so for you. Make sure you're ready to grab the bull by its horns and sit tight. I have faith you'll tough it out. Hell, you're the only one of my sons that stuck. Every other one couldn't put up with this life. Took off the second they turned eighteen."

"They're morons. Every one of the Compass Brothers. I wouldn't have picked anyone else to be my father. No other place to call home." Pride at the man's compliment filled him with awe and gratitude. JD put his sons above all else. To be counted among them meant something. Something huge.

They pivoted as if by mutual agreement, standing shoulder to shoulder against the rail so they didn't have to look into each other's eyes. "You and Victoria raised your kids right. Nothing like my shithead sperm donor."

JD grunted his agreement.

Colby had always suspected it'd been the head of Compass Ranch who'd kicked the living crap out of his father to encourage the asshole to leave town. The sick bastard had limped from Compton Pass, never to be seen again, abandoning his teenage son. An hour later Vicky had showed up to claim the malnourished, beaten kid Colby had been and welcomed him into their lives. She'd tamed him like a wild animal, inching closer until he finally believed in the reality of their generosity, kindness and love.

The Comptons had given him shelter, a job and so much more. Family. A home.

A life worth living.

"I'm not planning on leaving Compass Ranch anytime soon if that's what you're working toward. I would never abandon you or Vicky or Lucy. Not after what Silas put you all through. I'll give him a chance to heal up, but we're gonna have words about it. That I promise."

Another long silence followed, this one easier as the firm set of JD's shoulders relaxed a hair. As they often did while catching a break, they shared the silence, watching over the ranch as they kept their own company.

Colby had become fast friends with all four Compass brothers—as the locals referred to them—overnight. Still, there'd always been something about Silas and Lucy. The three of them would take off on adventures, exploring the land and the bond growing between them.

Until things had spiraled out of control.

"Remember Jack Newton?"

Colby searched the recesses of his memory at JD's random interjection. A lot of wandering men had worked the ranch a summer or two but...Jack?

"Tall, skinny like a bean pole, mean as a bear with a tooth ache?"

"Ah, yeah. I remember that fucker. Never did trust him." More like he'd hated the way the man had appraised him with lurid intentions blatant in his stare.

"When I fired his ass, he tried to throw it in my face how he'd seen you and my 'fag son' going at it in the barn. How little Lucy caught you and bolted the night before Silas hightailed it out of here."

"Son of a bitch." Colby crashed his fist into the rough-hewn rail, regretting it as a spike of sensation traveled through his knuckles. "I fucked up, JD. Shit, I'm sorry. All these years. It's my fault he left. You knew, and you didn't kick me out?"

"Don't go getting stupider than you've already been, son."

"What's that supposed to mean?" He shook the sting from his hand.

"You three kids have been pissing away time like it goes on forever." JD rubbed his side, a gesture Colby had spied him making a few times lately. "Quit screwing around and set things straight. Whatever it takes. You're only given so long around this place. Use it well."

A million other questions tumbled through Colby's mind, but by the time he recovered, JD had already handed his horse to Jake—who worked the stable this morning—then headed inside to his wife. Despite Vicky's spine of steel, she probably wished for her husband at her side. Colby hoped his marriage, and Lucy's attachment to him, was half as strong as the extraordinary relationship JD had forged with his woman.

Anything less would make the fledgling plans kicking around in his brain unravel in a heartbeat. Phase one entailed corralling Lucy alone. Isolated from the herd of folks gathering on the front porch bearing pies, and hoping for extra gossip, as the news spread.

Less than a half hour had passed since their lives flipped inside out yet several pickups already cluttered the yard. The drone of more engines approaching along the winding drive from the main road, a few miles in the distance, insured extra casseroles and gossip headed this direction.

Colby should have realized the flaw in his plan when he had to stop twice on the way to the house. "Is there anything I can do?" Cindi, the cute bookkeeper who worked from a little office in the barn, stepped in front of him, swiping a stray lock of hair beneath the pencil wound in her hair.

"How about putting together a list of supplies from Lucy? She might need equipment we don't have here and can't find in town."

"Good idea. I have it covered. We're expecting a shipment tomorrow morning from Laramie. I'll make sure anything else comes with it."

"Great, thanks." He accepted her hug but didn't make it more than ten feet before he bumped into Leah Hollister.

"Whoa." Colby snagged the covered dish about to smash on the rocky yard.

"Nice catch, foreman." Compton Pass's sweet kindergarten

teacher reclaimed the dish with a sad smile. She refused to let him help her carry it, always trying to prove herself. Someday he'd ask her why that was. "Are you hanging in?"

"Yeah. Need to find Lucy, though." He kept one hand on her elbow as they climbed the stairs. Such a tiny thing couldn't possibly see where she stepped around the comfort food she'd carted over in record time. How the hell did women do that?

"I think you missed her. She ran past while you were talking to Cindi. Said she was headed to the storage shed to dig out a few of Silas's things." The door opened before they reached it. Someone piled Leah's offering with the rest. The crowd swallowed her before he could slip another word in edgewise. He tried to break out, follow Lucy. No use. Someone else interrupted. Damn!

And so it went.

Despite valiant attempts, he didn't manage to isolate his wife until after midnight. All day, prying eyes and pointed comments had eroded his confidence. Lucy's infatuation with Silas had been no secret growing up. The entire community wondered what would happen if the chemistry zinged between her and Silas when the pair reunited at last.

Colby most of all.

What if she only wanted Si? Nothing—no one—more?

It had damn near killed Colby not to chase after Silas and beg him to come home. Survival without both halves of his soul would prove impossible. Only Lucy had made Silas's abandonment bearable.

Sometime in the last couple minutes his wife had sunk onto the floral-patterned sofa in Vicky's parlor and crashed. He studied her even breathing across the bar that opened into the family room of the ranch house while he finished drying glasses.

"I can clear these up." Vicky reached up to pat his back.

"I've got them." He smiled over his shoulder but couldn't hold her assessing gaze for more than a moment. "Almost done."

"If you squeeze a little harder you'll shatter it. I'm fond of that pattern." She *tsked* then applied pressure on the bunched muscles of his forearm until he paused. "Things will be all right."

He set the final cup on the counter then absorbed Vicky's hug. She didn't hound him to speak. Instead, she hung on until some of the tension seeped from him.

"There, that's better. Now, take that girl of yours home. She's exhausted herself."

"I can't believe she got Silas's old room ready so fast."

"That isn't what wore her out." Vicky stared at him as though he were slow. "Enough hiding, Colby. JD promised he spoke with you this morning. Maybe he didn't do a good enough job?"

"It's not fair for you two to gang up on me." He laughed then kissed her cheek. "JD did fine. It's just..."

"What?"

"It's been so long. If Si had taken her immediately maybe it would've been different. I wouldn't have known what I was missing. If I lose her to him now, I'll never survive it. But I want them to be happy. Both of them."

"So I guess you'll have to make sure all three of you win now, won't you?" She squeezed Colby as though she weren't condoning an illicit arrangement for her own son.

"How did you guess what I was thinking?"

She withdrew a fraction of an inch, one brow raised. "Why do men always think they're so subtle when they're after something?"

"You're okay with...?" He didn't how to describe the relationship he had in mind. He needed the three of them to be together, equals bonded permanently.

"It's called a triad, Colby." She chuckled when a blush heated his cheeks. "Plenty of people enjoy ménage. Shoot, in our day, JD and I—"

He choked. Christ, what was he, thirteen again?

"Yeah, well, you get the point." She grinned, relishing his discomfort a moment more before turning serious. "What's in your heart? Don't listen to anything else. A hell of a lot of people objected to JD and me when we first started dating."

"Why?" His head tilted as he absorbed the sincerity of her statement. He couldn't imagine two people better suited. What could society have possibly objected to?

"'Cause I was so young. He was handsome as sin, wealthy and nearly twenty years my senior. People couldn't believe affection or tenderness was involved." She grinned. "And he had quite a reputation for having a dark edge in bed."

"Okay, enough!" He didn't need to picture JD's dominant personality translating to sex. It reminded him too much of his dreams of Silas. He shook his head. "It's funny, I don't see any of that when I look at the two of you. I can't imagine either of you with anyone else."

"Exactly, Colby." She patted his cheek then nodded. "Folks might gawk or run their fool mouths at first. In time everyone else will accept you. I can't picture the three of you any other way."

"He's been gone so long." He wished he could kick his own ass when his whisper caused his surrogate mother to wince and the sheen of tears glistened in her eyes. "What if things are different?"

"If I know my boy at all, he'll be the same as ever. Headstrong, noble and hard-working." Vicky nibbled her lip as if debating whether to speak her mind. He waited her out, glad when she continued. "You needed this time, Colby. To grow into your own without Silas here. I think if he'd stayed, you never would have become so independent. You're a man to be proud of, honey. You earned your position as foreman and the other hands respect you. Lucy adores you. JD and I are lucky to have you. Silas would be too."

"Thank you." He hated the sting behind his scrunched eyelids.

"Now put your wife to bed right. She'll need her energy tomorrow."

"Yes, ma'am." He grinned as he rounded the bar and scooped Lucy into his arms.

She snuggled close to his chest and sighed, a perfect fit for his hold.

Chapter Four

Lucy blinked at the hairline crack snaking across the plastered ceiling above her and Colby's bed. How had she gotten here?

The foreman's lodge lay half a mile east of the main house. She didn't remember the trip home. They certainly hadn't raced their mounts along the well-used trail as they did when they couldn't wait to crash into bed—or onto the kitchen floor—together. Neither did she recall driving herself in her Jeep as she did when she returned from a long day of tending to her elderly or terminal homebound patients.

It would have been impossible to forget riding double with Colby in the moonlight and crisp air as they did on occasion to relax after a long day. The security of her husband's muscled arm around her waist, his powerful thighs bracketing hers and the promise of his hard cock in the small of her back always had her eager for attention by the time they walked his gelding—Couper—bareback out of the farmyard, never mind along the entire trail to their house.

Sometimes they had to stop along the route.

She smiled to herself as she realized Colby must have driven her home sometime after she'd surrendered, promising to take a miniscule five-minute break before washing the mountain of dishes that had piled up. Nearly the entire town of Compton Pass had swung by the ranch at some point to show their support. The whole day melted into one long blur of activity.

The brush of supple cotton sheets on her breasts as she lay naked confirmed Colby had tucked her in. Undressing her infatuated him. He'd peel her clothes off as though he performed a sacred ritual intended to worship her body. The man treated her like a goddess.

Running water caught her attention. She rolled to her side and checked the clock on her nightstand. Nearly two in the morning. She considered joining her husband in the shower as he soaped his ripped muscles, honed by daily manual labor.

Every ridge and line would gleam beneath the slick suds.

Memories of many shared washings had her humming her approval. Despite the stress of the day, she couldn't shake the low level buzz that had haunted her since the news of Silas's homecoming. Her thighs parted a bit, and she ran one palm low on her abdomen. Engrossed in the recollection, she didn't notice Colby had finished until he strolled into their room.

"What's going on out here, naughty girl? Can't leave you alone for a minute." The twinkle in his eyes as he emerged with a towel slung low on his trim hips proclaimed he'd caught her thinking of him. With one glance, he read everything she felt. Exactly what she needed.

He ruffled the terrycloth over his damp hair, granting her a world-class view of grade A beefcake.

"Like what you see, Mrs. Peterson?"

"Mmm. You're one mighty fine cowboy."

A glimmer of doubt crossed her husband's face. "Was it me you were thinking of?"

Lucy levered onto her elbows, the sheet pooling at her waist. Things were serious when her bare breasts couldn't distract Colby. He had a thing for her tits, especially when her nipples stood straight out as they did now. He would spend hours ravishing the sensitive peaks.

He didn't glance away from her stare. His throat worked as he gulped. She patted the bedspread beside her hip, and he crossed to her in two moderate strides of his long legs.

"I *always* dream of you." She took a deep breath then admitted, "But sometimes you're not alone."

Her husband slid beneath the jewel box quilt Victoria had made for their wedding present, gathering Lucy to his chest. The pounding of his heart drummed in her ear.

"You truly believe I don't want you anymore, Colby?"

"For tonight, sure. Once Silas is home..." Her cheek rose and fell when he shrugged. "You've always loved him. Shit, you only agreed to date me in the first place to make him jealous."

"You knew that?"

"I'm not stupid, Lu. It pissed me off when he shunned your affection." He drew a deep breath. "Like he'd always done to me. Acting like we were nothing but friends. I understood how bad that would sting you."

"Colby, we were young." Her sigh buffeted his nipple, hardening the dime-sized point, stealing her attention for a moment.

"Especially you. I wondered if Silas kept his hands off because you hadn't even turned seventeen yet. But I couldn't resist. I never was as honorable as him."

"Don't say things like that." She lifted her head to meet her husband's troubled stare. Her fingers stroked damp hair off his brow. "What I meant is that I was too inexperienced to comprehend all you had to offer. You're subtle where he's flash. You're steady where he's hot then cold. You're reliable, trustworthy and sexier than any man has a right to be."

"You're good for my ego, Lu."

"You're good for my soul."

When he dragged her close for a drugging kiss, she tasted the cherry candy he popped like mints when he worried. Didn't he understand?

"You were always spectacular and you've done a hell of a lot of growing since those days, Colby. No potential went to waste with you." She forced herself to put some distance between their torsos or she'd forget what she intended to say. Still, she couldn't stop herself from walking her fingertips up his chest, over the contours of his neck, to his lips. "I admire how you forged yourself into the man you are today. You didn't have all of Silas's advantages and yet you've become one of the most respectable leaders on the ranch and in Compton Pass. Hell, I heard rumors in town they're going to write you in on the ballet for trustee this year."

"Funny." He nipped her finger then sucked until the sting disappeared. "Victoria said something similar earlier. You didn't need any polish, Lu. You've always been perfect to me. Even when you schemed to use your pal Colby to make Si suffer."

"It didn't take long for me to realize I already had what I wanted." She leaned forward to taste his lips once more. No use in resisting. His palm landed on her ass, cupping her as they shared a deep, lingering kiss. She chuckled around his fluttering tongue then dislodged her mouth to whisper, "I think we dated all of one day before I begged you to take my virginity."

He'd refused.

She still couldn't say if it had been some misplaced sense of propriety or the fact that he'd lusted for someone else more than her. The sliver of doubt had niggled the far recesses of her mind for too long. Soon, she'd find out. Suddenly, she wasn't as eager for the answer. Her life here was perfect. She had everything important. Almost.

Colby bundled her into his arms then rolled onto his back, pillowing her on his gorgeous body. She rested their foreheads together until the creases that appeared on his brow when he discussed something serious crinkled against her skin.

"When we hooked up, you had s*ome* of what you wanted. Let's be honest, Lucy. You've always craved Silas. We both have."

The truth they'd tried to deny for so long reared between them. A tear leaked from her watering eyes without warning, dropping onto Colby's cheek.

"That doesn't mean I love you any less," she promised.

"Then you understand it's the same for me?"

She nodded. Ten years of Colby's easy companionship and generous passion didn't lie. Too bad Silas hadn't shown a glimmer of interest in her. When the object of her girlhood crush had clutched Colby to him, ravaging her then-boyfriend in the barn, the sight had sliced her in two. Jealousy had sickened her. She fled, praying she'd make it far enough that her ultimate disappointment wouldn't douse the sparks between the two men she adored.

Lucy hadn't done a good enough job of hiding her disappointment.

Silas had bolted the very next day, before she had a chance to guarantee him of her happiness for them. How much time had she stolen from Colby? From Silas? How callous did it make her that she'd savored her husband's devotion despite the cost?

She swore she'd set things straight and grant them the bliss she'd hoarded for a decade.

For one more night, her husband belonged to her alone.

"I'm not sure what tomorrow will bring, but if Silas is the same man we adored, you have to pursue your heart's desire Colby. For all of our sakes'." She couldn't bear to keep him from Si a moment longer. Colby would have chased the other man down long ago if it hadn't been for the responsibility he felt for her, the ranch and a million other real-life hurdles. "I won't be an obstacle to your happiness."

Her husband flipped her, rising over her supine form on straight-locked arms until he could peer into her eyes. She made sure only the hope for his bliss projected from them.

"Jesus, I'm crazy about you. I've stressed all day about how to tell you exactly the same thing, Lucy." He tangled his fingers in the curls at her temples and claimed her lips in ravenous kisses between vows. "I *will* fight for us. I promise. I'll do my best to convince him."

And then she'd be alone. No more sultry nights filled with familiar laughter and unending passion or the occasional disagreement resolved with gentle loving. Lucy reached for something to tide her through the lonely darkness to come.

A precious memory.

"Love me, Colby?"

"I'll always love you. No matter what comes tomorrow. Or the day after." He rubbed his nose against hers. "Or the day after that. I swear I'll never stop, Lu. I wouldn't have thought it possible, but I cherish you more for giving us this chance. For understanding."

Her heart broke. She nodded anyway. Us. Colby and Silas. Despite what her husband claimed, he wouldn't be able to deny his lust. She didn't have to have psychic abilities to predict the future.

Colby didn't waste any time in displaying his gratitude. He laid a trail of wet kisses down her neck, across the tops of her breasts, through the valley between them, along her center to her pussy. His hands lit her nerve endings on fire as he caressed her in tandem. He teased the edge of her mound with glancing swipes of his fingers before settling in the cradle of her thighs.

Her husband sighed as he inhaled the scent of her arousal then laid his cheek on her mound as though to ground himself before continuing. She petted his damp hair then nudged him toward her aching core.

"So hot, Lu?" He grinned up at her, his irises the shocking blue they turned when his desire took control. "What if I feel like going slow?"

"Jackass. You don't."

"Damn straight." Colby scooped his hands beneath her ass then raised her to his mouth. He sipped from her moist folds, feeding on every molecule of her arousal.

Lucy's hips flexed in his hold, her body undulating of its

own accord when he neared her clit with his roving lips.

"There." She buried her fingers in his hair to keep him still when he'd reached the perfect position. "Right there."

His smile spread against her slippery tissue. Of course he knew exactly how to touch her. He liked to tease, that's all. God, he made torturing her an art form.

Lucy shivered then smoothed the heels of her palms up her tummy to her breasts, planning to fight fire with fire. She cupped the soft swells in her hands, playing with her nipples using the tips of her fingers.

Colby paused his assault to stare. He groaned, vibrating her clit with his pleasure. When she winked at her husband, he slipped in some tricks of his own. One of his hands glided from her hip to her pussy. His broad middle finger nudged the opening, tracing her inner lips before delving inside.

Her hands fell to the mattress, her sweet torment abandoned. She slipped her legs from beneath his arms, propping her heels on his ridiculously wide shoulders. When her husband applied the perfect level of suction on her engorged bundle of nerves, her toes curled into his muscles.

"Ah!" She cried out when he added a second finger, stretching her pussy, preparing her for his cock. She couldn't decide if she'd prefer him to keep eating her or to fill her with his impressive length. Colby didn't ask. He pursued her nearing climax with a single-minded determination she found attractive both in and out of bed.

God help her when her man fixated on something. He'd go to the ends of the earth to make his desire reality.

His calloused finger massaged a hidden spot nestled deep in her body. He played her like a violin virtuoso with a Stradivarius. Lucy attempted to resist, to prolong Colby's seductive gift. When he added a third finger and rotated them all so he stimulated the clenching walls of her channel, she stood no chance.

Lucy slapped the mattress. The pressure building within

her required an outlet. She squirmed and shouted nonsense her husband understood on an instinctive level far beyond decipherable language. He took pity on her, sucking her clit into his mouth as he spread his fingers apart, triggering a climax of epic proportions.

She hadn't yet finished coming when Colby covered her with his entire frame. Her legs wrapped around his trim hips, opening her pussy to invite him inside.

Her husband tunneled into her clinging sheath, joining their bodies as tightly as their spirits entwined. The fit of their flesh impressed her every time. Though she'd never had another man, she couldn't imagine a match as perfect as this.

What would it be like to hold Silas inside her instead?

"Yes. God, yes." Colby shuddered over her. "Do that again. Clench my cock."

She thought of the responsible, brave and daring young man she'd hungered for all her life then pictured the man he'd become. She closed her eyes and allowed her imagination to run wild. In her mind, he claimed possession of her, fucking her without the restraint her husband insisted on for her protection.

"That's it, Lu." Colby grunted as he shuttled in and out of her with urgent glides. The contracted ring of muscle at her entrance caught the ridge below the head of his cock on every pass, preventing him from abandoning her pussy despite his quickening thrusts.

She wished she could taste the fluid leaking from his cock as it always did when he came this close to shooting. The salty emission mingled with her copious lubrication to facilitate his amplified motion. Colby fucked her harder, dropping his mouth to hers, whispering his affection against her skin.

He kissed her with a tenderness the pounding of his hips should have belied. Urgency overwhelmed them both, guaranteeing his care, his concern and his soul-deep adoration. Because she returned the sentiment, her open heart allowed her to sense the slight imperfection in their joining.

Colby needed something else to achieve the rapture flooding her in wave after wave. Familiar regret threatened their harmony. She couldn't satisfy all of his desires. Still, she would do her best.

Lucy nipped her husband's lip to get his attention. When his driving rhythm hitched, she shoved his shoulders, urging him to turn. He complied with a moan, rotating until he flopped onto his back. His spread fingers trailed from her ribs to her hips, confirming she'd settled herself comfortably before setting her loose.

Her husband relinquished control, handing her the reins. She tipped back, supporting herself with her hands braced on his thighs to give him room to do her bidding. He licked his fingertip then played with her clit, eager to serve.

Lucy rode him with a variety of motions designed to drive him insane. She rocked her hips in a series of short bursts that concentrated her tightest muscles on the head of his cock before grinding onto him fully.

The jerk of his erection inside her corresponded to the curses spilling from his lips. "Fuck. Ah. Shit. Yes. Damn!"

Colby slammed his hips upward with each utterance, his climax triggering a second wash of ecstasy in Lucy. He never could resist when she took charge. Spurts of his come splattered on her swollen tissue, filling her with his thick, white cream.

She raised herself until he shot the last strand on the outside of her pussy. Before she could rub the opalescent fluid into her flesh, he tugged her hip, forcing her to straddle his head. He surprised her when he devoured the pearly concoction.

Would he be so eager to ingest Silas's come?

The thought rocketed her to an instant orgasm. She ground her pussy on her husband's wriggling tongue. Before she could process what had happened, he'd tucked her into his solid embrace—face to face—so she could ride out the storm.

"Things are different already," he whispered into her hair. "That was..."

"Amazing." She panted, her breath impossible to catch.

"Wild." He massaged her relaxing muscles, sighing when she settled more fully against the contours of his body. "The same, but better."

"Exactly." Lucy couldn't stop touching her husband, petting every inch of exposed skin. "Scary."

"Why?" He cupped her cheek in his hand, tilting her face toward his.

"I'm afraid our relationship will never be the same."

"Only enhanced, Lu." His half-hard cock perked up when he communicated his optimism with a thorough kiss. "We'll never lose this."

They rocked together until the length of his erection firmed against her belly. He reached down and slipped inside her once more. They soothed each other with tender, lingering touches that focused on bonding rather than fucking for the sake of the prize at the end of the performance.

Lucy had never fathomed such an intimate exchange could exist. She couldn't say how long they held each other, hours maybe, before a gentle, reassuring warmth rained over her soul to match the heat flooding her womb. Ecstasy washed her clean of her troubles.

Colby stared into her eyes as he surrendered. The vocalization of their love became unnecessary as he communicated the value of their mating on a level far beyond words. She struggled to stay awake, to linger on the alternate plane they'd created with their exchange, but before she was ready, exhaustion and the security of his hold lulled her to sleep.

When she woke, Colby was gone.

Chapter Five

Silas groaned. He attempted to roll over to relieve the discomfort in his side but a canvas strap around his waist pinned him to a gurney. Fuck! He'd objected to being shipped home like a hunk of meat. Doctors had overruled his arguments. Crowded Alaskan hospitals forced them to release him despite his protests.

Once the insurance company found out about Lucy and the exceptional level of homecare she'd offered to provide, they'd assumed he would be thrilled. When he'd fought instead, the doctors had subdued him with a shot of something strong.

So strong he didn't remember anything else until this moment. Probably for the best.

Voices swirled around his clouded mind. He couldn't quite make out what they were saying. Then a beam of light stabbed through an opening to his left, illuminating the interior of a tiny plane, and hot air buffeted his face. At least it seemed steamy to him.

Silas didn't have to wonder where in the world he lay or if this stop were a transfer en route because fresh air enveloped him like a comforting hug, easing the pain he'd endured for the past month. No, since he'd left this place. His heaven on earth.

The smell of home—fresh mountain air, late summer flowers and hints of the cow pasture near the ranch's airfield—had him flaring his nostrils like a stallion scenting a mare in heat. He blinked and shook his head, struggling to stay awake.

Ironic, considering all the times he'd battled the intrusion of his alarm to linger in a dream of Compass Ranch a moment or two longer.

He might have thought it another vision, or maybe heaven this time, when a familiar woman called to him. "Oh, Silas."

The backlighting of the hatch caused a blurry silhouette, haloed by Wyoming sunshine, to materialize above him. Thank God for the buckles locking his arms by his sides or he wouldn't have been able to prevent himself from groping forbidden fruit. The lure of his personal siren's proximity after years and miles of separation overwhelmed all his logic.

"Lucy." The gruff bark seemed indecipherable but she came closer, dropping to her knees beside him. His frustrated bellows, not to mention the sedation the Alaskan interns had forced on him, acted like nettles stuffed down his throat.

"Si." The ragged gasps of her breath betrayed her weeping, though he still couldn't see her clearly. "Look at you."

Gentle hands stroked his scruffy face, his chest and his arms, stealing his ability to speak. When she entwined their fingers and laid her head on his shoulder, whispering prayers of thanks for his safety over his heart, he stared at her gorgeous mane of curls. Some things never changed.

"Come on, sweetheart."

Silas tensed at the inherent command radiating from the latest form, highlighted by the sun. "Let's take him home. We'll catch up there."

"Colby?" It seemed some things did change. The broad, filled-out form exuded power and a potent strength Silas didn't quite remember. Impressive. He hoped whatever blanket they'd covered him with for the trip hid the erection struggling to form despite the drugs lingering in his system.

His gut clenched, and he closed his eyes. Leaving had been the smart decision. He never could have controlled himself around these two. Reports of home from his brothers and his parents confirmed the couple's lasting happiness. He had no business intruding.

Colby crouched near his wife, one hand rubbing her back with an ease that made it clear he'd done it a million times before. Silas had never built familiarity with a partner. Other than Red, he'd forbidden repeat performances. His chest ached with regret.

For his friend.

For himself.

What would it be like to have that kind of unconditional support? He'd flown solo long enough to forget.

The tiny space grew cramped to the max when the weight of another passenger rocked the aircraft. This set of shoulders blocked the sun entirely. Lucy, Colby and JD came into view, the sight so overwhelming it almost knocked him out again. He swam toward the sunshine, the heat and the people he treasured. He couldn't bear to depart again so soon.

"Welcome home, son."

Surely, the rasp in his father's greeting had to do with his aging and not unbridled emotion. Right?

"JD." He couldn't say more but didn't have to. Three sets of hands braced him now, promising to lend him strength.

"Rest. We've got you," JD reassured him. "You'll need all your energy when your mama sees you. Prepare yourself. She's likely to squeeze you in half...or beat your ass with a wooden spoon. It's kind of a toss-up at this point."

Silas laughed, or tried to. The pain in his side dimmed his vision.

No! He scrambled toward the shimmering light but couldn't gain a firm toehold on consciousness. He spiraled into nothingness, everything in him straining to rejoin his family.

Lucy sat in the corner of the room, watching Victoria alternate sobs with shouts at her stubborn son, who occupied the king-sized bed in the center of his boyhood room. Colby stood by Lucy's side, his supportive grip on her shoulder helping to keep her relaxed.

Well, as much as she could be.

She'd anticipated that the jolt of desire Silas had always inspired in her would rear between them when they connected once more. And it had. But the intensity of the reaction had surprised her. It flared a hundred times brighter than the naïve infatuation she'd experienced as a young girl.

The injuries dotting his body, draining his alertness, had stopped her from mounting him where he lay. The wounds evident in his tortured gaze had broken her heart. She shivered as she remembered the undisguised agony she'd spotted in his dazed stare.

"Want me to find your sweater?" Colby whispered near her ear.

"No thanks." She capitalized on his nearness, stealing a kiss, needing the fortification to gel her insides, which threatened to dissolve into a pile of mush.

"He's going to be okay." Her husband sipped from her lips again.

"Are *we*?" She shivered again. "Did you feel it? The connection..."

"Did I?" Colby breathed hard though she doubted their kisses inspired his elevated respiration. "I still do."

Lucy couldn't help herself. She glanced at the crotch of her husband's ripped work jeans, sighing when she spotted the bulge there.

"Behave." He rearranged himself. The gesture didn't obscure the evidence. "I'm trying not to be obvious here, but it won't quit."

"Want me to take care of you?" Lucy squirmed in the chair. It'd been three hours since Silas had crashed into their lives again and already she thought she might die if someone didn't touch her soon. "I'll meet you in the bathroom downstairs in five minutes. I bet Vicky's good for another half hour of lecturing."

"At least." Colby winced.

They'd all faced the mama bear's wrath once or twice, but even the time Sawyer had gotten caught stealing from the general store for the hell of it his junior year of high school had generated less stern disappointment than this.

"When you have problems, you don't run from family. You *trust* the people who love you. I did not raise you to shirk your responsibilities. Your place was here. Always here. Not like your brothers, who dreamed of something else. What made you think the answer was lying to us? To yourself? To Colby and Lucy?"

"I feel kind of bad abandoning him. Especially for a BJ. Even one of yours, baby." Her husband hunched his shoulders and jammed his hands in his pockets when Vicky aimed her laser vision at him. He froze—like a deer in the headlights—until she turned back to her eldest son, disaster averted.

"...disrespectful..."

Lucy peeked up at Colby and grinned. Someday she hoped to have half as much command over her men and their children.

Men?

Oh damn, when had she gotten so greedy? Could it really be possible to keep them both? She had to try at least.

"...wasteful..."

Something about the energy surrounding the three of them when they'd touched in the ranch's plane, which they'd rigged to haul their damaged friend home from Cheyenne, had electrified her. Given her hope.

"...unhealthy..."

Lucy grimaced at the rising pitch of Vicky's diatribe. She thought she could hear dogs howling in the yard. When she shifted to leave the room, regardless of the danger from Silas's mom, the tirade stopped short.

"And I love you more than I can say. I missed you, Silas."

Vicky smothered her son in hug tight enough to break another rib or two. “Please, don’t ever do that to us, or yourself, again. This accident is a blessing in disguise. It’s brought you home, where you belong.”

“Is this still my place?” Silas broke his silence.

“Absolutely.” Vicky answered before either Colby or Lucy could interject.

“How do you know?” Their injured friend fiddled with the edge of the blanket covering him.

“Because I’m your mother.” She kissed his forehead then glanced toward the corner where Lucy and Colby waited. “You can still set things to rights. Be true to yourself. Make me proud, Silas.”

“I’m working on it.” He sighed. “I don’t blame you for not believing me, but it’s what I always tried to do.”

“Foolish boy.” Her warm tone betrayed the true feelings behind her criticism. “Don’t struggle so hard. The solution is easy if you let it be. Listen to your heart.”

Vicky rested her palm on her son’s bare chest before nodding then leaving the room, shutting the door behind her.

No one moved.

No one spoke.

Lucy couldn’t swear she breathed.

Colby acted first. He pried her white-knuckled fingers from the arms of her chair then helped her stand. Together they walked, side by side, toward the bed. Toward Silas.

The puffy slashes of fresh scars marring his skin threatened to distract her. He seemed so pale. Whether his injuries or his time hidden from the sun had leeched his color she couldn’t tell. It made him appear cold. So did his tight nipples, which stood proud above the line of the sheet. The bright cotton cover obscured the lower half of his body from her wandering gaze.

He hadn’t shaved in forever. The scruffiness worked for

him. Still, she couldn't wait for him to reveal his strong jaw and the other hints of masculinity he'd grown into well.

"Christ, you're so beautiful. More than I guessed, Lu."

When his compliment knocked her off balance, he covered the gap.

"Are you going to yell at me too?" The mischievous grin she recognized from their childhood made an appearance even if it seemed a little rusty.

"Not exactly what I had in mind." Colby answered for them both. He scrubbed his hands through his sun-bleached hair then cursed. "Hell if I know where to go from here, though."

Lucy opened her mouth to make a suggestion. Silas interrupted. "Can I ask you something first?"

She nodded.

"Are you happy, Lu?" He tilted his head when her eyes narrowed. "I mean, really happy. And Colby too. Please promise me those lonely nights were worth it."

"Jesus, dickhead." Colby filled in when no sound would pass the knot in her throat. "Did you listen to one word Vicky said?"

"Yeah, she told me to follow my heart." Silas's rugged face, stressed by years of hard living—and, if she wasn't mistaken, dented by the subtle unevenness caused by patches of frostbite—expressed his genuine interest. "All it's ever wanted was to protect you. Both of you. To preserve your happiness."

Lucy exchanged a look with her husband, enough to convey more than an entire conversation between most people. Colby nodded.

"Clearly, you didn't read a single one of my letters." Lucy plopped onto the mattress when her knees buckled. "Wow, that's probably a solid three months of my life wasted."

Maybe they'd deluded themselves all this time. Had Silas departed without a glance over his shoulder? Had his nobility supplied a convenient excuse? She scooted toward the edge, prepared to leave and reevaluate the situation, when his hand braceleted her wrist.

His hold sent electricity through her core.

"I couldn't." He coughed after the rush of air he'd expelled, his lungs still not fully recovered. When the fit extended, Silas's face flushing an unhealthy shade of purple, she reached for the pitcher of water beside the bed.

Colby wrapped his arm around Silas's shoulders then tipped their lost friend forward until she could touch the cup she held to his lips. He didn't drink for a moment, as though his pride rebelled at needing help to accomplish something so simple. Eventually, he accepted her offering.

The cool liquid soothed Silas. Lucy expected her husband to lower the man to the mountain of pillows arranged behind him. Instead, he stared at the expanse of their friend's back.

"You should see this, Lu."

"Does he have more cuts and burns there?" She nibbled her lip. Nurses couldn't be squeamish. She usually wasn't, but the extensive damage Silas had sustained wrung her stomach. "Should I grab some fresh bandages?"

"Yeah, he's pretty tore up. That's not what I'm talking about, though."

Silas met her gaze. He stared, offering no input. Close enough to kiss him, she watched him lick the last of the water droplets from his cracked lips. She opened a tube of balm she'd laid by the bed, part of her standard patient kit, and swirled some onto her finger. She'd applied the silky gel to many people in her career. None of them had made it seem like a dirty act. Tracing Silas's parted mouth inspired her to flush then avert her eyes.

They weren't ready yet.

Lucy forced herself to retreat, at least far enough to carefully straddle him as she crossed to his other side. Examining him from beneath Colby's supportive hold would prove impossible. She gasped when something hard and long brushed her thigh. "You're supposed to be sick."

"I'd have to be dead not to get a rise in my Levi's with you in my lap."

"Amen." Colby chuckled from where he kept Silas upright. "Except you're not wearing any pants, big guy. There's some serious crackage happening back here."

"I think I'm skipping down the yellow brick road in Oz about now. It looks like I'm on Compass Ranch, but I really cracked my skull in that explosion and I'm lying on the rig while the world burns around me."

"God, Si." Lucy couldn't stop herself from hugging him. She wrapped herself lightly around his torso and visualized absorbing his pain. Her touch seemed to break him from the memories assaulting him, at least long enough for him to make a joke.

"Any minute now flying monkeys are going to zoom past that fucking window. Keep the crazy lady on the bike away from me, okay? She gives me the willies."

"Is it impossible to believe you're home?" Lucy stroked his fuzzy cheek.

"It's either that or you're all insane. Most husbands wouldn't find it amusing when some random guy wants to fuck his wife."

"I'm not most husbands. And you're not any guy."

"That probably makes this worse." Silas arched his hips, grinding himself against Lucy's mound. She thought she might come on the spot. He desired her!

Relief poised her on the verge of tears and had naughty ideas screaming for attention.

Lucy scrambled to the other side of her patient before she landed them all in trouble. If he needed medical attention, that had to come first. They could figure out the rest later. It was enough that attraction zinged through him too.

When she spied what her husband stared at, she gasped.

"Oh, my God."

"Is it ruined?" Silas's frame heaved with the disappointment he couldn't suppress, shifting the image decorating his strong flesh. "Is Snake still around? Maybe he can fix it up for me."

"Hell, no. I mean, Snake's still kicking but..." Colby murmured reverently, "it's fucking great. Perfect. I wish I'd thought of it."

Lucy couldn't stop herself. She traced the compass spanning his shoulders with her index finger. "It's crazy, Si. There are slices, yellowed bruises, half-healed blisters and scrapes all around it. But nothing touched the tattoo. Not one single thing harmed it."

"Maybe Mom is right."

"Isn't she always?" Colby ducked down for a better look. "What is that, there, between the cattle brand and the barn? I see something in the shadows."

"No one's ever noticed before." Silas groaned. "Not even my brothers."

"It's your name, Colby." Lucy bent forward to kiss the patch of skin, honoring the bond that had driven Si to carry her husband with him always. She'd known the instant she witnessed their embrace in the barn, they were meant for each other.

"Holy crap. You're right. It is." Colby's shock might have been funny if the significance of the moment didn't ripple through their entire lives. "And yours."

"What?" She followed the direction of her husband's pointing finger. Then she saw it. The tail of the y in her name entwined with the o in Colby.

Her hand flew to her mouth. Her knuckles couldn't stifle her sob.

"Now you did it, Si. You made our girl cry." He settled the injured man against the pillows, allowing both guys to peer into her unfocused eyes.

Lucy touched her cheeks with trembling fingers. Sure enough, tears dampened the skin there. She couldn't resist them any longer.

When she held her arms out to Colby, he lifted her over Silas's torso, into his arms. Instead of burrowing into his chest as she usually did on the rare occasions she succumbed to the need for a good cry, she kissed his jaw then turned. Careful not to hurt Silas, she tucked beneath his left arm and rested her cheek on his chest.

He stiffened beneath her for a few seconds before her tears melted his rigid hold.

"Shh, Lu." He petted her hair with awkward pats. "Please, it destroys me when you're upset."

She couldn't stem the flood now that it had started. In the periphery of her blurry vision, she caught him shooting Colby a plea for help. Her husband knew how to comfort her. He lowered himself to the mattress behind her, snuggling up tight to whisper soothing nonsense in her ear while he bracketed her with warmth.

Silas curled his arm around them both, his grip faint yet discernable.

"I'm sorry, Lucy." His voice weakened, as though her misery sapped his strength. His agony increased the flow of her tears. She cried for all the nights they'd spent apart. For all the times he'd had no one to lean on. For so many wasted years.

"Do you have any concept of what you're apologizing for?" Colby sounded kind of pissed. She couldn't catch her breath long enough to referee.

"Not really." Silas went slack beneath her. "Anything that causes her pain. Everything I've ever done. All the stuff I've fucked up. For all three of us..."

He whispered the last.

"If you hadn't trashed her letters maybe you would have figured it out sooner. She told you every fucking day. How much she missed you. How much we needed you. The gaping hole you left behind never closed up. Never healed over." Colby found the strength to say what she couldn't. Not again. "She told you over and over that we care for you, and that we'd always be here, waiting for you to come home. You bastard."

Silas shivered beneath her.

"Kept them. Every one. In my duffle, have them all. Waited for them. Collected them. Slept with one under my pillow. Couldn't read them. Couldn't stand to hear about the one place I ached to be and could never go," Silas murmured, on the verge of losing consciousness again. It'd been a long day, full of stress and sedatives strong enough to knock out a horse. "I never stopped loving you either. Promise."

Silas's confession and the running stream of Lucy's tears consumed the last of his stamina. He faded into a restless sleep beneath her cheek. For a long time, she clung to the man she'd lost while the one who'd caught her did it again. The three of them stayed like that.

Together.

All night long.

Silas picked at the knot in the tattered ribbon securing the bundle of letters he'd received in the first six months he spent in Alaska. After Lucy had departed for the day to tend her other patients, amidst a slew of unnecessary apologies, Colby had set the bricks of correspondence on the tray at Silas's side then unplugged the TV in his room.

"You can stare at the wall all day, or you can read those."

How fucking demented did it make Silas that Colby's iron will turned him on? The innate authority his friend possessed made the prospect of topping the man that much more alluring. He'd give every penny of the wages he'd hoarded for the past decade to bend Colby over the edge of the bed and screw him senseless.

He could make the foreman enjoy it.

Beg for more.

Caught in the daydream of burying himself repeatedly in Colby's tight heat, penetrating the ass he suspected had never welcomed a stiff cock, he tuned out the rest of the frustrated man's rant until Colby grabbed his hair as though he might attempt to tug it out. Silas blinked, dissolving the lurid movie playing in his imagination. Torn between admitting his depravity and letting his friend assume he'd ignored him on purpose, Silas hesitated too long.

Colby started to say something but closed his mouth, opened it again then spun on the heel of his boot. He reappeared in the doorway long enough to toss a cordless phone onto the bed. "Lucy's one, I'm two and JD is three on speed dial. Your mom will be back from her lunch with Lydia Redmond in an hour or so. Sometimes they like to shop afterward, though I doubt she will today."

Colby clomped down the stairs and onto the front porch. The screen door slammed behind him. Good thing Vicky hadn't heard it. She'd have ripped him a new one, foreman or not.

Silas tried to doze, but the sweet oblivion of sleep eluded him. Hell, he'd spent most of the past month unconscious. His body healed exponentially now, fueling his impatience to be up and about again. Especially with the lure of Compass Ranch right outside these prison walls.

He idled another quarter hour testing the strength in his leg.

He'd managed to convince himself he might be able to stand without the crutches propped near the door, ten feet from his resting place, until he twisted something funny and delivered a bolt of agony up his spine. The resulting jerk of his torso tweaked his ribs. Sweating, cursing and grumbling, he resettled himself on the pillows. He couldn't achieve the level of comfort Lucy had provided when she'd tended him.

In an act of desperation, he stared at his laptop, willing the hunk of plastic and metal to levitate to the bed from the desk as though he'd mastered the Jedi mind trick.

No such luck.

The yellowed paper of Lucy's letters scared the shit out of him and tempted him at the same time. Sort of like the woman who'd authored them. He trailed the tip of one finger over their edges, noting the dulled corners on most from his frequent handling.

If he were honest, he'd admit he'd never opened them because he would have run straight home if she'd given him the slightest bit of hope. How stupid had he been all those years? What had really frightened him?

Would he continue on as he had, or find the courage to do better? Suddenly, it seemed as though the only person with a problem accepting the truth was him.

"Son of a bitch." Silas worked the knot until the faded satin unraveled. He plucked the first letter from the stack and slid his finger beneath the flap on the back. With one motion, he shredded the seal along the top then withdrew the lined paper from within.

Lucy's elegant script flowed over page after page.

Dear Silas,

I can't say how many times I've written that salutation yet never before have I meant it so sincerely. Today is the first day Compass Ranch is without you and the absence is horrifyingly apparent. Colby and Seth took your place, covering your chores and their own. Colby even made your run to town with the extra chicken eggs for the farmer's market since it's Tuesday.

I thought Sam and Sawyer might want a cut of the responsibility, but the twins don't seem to share the same love for this life as we do. For Colby, it's a golden opportunity. I can see how it might be more of a burden on your brothers. At least now. They're young and eager for freedom. Same as you, I suppose. As for Colby, well, something's different in him already. Without you here to lean on, he's growing minute by minute and you'd find his newfound confidence as attractive as I do.

Oh, Silas. How can I ignore it any longer? I suppose I'm writing to tell you how sorry I am to have stolen him from you. Please, come home. If you return, I'll leave him to you fair and square. You crave him as much as I do, that much is apparent. And he showed you more hunger than I've ever been able to coax from behind his restraint.

I suppose that's truth of why I ran. When I saw you...in the barn. It's important to me that you understand.

The sight terrified me. It's been the three of us for so long. How can I live alone? Separated? Hell, we are now anyway. It's not right, Silas.

The way you touched him, the way you both grappled to get closer, it knocked the wind from me. Not because your raw desire horrified me, quite the opposite, but because the passion on your faces convinced me I'd lost you both.

Neither of you has coveted me with such ferocity.

"The fuck we haven't!" Silas roared to the empty ranch house. "How could you think that, Lucy?"

Even as he asked, he rewound time and imagined viewing the past through her lens. He'd done his best to preserve her innocence—to protect her from the savage needs raging inside him. Time after time he'd fucked up by trying to shelter her and Colby when he should have admitted they were tough enough to take what he had to give.

He refused to insult them any longer.

He'd finish reading this letter. Then all the others, every last one. Ten years of history through the eyes of the woman he loved. Had always loved.

Tonight he'd come clean. He'd put his soul on display and stand naked before them, all faults exposed, allowing them to decide his future.

Their future.

Until then, he'd hope for a miracle. He'd need one to ensure it wasn't too late.

Chapter Six

Victoria called out as she climbed the stairs, giving Silas a heads up before she intruded on his thoughts. It wasn't as though Lucy, Colby, or both, entertained him. He should be so lucky. After the hours he'd spent reading, he doubted they planned to return this century.

He winced as he recalled one particular note he wouldn't forget anytime soon. Lucy had vented her anger, calling him every name in the book and some colorful variations he gave her kudos for inventing. The scathing rebuke followed a spur of the moment visit she'd made to the fishing hole he and Colby had often frequented. Truthfully, they'd done more goofing off than actual fishing. The secluded spot had sheltered them from prying eyes and ears when—in the early days—the burden of Colby's past had threatened to smother the teenager with darkness.

Lucy had described the anguish she'd witnessed on her fiancé's face when she'd happened upon him. She'd hidden in the brush, horrified, when the man she loved dropped to his knees and sobbed, begging forgiveness for moving on without Silas as part of their relationship. Her justified outrage had crackled throughout the missive, which included several scratch-outs deep enough to tear her pretty, floral stationary.

The worst of the damage to the note centered around her accusation that he'd tarnished the joy she felt every time she glanced at the token of Colby's fidelity and devotion. The engagement ring she'd prized studying in the sunlight seemed a little dirty after that day.

For that alone Silas owed her more apologies than he could utter in a lifetime.

"Silas!" His mother spoke as she rounded the corner. "Lucy and Colby are running late. Mr. Thead had to have an extra infusion and one of the fences in the west pasture needed mending. But your brothers would like to talk to you."

When she took in the pile of paper covering the mattress, she stutter-stepped but recovered quickly. She smiled, nodding in his direction.

"Are Seth, Sam and Sawyer online?" He checked the clock. With the wide variety in their time zones, it was rare they all were available to gather together for a quick conversation. They managed it when they could.

"I guess. Seth called. He said something about a web whatsit."

Silas barked a laugh. He'd done more of that in the last twenty-four hours than the past several years. "If you hand me my laptop, I'll show you."

Vicky passed him the computer then kissed his cheek while he got things up and running. "You're looking better already."

"Thanks. For everything." He smiled at his mother, unsure of what more to say. She understood anyway.

"Would you mind cracking the window?" He craved the fresh air he'd sampled yesterday and the sounds of the country at night. The cool breeze would help mitigate the raging inferno in his belly, ignited by the hundreds of letters he'd read today.

"Have you forgotten how chilly it is at night?"

"Are you kidding? Hell, most of the drafty places I stayed in were colder in the middle of a summer day."

She winced but didn't argue. Instead, she shrugged and did as he asked.

Silas logged on to the web conferencing service Sam used

for business. In the late evening, Eastern Time, no one in the New York office minded them hopping on the line. Hard to believe his little brother had become a powerful stock analyst on Wall Street. Silas had cracked up when he heard they called him The Cowboy.

A series of three dings proved Seth, Sam and Sawyer waited for him to join. He selected their names from the list onscreen then entered the conference.

"You should have seen them. Smoking hot quadruplets, Sam." Silas's brother out west bragged to his twin. "Two for you, two for me."

"Sawyer Compton, what kind of trouble are you digging up now?" Vicky laughed at the horror on her youngest son's face.

"Dude, a little warning would have been nice before you tossed Mom on the line." To see the Coastie blush made Silas's day.

Four pictures divided his screen. He'd placed the images of his brothers as they were situated around the country. His window on top. Sawyer—in San Francisco—on the left, Sam—in New York—on the right and Seth—in Texas—at the bottom.

"Hello, my sons." Vicky tried a finger wave, giggling at the reflection of herself on the screen.

"Hi, Mom." Funny how the appearance of one small woman could change them all in an instant.

"All right, I can tell I'm crashing this party. Just had to see my boys a second. Have fun and call me soon. I love you."

A chorus of "Love you too" echoed through the crappy, built-in speakers.

As soon as the door shut, Silas announced. "Okay, she's out."

"How much of that did she hear?" Sawyer adjusted his uniform. He must be on a dinner break.

"Obviously I missed a good story. Nothing but the last few words came across. You're clear."

"Holy shit, I almost had a heart attack."

"Her and JD aren't exactly prudes." Seth—kicked back in jeans and no shirt with a beer in hand after a long hard day—supplied some dirt. "I heard from Jim Spade they tore it up in the day. Plus, remember the time Sam walked in on them in the kitchen?"

"Gross. I could have gone my whole life without thinking about that again, fuckwad." Sam rolled the sleeves on his expensive shirt to his elbows. Knowing him, he'd planned to head out soon to wine and dine some sophisticate at a restaurant so exclusive, Silas could only imagine what it'd be like.

He'd probably hate it.

"Moving on..." Seth grinned. "How the hell are you, bro? Surly as ever, I guess. The mountain man beard is a nice touch."

"Better today than yesterday." Silas noted the real concern beneath the teasing. As the oldest brother, he'd always been the one to look after them, not the other way around. "Can't wait to climb out of this bed. Maybe take Rainey for a ride."

"Why not stay there? Give Lucy a go, instead. Hell of a lot more fun than a middle-aged horse." Sam laughed at his crass joke. No one else did. "Oh, fuck. Too soon?"

"Moron." Seth shook his head.

Silas growled. "Don't talk about her like that. She's married."

Not that he hadn't thought the same thing himself a time or two today.

"To a man who's as hot for you as she is." Sawyer didn't zip his big mouth despite the glare from Seth. "How long are we gonna pretend we don't notice them begging for scraps of information from us? How many times are we gonna let Silas fuck things up? One of these days it'll be too late. If I had that kind of love in my life, I sure as shit wouldn't waste it."

"It doesn't freak you guys out? The whole Colby thing?"

Silas had struggled with sharing his bisexuality with his brothers for years. Could it be that easy?

"I don't care to hear the play by play, but who you fuck is your business." Seth acted as the spokesperson. The twins nodded agreement. "If I can stand to listen to Sawyer go on about his whips and chains, I think I can handle you getting moony over a guy we all respect."

"I think it's kind of hot." Sawyer shrugged. They all knew of his penchant for BDSM. Power games appealed to their youngest brother. "Not my thing exactly, but I can see how having another guy submit would be a turn on. Don't act like you've never shared a woman with another dude, Sam. You have. And you liked it."

"Sawyer—"

"No, the kid's right." Silas shrugged when all three of his brothers stared, speechless. "I've done a lot of thinking lately. More today."

He grabbed a handful of crumpled envelopes and let them rain around him. "I won't hide who I am anymore."

"You read her letters." Sam's eyes went as big as silver dollars.

"Holy shit." Seth dropped his feet off his desk, leaning closer to his monitor to better inspect the background. "They're everywhere."

"What was in them?" Sawyer had always been curious. "I can't tell you how many Christmases, Thanksgivings and nights I spent on leave that I'd watch little Lucy huddled with a pad and a pen, writing like mad. She never gave me a peek, though. What did she write you?"

"Everything." Silas grimaced when his voice cracked a bit. "It's the best gift I could have imagined. A time machine. Every bit of the ten years I missed, it's all here. There were even some pictures."

He held up a few snapshots for his brothers to check out.

"Ohhh, did she include good bits too?" Sam wiggled his

brows. “Nasty stuff?”

Silas chose not to inform his brothers of the detailed account of the night Colby had taken Lucy’s virginity. Or the night he’d proposed. Silas figured if he kept reading straight through to tomorrow he might find their wedding night in the heartfelt notes she’d kept as religiously as a diary.

“Damn! She *did* write about that stuff. Look at his face.”

Before Silas could make them fuck off, a distraction deflected the heat from his revelation.

A sassy voice called out from somewhere, “Tell your brothers it’s not nice to kiss and tell. Well, I suppose this Lucy did, but sharing a note with a lover is different than tossing those fantasies to a pack of rabid, ungrateful, fickle cowboys.”

“Who the hell was that?” Sawyer jumped at the rebuke.

“Only the cowgirl your fucking asshole brother is keeping prisoner in this godforsaken shack. Will someone please call 911?”

Seth grinned into the camera before tossing over his shoulder, “Don’t make me gag you, darlin’.”

“Holy shit.” Sam leaned closer to the camera. “What is that in the background? Do I see pretty ankles tied to the end of your bed, Seth?”

“I’m Jody Kirkland! My dad is your brother’s boss. He’ll probably also be the man to murder this piece of shit, arrogant, limp dick when he finds out what he’s up to.”

“I’ll give you arrogant, but I’m guessing Seth’s anything but a limp dick right now, honey.” Sam braved his brother’s wrath.

Silas agreed. A woman that spirited would be worth a black eye or two.

“Argh! You’re all alike. I can’t believe there are really *four* of you. Thank God you spread yourselves out. No state should have to house that many Compass brothers. Especially if you’re all as dense as Seth.”

“I like this girl.” Sawyer grinned in response.

"So, you're calling the police?" The legs thrashed at the corner of the mattress.

"I don't think my mom would appreciate Seth missing out on the next ten Christmases because he's in jail." Sawyer winked at his brothers. "Sorry, honey. I bet he could help you make the most of the situation."

"You're all bastards. Every one of you asshats!"

"Jody. Give me two minutes. Then we'll talk, okay?" Seth's exasperated groan spoke volumes. Silas didn't try to hide his enjoyment of his brother's frustration. At least he wasn't the only one who did stupid shit when his guts were in a knot. "Si, I swear I thought I'd crapped my pants when they told me you'd almost blown up. So I'm going to say this flat out. I know you're still on the mend but ignoring what Lucy and Colby are offering would be ridiculous."

"Says the man talking to his brothers instead of playing with the sexy woman tied to his bed, about to escape."

Silas enjoyed the hell out of the surprise on his brother's face. Sam and Sawyer showed their appreciation with whistles and catcalls.

"What!" Seth spun in his chair. When he spotted Jody—naked, in the camera's line of sight as she undid the last of the knots—he lost it. He snagged a blanket off the foot of his bed then wrapped it around her. "What the hell do you think you're doing?"

"Leaving, moron!" She thrashed in Seth's embrace until his brother hefted her over his shoulder, bundled in the blanket.

"Okay, as fun as this is, I have to be on deck in five minutes." Sawyer grimaced. "Someone better fill me in later."

"No, there will be no filling in!" Seth marched to the camera, blocking it with his palm. "I have to go, Si. We'll talk more. Soon."

His connection terminated with a generic beep, leaving Sam and Silas alone on the line. They looked at each other and laughed.

"Almost time for me to hit the city, bro." Sam stretched, taking his suit coat from a hanger behind him.

"Hot date?"

"Sort of. Been spending some time with a girl I work with." His grimace promised it could spell disaster. "I think she's worth the risk."

"Trust your gut, Sam. I should have done the same a long time ago."

His brother nodded. "I'm glad you're home. Safe."

"When are you coming to visit?" Sam made it out to Compass Ranch almost as infrequently as he had. "It's not the same without you three around to piss me off."

"Too hard to fit in a trip. I'm in the running for VP, Si." The corners of his brother's mouth kicked up. "I'd be the youngest in the history of the company."

"We all have our dreams, Sam." Silas couldn't begrudge his brother a shot at his. "Good luck."

"You, too." Sam smiled. "I think you're going to need it."

Colby slid from his horse, exhausted and sweaty. Dozens of snags had mutated his light day into a saga of never-ending hassles. From cowboys fist-fighting over a woman, to a handful of sick steers, to a busted fence, the ranch had conspired against him quitting early. He couldn't wait to find out how Silas had spent his time alone.

"I can take care of Couper for you," Jake offered when he caught Colby peering at the house. "I don't mind, foreman."

"Thank you." He slapped the man on the shoulder. "I'll cover you next time, deal?"

"Deal."

Colby glanced at the light shining from the upstairs window. Was Lucy in there, comforting their man, already? A twinge of unease ran through him. What if Silas only chose her? What if Colby fooled around with Silas and it didn't make him as hot as he thought?

Okay, really, now he was being ludicrous.

Colby had never sought the company of another man, but he and Lucy had talked frankly about how much the idea fired him up. Big time. They'd even played with some toys. It hadn't seemed the same, so they'd stashed the gadgets in their nightstand drawer.

Every now and then, when Lucy treated him to one of her spectacular blow jobs, she'd ream his ass with one of the moderate dildos. The combination spurred him to shoot so hard he feared he'd hurt, or worse, scare her. He never did. She would peek up at him with an evil grin then swallow the huge load he'd pumped down her throat.

Speak of the devil. The high-beams of his wife's Jeep surprised him as they flooded the yard. He strode to greet her with one last tip of his hat to the ranch hands. "Looks like you had the same kinda day I did, baby."

He handed Lucy down from the vehicle, taking her into his arms despite the fact that he stunk to high heaven. She didn't seem to mind.

"If you mean a royally sucky one, then yep." She rested her head on his chest, as though she absorbed strength from his embrace.

Colby adored providing for her.

He wrapped his hand around her elbow then escorted her into the house. As they passed through the kitchen, Vicky removed plates from the warming drawer and put them on a tray along with several beers. He studied the contents as he balanced it on one arm. "Three dinners? Silas hasn't eaten yet?"

"Stubborn boy insisted he'd wait for you two." Vicky smiled then kissed Colby and Lucy on the cheek. "JD and I are heading into town for a movie if you don't need us. Rick and Janice Lowell have been asking us to stop by for ages to check out their new guesthouse, too. You know how it is when JD and Rick start tossing back and shooting the shit. If they talk us into staying, we might not see you kids until tomorrow."

Colby hugged her extra tight. He was nobody's fool anymore than he was still a kid. "Thank you, Vicky."

"Welcome." Silas's mother squeezed Lucy's hand. As he and his wife climbed the hardwood stairs together, they heard Vicky calling, "JD Compton, get your ass in gear or we'll be late."

The threat worked. JD insisted on being on time for things. Before he and Lucy paused outside Silas's door, the engine to JD's truck turned over. Colby exchanged a long look with his wife. She smiled and nodded. They were ready to discover the possibilities together.

They held hands as Lucy knocked softly on the paneled door. "Silas?"

"Come in."

Lucy opened the door since Colby carried the tray. She stopped short in front of him, nearly causing him to smash their dinners between them. When he'd managed to control the wobble and rebalance his cargo, he noticed what had captured his wife's attention.

"You read them." A grin spread across Colby's face.

"Yeah." Silas patted the bed next to him. "Come here, sweetheart."

Lucy glanced over her shoulder for Colby's nod before sprinting across the small space and hopping onto the mattress. She laughed and dove through the crumpled envelopes as though they were a pile of fall leaves.

Silas tugged her closer, limiting her movement.

"Oh, shit, sorry. Did I jostle you?"

"I'm not delicate, Lu." Silas sat up straighter and hugged her. He kissed her cheek with infinite tenderness that threatened to close Colby's windpipe. How long had he waited to witness something like this?

"You look better today." His wife fit so well in his best friend's hold. She leaned back a little to study Silas.

"Feel better." He smiled into her eyes. "All because of you. These letters. Colby's understanding. All of it. I can't figure out where to start."

"How about with dinner? You need to eat, and so does Colby."

"I think I better hit the shower first or I'll ruin the chair." He did a quick sniff check and nearly passed out. "Definitely a shower."

"Want me to run your jeans through the wash?" Lucy offered.

"That bad, huh?" Colby examined his soiled clothes. "Yeah, I guess we better."

"There should be a pair of gym shorts in my duffle." Silas jerked his chin toward the bag on the floor. Then his eyes turned dark, hungry. "Or you could go without."

A tiny moan escaped Lucy, breaking the moment and making them all laugh.

"How 'bout you two concentrate on eating dinner and we'll see where things go from there?" Colby grinned when two gazes followed his progress around the room. He couldn't help but rile them further.

He toed off his boots then sidled into the bathroom to flip on the shower. When he'd adjusted the water, he shouted over his shoulder. "I'll leave the door open so I can hear in case you need anything."

Dual stares burned into his back as he shrugged his cotton button-down shirt from his shoulders. He dropped the garment into the hamper then ripped open his fly. Thank God. The pressure had been strangling his hard cock all day.

He peeled off his socks then tucked his fingers into his waistband and nudged his jeans until they dropped to his ankles. He stepped out of the denim then bent to deposit the rest of his dirty clothes in the laundry.

"Jesus!"

A girly giggle followed Silas's rough exclamation. "Hungry, Silas?"

"Starved."

"Go ahead and eat, then Lucy and I can swap." Colby called out. He couldn't resist one peek over his shoulder as he stepped into the shower. The naked lust on Silas's face matched the longing on his wife's. His cock jumped at their attention.

He slathered himself with suds, taking a world-record breaking shower. He made sure to wash all the important bits but forced himself to stop soaping his shaft when it would have been easy to lose control. So easy.

Colby rotated, allowing the water to sluice down his back and run between his ass cheeks. He canted forward, taking the spray against his sensitive hole, imagining what it would be like if it were someone's fingers—or tongue, or cock—caressing him instead.

Precome dripped from his crown onto the shower floor where it swirled in the eddy before disappearing down the drain. His plan almost backfired when he cupped his balls with one palm, fitting the other over the head of his cock.

"You're taking an awfully long time in there, foreman," Silas shouted from the other room. "Your dinner is getting cold."

The strangled sound that emerged when he tried to yell a retort betrayed him. Lucy and Silas laughed between the clinking of forks and knives on their plates. He shut the water off with a snap then toweled dry. He didn't trust himself to tempt them more than he already had.

Not yet.

When Colby wrapped the terrycloth around his waist, he realized hiding his erection would be impossible. He debated for all of ten seconds before deciding, what the fuck? No time like the present. He strode from the room, completely naked and obviously aroused.

"Is that our dessert?" Lucy collected Silas's empty plate, stacking it on her own, before kissing his cheek and heading toward the bathroom.

"Could be." Colby smiled, a little unsure of how to proceed.

"Why don't you tuck under the covers and eat your dinner while Lucy cleans up?"

The chill in the room couldn't account for the shiver that shook him at Silas's suggestion. He did as directed, twisting the top off a beer from the tray then digging in to his food. Sitting side by side with Silas, their shoulders leaning against the headboard, seemed surreal. He focused on the home cooking filling his growling stomach.

"I'd do just about anything for a big swig of that." Si reached toward the bottle. "Do you mind?"

"Should you drink when you're taking pain killers?"

The other man hesitated with his hand wrapped around the dewy brown glass.

"I haven't used any today. I won't be doing that again." Silas shook his head. "Between you and me, I'm done with *all* the hard stuff. Booze included. Kick my ass if you see me slipping, but I need a sip or two to make it through the next hour."

"I understand." Colby put his hand over Silas's on the beer, squeezing. He couldn't imagine how hard it had been for the other man so far from home. Lost in thought, he left his fingers there a little too long and things became awkward. He laughed, hating how nervous he sounded. "This is kind of weird after all this time."

"It is." Silas rounded on him, the newfound honesty he'd sworn to live by evident in his stormy eyes. "But we'll work it out. It'll become normal. Natural."

"You've done this before?" Colby hated the jealous prickle that climbed the nape of his neck. Hell, he'd spent the last ten years making love to Lucy every chance he found. Silas had to have had someone to turn to for companionship, for relief.

"With another guy?" Silas scrubbed his hand over his face then took a gulp of beer. He placed the bottle on the far side of

Colby's tray, away from himself. "Yeah. Lots of times. Would you hand me my shaving kit from my bag when you're done?"

Colby shoveled the last bite of mashed potatoes into his mouth to keep from cursing or having to answer at all. He couldn't risk blurting the wrong thing. His appetite diminished, he swung from the bed to retrieve Si's razor and the warm bowl of water sitting nearby.

As Silas removed layer after layer of whiskers, exposing his bare skin to the elements for the first time in a long time, Colby stewed. He picked at the blankets, trying not to stare at the familiar visage Silas revealed. Without facial hair, he reminded Colby of the young man he'd known. The friend he'd lost. The guy who'd left them to fuck a swath across the Arctic.

Was he angry? Jealous? Envious?

Lucy saved the day when she reappeared. Nothing obscured her beauty.

"Son of a bitch." Silas gawked so hard at the seductive curve of her pert breasts and the dip of her trim waist, Colby expected drool to gather at the corners of his mouth. The other man groaned when his wife did a sultry turn in the middle of the floor, shaking her ass and running her fingers down to her bare mound.

"I guess we both did a little trimming." She giggled. "You look handsome, Si."

"You're even sexier than I imagined, Lu. And I fantasized about it a lot."

"You did?" She nibbled her lip.

"Yeah, almost constantly." Si held out his hand and she approached to accept it. "I read those letters today, Lucy. I couldn't believe, all this time, you were scared I didn't find you attractive."

"What?" Colby's jaw dropped. "Baby, how could you think that? He used to lose it every time you came near."

"I know, right?" Silas's mouth twisted. His smile held a huge dose of cynicism and disgust. "I guess I did a great job of hiding my lust from her when she was too young. If she hadn't been so damn innocent she would have seen right though me. Like you did."

"All I could think about was how you two looked together." She probably didn't realize her hand had wandered to cup her breast as she recalled the fateful evening. "You were so wild, so hungry, so perfect."

"Would you like a repeat performance, now that we're all clean and fed?" Colby noticed Silas's cock tenting the sheet as much as his own did.

Lucy blinked, as though trying to concentrate on practical matters. "I didn't have time to do more than eat while you were in the shower. I didn't give him his medicine or help him clean up. Are you okay, Si? Do you need pills? Do you feel clean?"

"No."

"I can give you a sponge bath."

Both men groaned.

Chapter Seven

"While that's tempting, it isn't what I meant." Silas hung his head, something Colby didn't remember the proud man ever having done before.

His wife carried a porcelain basin to the sink in the bathroom and filled it with hot, soapy water. Colby swung his frame from the bed and toted the heavy load for her.

Damn woman never asked for help.

She whipped the quilt and sheet from the bed, exposing Silas to their roving stares. Despite the dozens of marks dotting his skin and the immobilizing brace keeping his femur in line, his physique still stole Colby's breath. "Holy shit."

"What he said." Lucy ogled Silas's thick cock, licking her lips, but their friend didn't seem to understand at first.

"They put a metal rod in my thigh. If someone leaves my crutches where I can reach them I might try them out tomorrow."

"Not by yourself. You'll wait until Colby can spot you." Lucy still didn't avert her gaze. "Roll over, Si."

"If I do, you won't be able to stare at my cock anymore."

She had the decency to blush. "It's more important to wash you clean."

"It'll take a hell of a lot more than a sponge bath to do that, sweetheart." Silas accepted Colby's hand as he scooted lower on the mattress then sprawled onto his front. He lifted his hips to arrange his enormous package.

The motion wiggled his ass, making Colby groan.

"Tell us about it, Si." Lucy dunked the sponge in the warm, soapy water then drew it over Silas's shoulders. She spent extra time swirling the moist material across the tattoo of Compass Ranch. "We're here. We're listening."

"I'm afraid I'll scare you both off."

"We'd never judge you." Colby watched, mesmerized, as his wife continued to soothe the man they both cherished. After she'd finished washing and drying a portion of Silas's skin, Colby couldn't help himself from joining in. He massaged the spaces between Si's injuries, gratified when tension left bunched muscles where he rubbed.

"The more I read today, the more I realized how *wholesome* you both are." He sighed deep enough for the persistent rattle in his lungs to echo in the room. "Colby, you messed around with a couple girls in high school, but once you hooked up with Lucy, she was all for you."

"And I've only ever been with Colby." Dunk, swish, dry. This time across Silas's lower back and the upper swells of his ass.

"Damn, sweetheart. That's so hot to me." Silas's hands started to fist on the sheets until Colby flattened them once more. "I'm not proud of it, but I spent a lot of nights trying anything to warm up inside. I fucked a ton of women. And men. I was always careful, always used protection, still..."

"You think we'd reject you because you've had a lot of partners?" Lucy tilted her head as she moved on to Si's powerful thighs, careful not to press too hard around the area of his fracture.

"I think you should. Not only because of how many there were but also because I did it without an ounce of caring."

"Not even for Red?" Lucy concentrated on washing Silas's feet.

A strangled groan burst from him when Colby followed in

her wake, massaging Silas's heels, pressing into the fleshy part of the soles with his thumbs.

"How do you know about Red?" Silas's question crackled with all the emotion he claimed not to have felt.

"I spoke to him on the phone a few months ago. I, sort of, called you every once in a while. Sorry for all the hang-ups." Lucy nudged Silas's hip. "Over."

Colby helped him roll onto his back. Silas's hard cock flopped onto his belly with a thud. "Okay, Red was different. Maybe, if I hadn't already loved you both, I could have been happy with him. I should have made him leave."

"You aren't responsible for what happened, Silas." Lucy paused her nurturing to kiss his scrunched eyelids.

"Maybe."

Colby rubbed Si's scalp, helping him relax again. Without pain pills, sitting in bed all day had to rip up such an active guy. "Look at me, Silas."

When the man complied, Colby leaned close. "We accept you despite your faults. If abandoning us for ten long years didn't tear us apart, then you sleeping around to fill the void won't do it either. If I hadn't had Lucy all this time, I have no idea what I would have done. At least you used protection."

"And I got tested. Every month." He winced. "There was a lot of shit circulating in those bunkhouses. I made sure I'm clean. I'd never put you at risk like that. Either of you. I just... needed to share. In case you're still interested in something more."

Colby couldn't stop himself from eliminating the gap between them. He fused his lips to Silas's, half-braced for rejection even now. He shouldn't have worried.

Si buried his fingers in Colby's damp hair and tugged him closer, devouring his mouth. Lost in the moment, he didn't realize the pressure on his cock was caused by more than the throbbing he'd experienced for two days straight. When Silas moaned into his parted lips, Colby cut his eyes toward his wife.

Lucy held a cock in each hand, pumping in time to the thrust of her men's tongues between each other's lips. Fuck, that was hot. He broke the kiss, needing a breath of air.

Silas coughed beneath him.

"Are you okay?"

"Fuck, yes." Si's head dropped against his pillows when Lucy finished scrubbing his chest and abdomen.

She trailed the sponge and her wet fingers along the ridge of muscle leading from Silas's hip to his groin. "This has to be the sexiest muscle on earth."

"Hey, I have that one too." Colby grinned.

"Maybe you should let me compare them side by side."

"I think your wife is up to something wicked," Silas warned.

"I learned a long time ago it's best not to put up a fight when her eyes have that glint to them." Colby beamed at her as he lay beside his best friend. The heated length of their fit bodies tucked together.

"You're so warm." Silas panted. "Finally, warm."

"Spread your legs. Both of you."

They obeyed without question. Without hesitation. Colby draped his left leg over Silas's right, the uninjured, thigh. Lucy knelt with one knee on either side of their stacked legs. The position spread her pussy, which pressed against Colby.

"Oh, shit." He groaned. "You should feel how wet she is. Scorching my thigh."

"Lucky bastard." Silas grinned. "But I can smell her arousal. Sweet. I bet she's delicious."

"She is." He smiled up at his wife, recalling the feast he'd made of her two nights before.

"Sweet and dirty too." Lucy laughed. "We're about to play a game. I'm going to suck you both. Whoever holds out longer gets to fuck me. Feel free to sabotage each other however you like."

Silas turned to Colby and growled, "You're going down."

"No, I am." Lucy chuckled around Silas's shaft as she pumped Colby with her petite hand. Her soft skin always had him harder than a rock in seconds.

"Oh, damn." Si shuddered. "You don't play around. She took me balls deep on the first pass. Not many women can do that."

"I've been training her for you." Colby grinned. "You're welcome."

"I owe you. Big time."

"Then show me what *you've* learned. Teach me how to be with another man. What do you like, Si?"

The man beside him hesitated. "Uh..."

Lucy pulled her mouth off Silas's cock with a slurp. Her familiar touch engulfed Colby's hard-on, pushing him dangerously close to the edge within seconds. Lying with the two of them ranked high on his list of fantasies.

Less distracted, Silas focused. "You don't understand. I never made love to another man. I've fucked them, sure. Nothing more. I, uh, I've never kissed a guy before. Or any women while I was away for that matter."

"Give me more then." It thrilled Colby that Silas had saved something for them alone. He tipped toward the other man, sucking on the tongue plundering his mouth with rough thrusts. Thicker, stronger than Lucy, the differences excited him. Silas's unique taste thrilled him.

His balls gathered, drawing close to his body.

Lucy switched back to sucking Si's cock, her hand teasing Colby's hard-on with expert handling that kept him from losing it while maintaining his pleasure.

"Yes, baby." He encouraged her to take Silas deeper, faster. He needed the man to abandon himself to the desire they inspired. "Suck him harder."

"Yes! No!" Silas's hips flexed, fucking his cock farther into Lucy's eager mouth.

Colby added to Si's rapture when Silas guided Colby's hands to the hard nipples decorating Silas's action-figure chest. Colby flicked his fingers over the sensitive nubs. Silas nipped Colby's lip, encouraging a more aggressive touch, so he pinched the dense, gathered skin and accepted the resulting groan and curse as reward.

Lucy lifted off Silas's cock with a pop. "I think he's close, Colby. I can taste him and the head of his cock is more defined against my tongue. Help me make him explode. I want to drink his come."

His wife's dirty talk had unintended consequences. Aching desire bubbled in Colby's balls. The base of his cock tingled. He was done for.

"Ungh." The first contraction of Colby's orgasm felt like it harvested seed from the tips of his toes. He moaned several more times in rapid succession.

"Oops." He heard Lucy's hybrid laugh and moan when jets of white fluid sprayed over her hand and his abdomen.

"Oh, shit." Silas knocked her fingers aside and milked the rest of Colby's ecstasy from him. All the while they kissed, long and deep, until Silas wandered along Colby's jaw, down his neck, to stare at the evidence of his lust pooling in the dips between his honed muscles.

Colby had never been as proud of his body or his orgasm as he was now. His two lovers radiated appreciation from every pore. Lucy leaned closer and lapped at the opalescent fluid dotting his still-heaving torso.

"Come here." Silas's command would have been impossible for either of them to resist. Lucy turned, her lips glistening in the light from the table lamp. Silas reached for Colby's wife, guiding her up until he could capture her mouth and sample the product of his efforts. "Fuck, yes."

Colby decided to go for broke. He swiped his forefinger through the thickest of the gel then raised it to his partners. Silas ingested his come, leaving Lucy searching for relief.

"She needs your cock, Silas."

"Find me a condom."

"No." Lucy rebelled. She carefully positioned herself above Silas's hips. "I want you bare. You said you're careful. Tested. Clean."

Silas nodded. "But I'm still not your husband. What if you get pregnant?"

She cut her eyes to Colby, who agreed with her. "You're planning on sticking around to raise our kids, right?"

"What?" Silas's purple hard-on flagged a little. "You'd want that? What would people say?"

"I only give a fuck what you and my wife think." Colby reached between the two people he loved most and took hold of Silas's cock. He positioned the hefty tool between his wife's legs. "Lower yourself onto him, Lu."

She dropped a bit, until the blunt head spread her delicate lips. Silas's girth would stretch her more than his. He hoped it wouldn't cause her pain but, even if it did, she'd relish every moment. So why did she hesitate?

"What's wrong, Lucy?"

"I'm afraid I'll injure him." She rotated her hips, teasing. The motion didn't make much progress in fitting Silas inside her.

"You're killing me. Right now." Silas had forgotten his objections. "Don't stop. You could never hurt me. Not like this. Needed this for a lifetime."

Colby rubbed the remaining traces of his orgasm into his six-pack then knelt behind his wife, between Silas's spread knees. He banded his arm around her waist. "I've got you, Lucy. He's not bearing your weight."

Colby whispered in her ear, loving the goose bumps breaking out all over her peaches and cream complexion. "I'll make sure you don't jostle his thigh. Hang onto my arm and you won't brace yourself on his ribs either."

"I trust you." She angled her head to kiss Colby sweet and slow. While their tongues tangled, he lowered her, a fraction of an inch at a time, onto his best friend's cock, lifting when the resistance grew too strong only to snug her deeper on the next pass.

"Oh, yes. Yes. Finally. Dreamed of this forever," she whimpered into his mouth. "He's so big."

"She's so tight. Can't believe it's real this time." Silas had fisted his hands in the sheets at his side. "I was close already. I'm not going to last long."

The panic on Silas's face caught Colby's attention. "I'll make it good for her. Don't worry. Lie back and enjoy, Si. I want to give you both this."

Colby's cock stirred a little when he raised Lucy then lowered her again, using his wife to fuck their lover. He shifted his grip so he could rock her faster, while the fingers of his other hand danced over her clit.

Her breasts bounced, the bottoms of the soft globes bobbing on his forearm.

Lucy stared at Silas and the other man returned the gaze, never even blinking. "Perfect. Better than I imagined. Oh, God, Lucy."

His wife started making the tiny mewling sound in the back of her throat that meant she'd explode any second. Colby picked her up—forcing the tip of Silas's cock to fuck her entrance a few times —then impaled her on their lover's thick, veined shaft.

Colby wondered just how good that felt.

Penetrated. Stretched. Stroked from the inside. Hopefully, he'd find out soon.

He tipped his head to nip her neck in the exact spot she preferred. She cried out, "Please!"

"You ready?" he asked Silas.

"Can't stop it." The man shouted and drove his pelvis

upward, grinding the muscle covered bone there into Lucy's clit. "Coming! Inside her. Yes. Lucy! Colby! I'm coming."

Colby held on tight while his wife spasmed. Her orgasm seemed endless, enduring. Silas roared their names as he pumped Lucy full of his come. After several minutes, their moans faded to sighs and whimpers.

Colby stopped the gentle sways he'd maintained for his wife, lifting her off of Silas's softening cock. A glistening strand of their mingled fluids dribbled from her spread pussy. He placed her on her back beside the nearly comatose man who'd welded himself to their hearts and souls in a shower of sparks.

He had to show them how much sharing this night with them had meant. He wanted to tend to them. To care for them. To provide all they needed. Instead of reaching for the sponge to clean them, he nuzzled between his wife's legs. He blew on her gently, desensitizing her engorged tissues.

Slowly, he licked her tender folds, lapping up the familiar taste of his wife and the exciting new flavor of their lover.

"If you hadn't drained me already, that would make me come again." Silas coughed as his breathing returned to normal. He'd barely confessed when Lucy cried out, bucking in Colby's hold.

Silas angled himself toward her as best he could, cradling her in his strong arms. "Yes, sweetheart. Like that. Just like that. Come for us. Push it out, give him more."

Wetness flooded Colby's mouth. He devoured her with eager swipes of his tongue. When she finally quieted, he kissed her inner thigh then turned his attention to Silas.

When Lucy realized what he intended she cried out, attracting Silas's attention.

"You want to taste me too, Colby?" The other man arched his hips. "Go ahead. Take what you need."

Colby paused, a hairsbreadth from unexplored territory. This was it. He surged forward and licked along the other man's balls then down the length of his shrinking shaft. He wasn't sure what he'd expected but the silky-smooth skin surprised him. It shifted over the core of lingering firmness. He opened his lips then sucked Silas down to the root of his cock.

"Mmm," Silas hummed.

"Oh, yes!" Lucy's delicate frame was wracked by another set of spasms as she watched her husband clean their lover's cock, stealing his first taste direct from the source. Silas held her, soothed her, massaged her clit until all three cried uncle.

"I can't take any more." His wife laughed, the lighthearted sound cheering his soul. "Not for at least five minutes."

Colby smiled as he repositioned himself beside her, sandwiching her between him and Silas. Despite their long day and the utter relaxation permeating them all, none of them seemed sleepy. After a lengthy silence, Lucy faced Silas. "You've read some of my letters. Now, share Alaska with us. Tell us about where you've been. Was it as beautiful as it looked on all the documentaries I've watched since you left?"

"God, yes." Silas launched into a description of the landscape. The beauty and the terror. Together, they talked long into the night, finally surrendering to exhaustion only when the sun's rays painted the horizon pink and roosters crowed in the distance.

Chapter Eight

Silas swung into the stable slower than he would have liked. Crutches and barnyards went together like toothpaste and coffee. Sprinkle in a handful of mostly healed, yet still tender, cracked ribs and molasses probably moved faster than he could right now. His muscles burned and he struggled not to hack up a lung. Fucking smoke. A couple hundred feet had never seemed so far.

Still, he hadn't busted his ass on the hike over from the main house. He'd take that.

"Oh, crap!" A cute blonde in a flirty sundress did a double take when she spotted him hobbling along the aisle between the stalls. Someone had converted one of the old tack rooms into an office for her. His savior hustled from the tiny room with a beat-up folding chair before he could object.

"Sit."

"I'm not a dog." Silas grumbled but accepted her surprisingly steady shoulder to lean on while he lowered himself to the rickety seat.

"Worse, you're a man. A mutt would have more sense." She shook her head then jogged to the open doors facing the pasture. He made idle mental notes about the sexy curves she attempted to obscure beneath the floral-print cotton. If the disguise fooled any man he'd be surprised. "JD! Visitor!"

She trotted over to check on him.

"I'm Silas." He held his hand out and she grasped it with a

firm shake.

"I figured. Not too many walking wounded around these parts." She flashed a bright-white smile. "Plus, you resemble your dad."

She pushed her thick glasses up her pert nose with the tip of one finger. "I'm Cindi Middleton. I do the books for Compass Ranch."

"And we couldn't set you up someplace a little nicer? Less dusty at least?" Silas swiped a smudge from her cheek, his eyes slitting when the skittish accountant flinched. He'd been back less than a week but his big brother instinct had defrosted already. The young woman tempted him to offer a hug. Something painful lurked in the depths of her light green eyes. She stayed too still, kept her back to the wall. He'd have to remember to find out the scoop from Colby later.

"She won't hear of us building her a real office." JD tucked a pair of leather work gloves in his ass pocket as he strode into the building. "Enjoys being near the horses. Or so she says."

"It's true." She sighed then drew a deep breath. "Something about the smell of the hay and the animals relaxes me. I like the small noises they make and the barn cats keep me company. Have you met the new kittens, JD?"

Cindi beamed as she pointed to a basket in the corner next to her desk. Tiny balls of orange and black fluff tumbled over each other.

"Yeah, I noticed them yesterday. Actually, I was heading over here to bring you this." He held up a mason jar brimming with fresh milk. "Colby told me you haven't been able to find Tweety."

"Not since two days ago." She worried her lip. "I don't think she's coming home. There was a lot of blood."

"Sorry, hon. You loved that fur ball." JD did hug her then. "Sometimes it's better like that. They go out on their own terms, no suffering when there's nothing you could do to help."

Cindi nodded. She accepted the food for her pets, kissed JD

on his tough cheek then pivoted before scrubbing her eyes.

"Better hope Lucy doesn't catch you out here, son. Or Colby for that matter."

"Couldn't stay inside a minute more. Too much restless energy."

JD studied Silas with an appraising stare. "Any left after that hike? There's something I need to talk to you about."

When Silas levered himself to his good leg, JD handed his son his crutches then motioned with his chin. "Come say hello to Rainey. I'm guessing it'll be quite a while before you're back in the saddle but at least you can reintroduce yourself."

"Yeah, doctor said it would be at least another two months, maybe as many as four, before I can ditch all this crap." Silas thanked JD silently when the man paused to fiddle with the hardware holding a feed bucket halfway across the barn. He suspected the gesture was all for show. "Then I'll probably need a freaking cane for another six months. Physical therapy for at least a year."

"Could have been worse."

"Don't I know it?" He thought of the email he'd sent to Red's mother earlier, offering the only solace he could. Her son had intended to return. The woman had responded within minutes, thanking him for the gift of knowledge and offering him shelter if ever he needed it. She seemed to think he'd meant something to her son and that Red would have been pleased his exile had ended—something positive had resulted from the disaster.

Silas grunted as he reached Rainey's stall and leaned on the wall. The gelding snorted then nuzzled him as though they'd come in from the hard ride from his brothers' campsite minutes, not years, ago. The set of the horse's ears displayed his excitement as he lipped Si's outstretched hand, eager to welcome his rider home. He wondered if the horse could tell from his grin how happy it made him to lay hands on the animal again.

"That horse never turned one bit friendlier while you were gone. Grumpy as shit."

"Seems awful nice to me. Always was." Silas cleared his throat and patted Rainey's neck as the animal leaned into his touch.

"He's clear on who owns him. Most creatures are. That bond and respect never change once earned."

"We still talking about Rainey?" Silas would have shuffled his booted feet if he could have.

"Not likely." JD rubbed his side then helped Silas to the chair before sinking onto a bale of hay. "The hell you've been through changes a man, Si. When you brush death like that, up close and personal, you learn quick to quit fucking around. Time is too precious to waste. We're only given so much and then we're gone."

Silas nodded, wondering how his father understood.

"And that's why I'm gonna ask you straight up. What are you planning to do? Stick? Run? What?"

"I can't leave. Never again." Silas sighed and closed his eyes. "I'm afraid to believe but it seems like this could work. Me. Lucy. Colby. It's insane and flawless. Unless..."

"What now?" His father glared at him.

"Do I embarrass you? There won't be any hiding things. Not around here. The ranch is too close-knit for that. I can't keep it under wraps. After all this time, I can't hide anymore."

"I'd rather you didn't try to pretend at all." JD tilted his head. "There's no shame in honest love, Silas. I thought we raised you better than that. Don't you dare dishonor the patience and pure adoration those kids have kept burning for you. That'd be far worse than the shit-storm of gossip that'll fly for a while. Everyone has a kink."

"Oh, yeah?" Silas laughed, pointing discreetly at the young woman dribbling milk from her finger into a kitten's mouth across the barn. "You think Cindi enjoys things rough and nasty? Likes to be spanked or take it from behind maybe?"

"As a matter of fact, I do." JD shrugged. "Not that it's any business of your disrespectful ass, but you're not the first or the last guy to take a roll in the hay in this barn. Hell, these walls have seen a lot of damn action, and I'm not talking about the horses. Sweet Cindi likes to play with the cowboys. Jake and Ray at least have had the pleasure of double-teaming her. I can tell by the way they touch her and, unless I'm off the mark by a long shot, I'd guess there are two or three more who could say the same. Heard whispers she takes 'em all on at the same time. Keeps her from ending up too close to any one of them. Rings true to me, more than cowboy trash talk."

Silas stared at his father, unsure of what disturbed him more—hearing the man speak so frankly about sex or the shattering of the illusion of innocence haloing the timid bookkeeper. "Her? She acted afraid of me. Not the kind of woman to submit to four or five guys, especially not those hulks."

"Not the type. Huh. I imagine a lot of folks would say the same about Lucy. Doesn't make it any less true." JD laid it on the line. "You can't judge what people need until you know them, Silas. Really know them. From what I pieced together, Cindi likes to surrender, once she's satisfied she's in capable hands. If I ever find the bastard who put those shadows in her eyes, I'll kill him myself."

"I'm starting to think our family has grown while I was gone." Silas regretted every minute he'd missed.

"It has. Still, no one could replace you or your brothers. This ranch is your legacy, son." JD looked straight into his eyes. "Are you ready to man up?"

"Sure, with you at the helm and Colby as foreman. I'll work twice as hard as anyone else. I swear I'll do my best to make you proud."

"You always have, Silas." His father sighed. "But you're gonna have to speed things up some."

"What do you mean?"

"I wish I could give you time to settle in. Heal. Take a honeymoon with Colby and Lucy." JD hunched forward, bracing his elbows on his knees. "I can't. *I* need you Silas. Your family needs you. Compass Ranch needs you."

As though a curtain had lifted, Silas noted the slight sheen of sweat on JD's face. Brackets around his father's mouth caused not by age, rather by persistent pain, drew his seeking gaze. Bloodshot eyes and a yellow cast to JD's skin Silas hadn't noticed beneath the tan appeared in the wake of his scrutiny.

"You don't feel well? Head to the house, I'll call Lucy."

"No point, Si." JD shook his head.

Was it this annoying when he went stubborn? Jesus, why had no one kicked his ass by now?

"And I'd prefer to keep this between us if you don't mind."

Silas's heart hammered when JD's solemn stare locked on him. This was bigger than the flu or some spoiled food at lunch. No!

"I heard you telling Colby about the fire last night."

The two men had sat out on the porch long past midnight while Lucy dozed on the whitewashed swing. He couldn't hoard enough of the fresh air or their company.

"I guess I'm at the point where I realize the alarm bells in *my* system are not caused by some false alarm." As though he'd summoned his own personal demon, JD coughed. When the man yanked his handkerchief from his pocket, Silas noticed tiny flecks of blood spotting the fabric.

Terror spiked through his brain. His invincible father could not be ill. Not like that.

"I'm not ready to call it quits. Or even to start blabbing about what I suspect. But I'm damn glad you're home. Takes a huge load off my shoulders. I've considered calling you back for a couple months now. I only wish, for your sake, that I'd picked up the phone sooner."

"Wait." Silas tried to process everything happening at

lightning speed. "Have you been to the doctor? What's wrong?"

"I don't need fancy medicine to discover what I already know." JD sat straighter. "I'm not willing to drag this out in some slow progression that steals every scrap of my pride."

"You can't throw in the towel without trying. You have to make an appointment, get a professional opinion. What if it's something simple? Something easy to fix? Don't be ignorant." Silas raged inside and out. "I may be on crutches, but I will make you do this if I have to knock you unconscious with one and haul your ass there myself."

"I truly did miss you." JD laughed so hard he clasped his side again. "I appreciate the concern. I'm past the point of no return. I'm not gonna waste any of the time I have left on nonsense. Tomorrow morning we'll begin reviewing information, starting with inventory and my five-year plan for operations."

His father checked his watch then made to leave.

"I suggest you wait here. I'm expecting Colby in the next ten minutes. I'll have him help you to the house." JD dropped his hand onto Silas's shoulder. "We can't afford you getting hurt anymore."

His father ambled into the setting sun, his silhouette shrinking as he moved farther away. Silas gasped hard through his open mouth, willing himself to calm. He had to call Seth. Together, maybe they could talk some sense into their crazy old man.

He cursed at the ceiling, his fingers gripping the stall door. Rainey nudged his hand until it rested on the gelding's nose. He stroked the white spot there over and over as he thought of all the possibilities.

Too few of them were positive.

"You've really fixed this place up."

Colby beamed. Silas inspected his handiwork as they leaned against the front bumper of his truck. Colby gave his friend a couple seconds to steady himself before heading inside his and Lucy's house. They'd convinced Victoria and JD it'd be safer for Si to stay at their place, where all the rooms were on one level, rather than risk their stubborn lover tumbling down the stairs if he had trouble sleeping and could no longer suppress the urge to wander.

The trip to the barn and back earlier seemed to have exhausted Silas. Granted, he hadn't undertaken much physical activity since the explosion but, still, it seemed odd for someone as toned as Si. He hadn't suffered from lack of manual labor during his exile—that much was clear.

Colby flexed the well-developed muscles in his back. He couldn't imagine his strength stripped from him. He took the body he'd grown into for granted sometimes. He'd earned every sculpted inch his wife often admired. "I've been finishing projects as I can. Replaced the roof this spring and built the wrap-around porch last fall. Lucy likes to slip on a bathrobe and drink her tea out there in the morning. Not like there's anyone to see."

"I hope you've taken advantage of that perk." Silas grinned at Colby.

"I've had to haul ass to meet the rest of the hands plenty of mornings." He wrapped his arm around Si's waist and helped the man up the stairs, practically carrying him. "Not gonna lie, making love to Lucy on the dewy planks before heading off to early chores is worth sacrificing breakfast, no matter how delicious her omelets are."

Colby ensured Silas had his crutches under him before he knelt to remove Si's boots then kicked off his own. Lucy would kill them if they tracked mud onto the precious maple floors he'd installed for her five years or so ago.

"Jesus. I can imagine." Si still seemed sluggish as they crossed the threshold, but the lascivious thought perked him up. "One taste of her and I'm addicted. She's so hot, so tight. So eager to play."

"Mmm." Colby settled Silas on the wide leather sofa,

elevating his braced leg using the ottoman and a few pillows as Lucy had mandated, then shifted the hard-on forming behind his zipper. "I love her so much, it's terrifying."

"Same here." Silas stared straight into Colby's eyes until he couldn't bear it anymore.

He cleared his throat then gestured to the bright plaid curtains and the plant stand overflowing with greenery. "Lu did all the decorating."

"It's nice. Really comfortable." Silas nodded when Colby sank beside him, their hands almost touching where they rested at their sides.

The injured man glanced at the clock above the piano, which no one played, but Lucy refused to sell. A ridiculous prop he tolerated. Anything to make her smile. "When does she call it quits? I don't like the thought of her driving on those deserted roads, alone, after nightfall."

Dusk encroached on the quaint home, sapphire blue sky replacing the orange streaks of the sunset lingering outside the picture window in front of them. "She's usually here by now. It depends on the day and the patients. She carries a cell phone despite the spotty coverage. I've gotten better at beating the worry into submission, but thanks for reminding me."

"Shit. Sorry, Colby." Silas winced. "Believe me, I appreciate how stress can suck the life out of a guy."

Could it be more than physical exertion draining Silas this evening?

"Anything you care to share?" Colby didn't quite know how to be with Silas. Not yet, anyway. So he waded through memories to the times Silas had shouldered some of his burdens. When nightmares of his father's abuse had seeped into his waking hours, Si had noticed and listened. Or distracted him. He'd forged a loyalty strong enough to last a decade, a thousand decades.

Maybe Colby could return the favor.

"Supposed to keep my mouth shut." Silas shook his head.

"Oh, I like secrets," Lucy called from the other room.

How had they not heard her arrive? She must have ridden her mare from the main house. He should have informed her he'd transferred Silas home.

"Tell me?" When she hung her bag on the hook by the door and pranced into the living room, Colby sighed. His wife would fix the lost look haunting Silas's eyes. She hesitated when she spotted the marked difference in their lover.

Lucy understood immediately. This had nothing to do with Si's injuries. Unlike Colby, she saw straight to the heart of the matter in an instant. "What happened?"

She dropped to the floor on her knees between Silas's spread legs, laying her cheek on his good thigh. Her arms banded around his waist, surrounding him with her gentle care. Colby angled himself to face them better, laying one hand on her trembling back and the other on Silas's shoulder.

Si groaned. He buried the fingers of one hand in Lucy's pale hair, kneading her scalp so her silken waves caressed the sensitive span of his palm. His other hand gripped Colby's knee. The ferocity of his hold convinced Colby he clung to sanity by his fingernails.

"We're here for you. Let us help. You're not alone anymore," Lucy whispered but her concern ricocheted around the room with the force of a rifle shot.

"Fuck. And thanks." Silas dropped his head against the cushion, his eyes closed as though blocking out the world would improve his odds of winning his struggle to maintain composure. "It's different. Hard to adjust. Everything in my life is chaos. I'm used to order, black and white, right and wrong. How can I be in control when everything is gray? My whole life has fucking changed."

"Some things for the better, right?" Lucy peeked at the man she consoled.

Bad day or not, Colby would crush Silas if he hurt his wife.

"Yeah. Shit, yes." Si didn't disappoint. "You're amazing.

Both of you. I couldn't do this without you."

"Do what?" Lucy petted his solid abdomen as it flexed with his elevated respiration. Colby fluffed his collar to release some steam despite the dread swirling around them like a cloud.

"Fuck it. JD knows what you mean to me. I don't intend to turn from you ever again. He has to suspect I'd tell you."

"What does your dad have to do with this?" Lucy raised her head, her eyebrows scrunching together as she tried to decipher Silas's ramblings.

The answer became clear as the mountain spring in the west pasture to Colby. All the times he'd caught JD rubbing his side, the persistent cough he played off as allergies, the gruff determination to teach Colby the strategic side of ranching this summer when he'd focused on operations for a decade.

Oh, son of a bitch.

"JD's sick." Colby swung his gaze to Silas's grateful stare. Si hadn't had to break his father's confidence yet he didn't have to tow the line alone. Never again.

"What?" Lucy started to stand but her men kept her in place. "I'll go to him. I can help. I was just at the house. No one said anything."

"They don't know. It's worse than a simple cold or a broken leg, baby." Colby hated the terror in his wife's eyes. She thought of JD as her own father. They all did.

"He's convinced he's dying." Silas stated the facts in a cold, distant tone.

"No!" Lucy struggled until Colby worried she might hurt Si. He tugged her into his arms, cradling her between his body and Silas's. "It can't be true."

"Nothing's for sure yet." Silas shook off some of his gloom to reassure her. Having a purpose seemed to help the commanding man. "Somehow I have to convince him to see a doctor."

"Between the three of us, we'll wear him down." Lucy's half-hearted attempt fell flat.

"You don't believe that. Unless I missed a shitload more than I thought, my father isn't the kind of man to succumb to badgering."

"Maybe it's time for Seth to come home." Colby spoke softly, serious. "He's learned tons from Kirkland's ranch. If the three of us can prove we have things under control here, it could take some of the pressure off JD. Then I bet he'd consider it."

"You have a point, but Seth has some...*issues* of his own." Silas rubbed his temples. "Let's wait a bit. We might work a miracle. If not, I'll make the call."

"It could be nothing." The rain cloud darkening Lucy's natural glow lifted.

Colby debated correcting her. He couldn't allow them to live with false hope. "I'll be praying, like everyone else, it's something minor. But I can't ignore the signs. He's never slowed down a minute in all the years I've lived here. This summer... I should have put it together. Should have caught this sooner."

"We all should have. I've noticed he seems tired." Lucy whimpered, and Silas stroked her cheek. "I assumed the heat affected him more this year, now that he's a bit older."

"He's such a badass. He makes it easy to forget he and Vicky have so many years between them." Colby nuzzled his wife's neck. "He's close to seventy."

Lucy nodded. "Vicky grumbled about her fiftieth coming up next year."

"Whatever happens, Silas, we'll handle it together." Colby met his friend's gaze over his wife's bowed head. "No more secrets between us. We're one unit, unconventional or not. Aren't we?"

Lucy perked up in time to witness Si's response.

"Fuck, yes." Determination blazed in the man's eyes. "If you'll have me. If it won't interfere with what you two have built. Nothing can tear us apart. I need you. I need what we have together."

"That's right. When the world is crazy outside, we're here." Lucy leaned in Colby's grip to place a calming kiss on their partner's lips. "Never forget. With us, you're in control."

Colby's cock lifted at the implication. Could the time finally be right?

"I've waited a long time for you to claim what's yours." Colby hesitated until Lucy smiled up at him, encouraging. "Take me, Silas? Find peace with me. Please?"

"I can't." Si threatened to splinter his soul.

"Why the hell not?" Lucy jumped to his defense. He didn't think he could beg twice.

"I won't be gentle. Not now." Silas shook his head. "Not like this."

"He didn't ask you to treat him with kid gloves." Lu took Silas's face in her palms, forcing him to meet her determined stare. "He's strong, Si. So strong. He wants all of you. He needs the unbridled passion only you can give him. Show him who owns him. Owns us both. Prove to yourself, you *can* take control."

Quick as a flash flood, and with all the same elemental power, Silas snapped.

He roared, "Bedroom, now."

Chapter Nine

Lucy wiggled from between the two men sandwiching her on the couch, impatient to obey Silas. With her on one side and Colby on the other, they ducked beneath Si's arms, which bulged with muscle, and helped him the short distance to their bedroom. Her hand swept from his waist over his tight ass, covered with soft cotton sweatshorts, when she released him to stand on his one good leg with Colby for support.

Without waiting for instruction, she knelt before him.

Lucy tucked her fingers into his waistband and stripped the light fabric from his trim hips, down his powerful thighs, careful not to snag them on the immobilizing brace. The ridge of his calves drew her fingers. She explored the furred skin a moment before raising her gaze.

His thick cock dangled, half-hard against his thigh. A flashback to the other night, when he'd packed her full, assaulted her senses. She shivered. An entire lifetime of fantasies hadn't come close to the real thing. She couldn't resist tasting him.

Lucy licked the broad crown capping his cock, sucking him to the depths of her mouth.

"Fuck, yes." He hissed when she flicked her tongue over the sensitive underside of his shaft. "Get me good and stiff, angel. I'm gonna need one hell of a hard-on to penetrate your husband's virgin ass."

She shivered, moaning around the cock inflating by the

second. Her gaze cut to her husband, afraid for a split second of what her abandon might inspire in him. She shouldn't have worried. Lust burned in his gorgeous eyes. And, if she read him right, a little envy.

Colby licked his lips, and she moaned.

When Silas descended onto the bed, she followed him, devouring his shaft while she could still fit the whole thing in her mouth. Wouldn't be much longer until he outgrew her. Already his thick shaft stretched her lips into a tight ring and she couldn't help but graze her teeth over his hard-on.

"Just like that." Silas stroked her cheeks around his embedded cock, smiling into her eyes.

Colby's hand broke her line of sight when he reached between her and Si to peel Si's T-shirt from his ripped torso. Her husband's spectacular muscularity seemed lean compared to Silas's bulk. How much hard living had he done to earn this ideal physique?

"Stand." He tugged her hair hard enough to sting. Her pussy gushed. She released him from her mouth reluctantly.

As much as she savored Colby's gentle loving, she'd be lying if she claimed she never longed for something a little more raw. A teensy bit rougher.

"Undress each other." Silas leaned on one elbow like a sultan observing his harem. He used the other hand to stroke his raging erection.

She didn't react immediately, fascinated with how he touched himself—firm yet gentle in places. Colby must have suffered the same distraction because Silas growled.

"Don't make me repeat myself." He swiped the bead of precome from his tip with his thumb then massaged it into his engorged flesh as he threatened, "I can still put you over my good knee."

A flash of heat rushed up Lucy's chest, neck and cheeks at the mental image of Silas pinning her to the mattress with one broad hand while the other delivered spank after spank until her wetness ran onto his fingers and Colby cleaned them both.

"I don't think that was an effective deterrent, Si." Colby groaned and took a step closer.

"Then how about this..." The injured man's hips arced off the mattress, thrusting his cock through the ring of his fingers to the base. He looked huge. Long and wide. "If you don't get naked quick, I'll take care of myself."

"No!" Lucy clapped her hand over her mouth, horrified. How could he play her so well?

Colby chuckled as he edged closer, nipping her neck before whispering, "Don't worry, baby. He wants us as bad as we want him. Let's put on a nice show for Si."

She couldn't think clearly enough to do anything more than respond to her instincts, which screamed to touch her men skin on skin. She crumpled Colby's button-down shirt in her fists, one on each side of the center, then yanked. Plastic pinged off the window, the floor and the furniture as the gap revealed his sleeveless undershirt.

"Much better." Silas abandoned his thick shaft, which thudded onto his flexed abs, in favor of cupping his balls. They filled his palm as he rolled them back and forth. "Keep going. Show me every inch of *my* lovers. You are mine. You understand that, right?"

"God, yes." Colby answered in unison with her. They looked at each other and grinned.

She decided to get down to business. The throbbing in her core wouldn't tolerate her torturing her men much longer. Every instant she tormented them withheld her own pleasure.

Lucy grabbed the hem of her dress and whipped it over her head, leaving her standing before her husband and his ravenous best friend. She wore nothing more than a few scraps of delicate lavender lace.

Colby clutched his chest and Silas's cock twitched on his belly. She smirked over her shoulder as she pivoted then bent at the waist and grabbed her ankles to present her ass. The sight kicked her husband into action. He fell to his knees behind her then stripped the thong from her hips. The tiny line of drenched fabric between her legs brushed her pussy as it separated from her body, making her cry out.

"So beautiful." Silas approved of the goods on display.

His lust spiked her arousal higher. A trickle of moisture ran down her thigh.

"You better not waste that, Colby."

Lucy's knees almost buckled when her husband licked a trail from her knee to her pussy at their lover's instruction. He supported her as he nibbled on the puffy lips bracketing her opening. She arched her hips, hoping he'd spear her with his broad fingers.

"Go ahead, give her what she's asking for." Silas granted her husband permission to stuff her. "Spread her ass. Open her until there's no doubt she's, ready. Then slide in deep."

Her husband followed orders, making her blush as he exposed her to Silas's laser stare. When he penetrated her, all other thoughts fled. She squeezed him, hugging his hand as she welcomed him inside her body.

"Do you ever fuck her ass? Is she into it?"

Lucy wasn't sure what it said about her that she enjoyed them discussing her as though she weren't right there in the room. She couldn't wait to serve them both, making their fantasies come true as they did the same for her.

"Once or twice." Colby curled his fingers, rubbing a sweet spot inside her. "She came, but I think she prefers when I fill this sweet pussy."

"Someday she'll take us both." Slick slapping sounds reached her ears as Silas jerked himself faster. "I'm gonna fuck that ass while you bury yourself in her pussy. All of us, linked together."

Lucy moaned, a shockwave traveling out from her center to the tips of her fingers and toes.

"She'll come if I'm not careful." Colby kissed her hip, withdrawing a fraction of an inch and easing his knuckle from her clit.

"Already?" Silas groaned. "So responsive. Perfect. Take the edge off, Colby. Grant her release so we can take our time. She can come more than once in a session?"

"Hell, yes." As though Colby couldn't help it, his fingers bottomed out in her rippling sheath. "I think the record stands around a dozen times."

"Sounds like a challenge to me." Si grinned. "I fucking love a competition. As soon as I'm healed, we'll find out who can make her shatter the most."

Lucy couldn't help herself. Her pussy spasmed around her husband's fingers. He spread them, resisting the compression of her climaxing body, even as she clamped down. He extended her pleasure with short jabs through saturated tissue. She didn't realize she'd gone lax until he bundled her in his arms and lowered her to the bed beside Silas.

"Come here, angel," he murmured to her as the world returned to focus. "Did our Colby do a good job? Did he make it sweet for you?"

"Always."

Silas lowered the cup of her bra until her full breast spilled from the garment. He surrounded the heavy mound with his hand, her hard nipple poking his palm, when she rolled onto her side. She jerked in his hold as aftershocks continued to zip along her spine. Unable to speak, she couldn't express how much it meant to share this with them both. He didn't need the promise. The appreciation for their gift must have shone from her eyes.

"This is just the beginning, Lu." Silas slammed his mouth over hers, drawing her tongue between his lips then sucking hard. He overwhelmed her senses with pure greed before breaking away to stare at Colby. "My turn for a taste."

Her husband put one knee on the mattress then extended

his fingers. Silas lunged upward, nipping the digits before devouring her juices from them.

"So fucking sweet," he groaned as he collapsed onto the bed. "But we're going to have to work on following directions. Why do either of you still have clothes on?"

Lucy had never seen Colby move so fast. Stitches popped, filling the room with a soft tearing sound when he shed his tank. She didn't realize she'd shifted her hand to her pussy at the sight of all that tan skin until Silas grasped her wrist.

"Did I tell you to play with my pussy?" he rasped.

"Please." She couldn't believe she begged to touch herself. She'd orgasmed not two minutes before for crying out loud.

"No." Silas set her arm at her side, clearly expecting it to stay there. He wedged his hand beneath her, unhooked her bra then removed it from her with one deft movement. "If you need to come again so soon, you'll take pleasure from me this time. If you like, you can stroke my cock while Colby strips for us."

He guided her head to his inclined shoulder as they both lay on their backs, side by side. Their arms crossed as they reached for each other.

"Oh, God." She gasped at the first contact of Si's fingers on her wet slit. Her hand fisted around his steely cock in response. She'd dreamed of this for so long, it almost didn't feel real.

"Mmm." He kissed her forehead before lending his attention to Colby. "Turn around. Wiggle that ass as you strip out of your jeans. When you're naked, I better see a stiff cock, ready to drill your wife. I think she's in need of a more vigorous ride than I can give her with this stupid leg busted up."

"Not a problem." Colby's reply sounded as though it were drawn through a shredder.

Lucy grinned at Silas. No doubt he controlled them. She counted the moments until he healed enough to place her face down, ass up, and deliver on his promises.

Si winked at her then nudged aside her swollen lips. The tip of his finger dipped into her slit and sought her ripe clit.

"Ah!" She angled her head and bit his pec when ecstasy washed through her. Her lingering orgasm rekindled beneath his inflaming touch. "Hurry, Colby."

Her husband swayed from side to side as he worked at the oversized buckle on his belt. She thrust against Silas's hand. Leather hit the floor and the rip of a zipper unknitting reached her ears. Colby hooked his thumbs in the waistband and shimmied from his jeans and boxer briefs simultaneously.

"Gorgeous, isn't he?" Silas asked her.

"Amazing in every way." Tears stung her eyes as she considered how lucky she was to have two men like this in her life.

"Horny as hell too," Colby grumbled but he didn't stop enticing them with the play of his golden form.

Her husband's heavy balls swung between his legs. From the position of his elbows, she assumed one hand played with his cock while the other rubbed his chest. He went bananas when she stroked him there, or licked his peaked nipples, while he fucked her.

"Enough," Silas barked, his erection throbbing in her palm. "Lucy needs your cock inside this slippery cunt. Are you ready to give it to her?"

"I was ready ten minutes ago, Si." Colby spun then, his hard-on jutting from the trimmed brown hair between his legs. "

Silas rolled to his side, his injured leg on top. He cradled her shoulders on one arm while the other played with her body. "I can't wait to watch you together. I need to see how it's been."

"I didn't think it could be any better." Lucy cupped his cheek in her hand. "But it is."

Colby nudged the inside of her knees until she spread her legs wide to make room for him. He didn't waste any time in aligning the head of his cock with her pussy. Though he could have thrust into her soaked folds, he glanced to Silas for approval.

"Fuck her slit first. Make your cock dance over her clit."

Lucy wouldn't survive. The glide of her husband's dense, heated hard-on over her delicate nub drove her insane on the best of days. Ultra-erect now, he had to force his cock down with two fingers on the top of the shaft.

"Need a hand?" Silas reached between them to aim Colby's shallow thrusts. The blunt head of her husband's erection tapped her clit, making her eyes roll.

"Yes!"

She wasn't sure who'd shouted it, but she agreed one hundred percent.

"Do you two keep lube around?" Silas grunted when Colby fucked through his fingers harder.

"Nightstand drawer," Lucy cried out when her husband seemed speechless.

"Grab it," Silas ordered Colby, who reached to the side without pausing his pattern of lunges. Her husband handed their lover the mostly-full tube. Knowing what he intended to use it for had her thrashing beneath her man.

"You like the thought of my cock sinking in your husband's ass, don't you?" Silas teased. She responded with something more convincing than a verbal affirmation.

Another orgasm gripped her. Her husband played with her clit, slapping his cock against it as Silas bent to suck her nipple into his mouth. He bit the tip lightly, soothing the sting with his tongue when the prism of light began to fade behind her eyelids.

Colby bent to kiss her, the simple gesture sweet and every bit as enticing as Silas's wicked play. While both men feasted on her, Silas's hand moved between them. He altered the angle of their connection so the next time Colby's hips shuttled forward, his thick erection tunneled inside her humid flesh.

"Ah, God." Her husband rose on straight-locked arms above her, his spine arched. He forged deeper and deeper as though he had no other choice.

Silas patted Colby's flank, encouraging him to work his substantial shaft into her body until they were joined as completely as possible. "There you go, Colby. Right where you want to be."

"Always." Her husband smiled at her before facing Silas. "With you both."

The men leaned toward each other until their mouths brushed. Their initial hesitance evaporated at the bare connection. Si wrapped his hand around the nape of Colby's neck and welded their lips. They ate at each other with more intensity than she might have found comfortable, but neither let up. Their tongues twined around each other and still her husband fucked into her.

Her body seemed to ride one peak to the next, never dipping into the valley she associated with prior extended loving. Instead of multiple orgasms with a period of rejuvenation, wave after wave of pleasure caught her in their flow. Everywhere she looked—every touch, every sound—was fuel for the fire threatening to consume her.

"Oh, shit." Colby ripped his mouth from Silas. "She's coming. Again. And again."

"Such a good girl, Lucy." Si beamed at her as though she had any control over her body at this point. "You love his cock, don't you?"

"Yes!" she shrieked when another burst of pleasure wracked her.

"Hurry, Silas." Colby fucked her as commanded. Tension drew his shoulders tight. "I can't hold off forever."

"I'm impressed you've lasted this long." Silas laughed. "I gave you less than ten minutes in my mind. This is better. We can all come together. Concentrate, Colby. Don't let us down."

"Low blow, Si." Her husband gritted his teeth and fucked. His head hung between his shoulders.

Silas uncapped the lube and slathered it over his fingers. When he reached behind her husband, Colby's brilliant blue eyes widened. "Oh God, Lucy. He's playing with my ass, teasing my hole, stretching me open."

Another ripple of delight passed through her cunt, squeezing her around her husband. She must have screamed because Silas glanced over at her and grinned.

"Keep going."

Colby grunted, whether because Silas sunk his glossy fingers deeper in his ass or because she wrung his cock with her twitching pussy, she couldn't say. She began to float, to observe as though having an out-of-body experience. The three of them fit together so perfectly, anticipating each other's desires. She couldn't imagine anything more beautiful.

"His ass is so hot on my fingers. You tried this with him. Didn't you, Lucy?"

She nodded, her hand gripping Colby's arm.

"I bet my fingers feel different. Don't they, Colby?"

"Thicker. Longer. Damn! So much bigger." Her husband panted, not complaining about the upgrade.

"Wait until you take my cock." Silas bit Colby's shoulder.

"Oh!" The intensity of the pleasure whipping through her increased again. Her clit throbbed where her husband's pelvis brushed it. Nothing had ever felt this good. Nothing.

"Now." Colby shuddered above her when Silas's arm increased its speed. Silas rammed his fingers in her husband's ass harder and harder. "No more waiting. Right now."

Silas laughed, the sound easing her spirit. "Greedy. I like it. You're ready."

"Been ready!"

"Roll onto your side, facing away from me."

Colby lifted her and rotated, his cock never abandoning her sheath. He settled them on the pillows then snugged himself toward Silas. Lucy threaded her hand between Colby's hip and his top arm to rest on Silas's side. She had to feel him. To maintain their connection.

"Push out. Breathe deep." Silas's worried face appeared over her husband's shoulder as he slicked his cock with excessive lube. She gripped her husband's ass and spread him wide, inviting Silas to take what belonged to him. "This might hurt."

"Nothing could be more painful than not having you," Colby answered for them both. Her heart concurred. She kissed her husband with every ounce of caring she possessed. Every molecule of the longing they'd both suffered through. She lent him her strength and courage. Silas gave her a play by play as he fit the head of his cock to the pucker in the valley of Colby's ass and broached her husband's virgin hole, joining them at last.

"Ah!" Colby went stiff in her arms. His erection wilted a fraction in her pussy. "Christ, you're huge. So fucking bulky."

When Silas would have backed out, she clamped her hand on his hip and drew him tighter to them instead, impaling her husband on their lover's shaft. She rocked her hips, stroking Colby's cock with her pussy even as she coaxed him to kiss her again and ride out the pain.

From the few times they'd played like this, she realized blazing passion would soon eclipse the discomfort.

"That's it. Relax, Colby." Silas moaned. "You're holding me nice and deep now. Almost buried to the balls. You're doing great. Just a little more. So fucking hot. Tight. Sexy."

Lucy shrieked when another mini-orgasm flooded her pussy. Hearing Silas's filthy yet reverent whispers destroyed her restraint. Her husband opened himself to another man even as he took her.

"Oh, yes." Colby's smoky tone returned and he began to pound inside her, fucking himself onto Silas as hard as he fucked her. "Her pussy is so hungry, milking me. She loves listening to you, Silas."

"Both of you. Together. Love you both." She stared into her husband's eyes, permitting him to observe the eternal joy he inspired in her.

"I love you too, Lucy." He kissed her long and slow as Silas began to fuck him harder, forcing Colby's cock to glide deep into her. They surrendered, allowing Silas to control the encounter along with their pleasure and their hearts.

"Silas," she cried out as she met his gaze over her husband's shoulder. "God, how I need you."

"We both do," Colby rumbled as Silas plowed into him, his injuries forgotten.

Silas reached over Colby to hold her hand, their fingers entwining as he captured Colby's mouth once more. Then he paused for a split second. He shifted his gaze between them. "I love you too. Both of you. So much."

He slammed his hips into them so hard she was sure he rammed his cock to the hilt in her husband's ass. Once. Twice. Three times. Then he roared the declaration. "Forever."

"He's coming. Lu, he's coming in me." Colby fucked her as he drew the seed from Silas's balls. "Spurt after spurt. So hot. Oh, fuck. Yes!"

The combination of the graphic commentary and her husband's expert loving amplified the extended pleasure swamping her senses. Her entire body gathered, her toes curling. Then she shattered. Colby gripped her tight, fucking her through the storm.

"Give in, Colby." Silas nipped her husband's neck. "Come for us. With us."

Her husband stared into her eyes then surrendered. "Love. You."

He howled as he emptied his longing, fear and hope into her along with jets of scalding come. She thought it impossible, but her body couldn't resist the lure of his capitulation and joined him in one last bout of rapture.

White light flared behind her eyelids and she sighed, unable to find one single reason to move from the shelter of her men's embrace. Exhausted. Sated. Complete.

Lucy relaxed, slipping into a state of unconscious bliss.

Chapter Ten

When Lucy awoke, stars shone through the open curtains, which billowed in the breeze Silas enjoyed so much. She lay in their bed, alone. Not acceptable. She glimpsed at the clock, shaking her head. After midnight. The growl of Colby's truck engine had roused her a while ago. She'd been too dazed to investigate.

After blinking a few more times, she grabbed Silas's discarded T-shirt from the floor and ducked into it. The supple gray cotton reached almost to her knees. She climbed from the king-sized bed, surprised she didn't experience more discomfort from their reckless fucking.

Silas could have reinjured himself. If he'd endured any pain he hadn't showed it. The memory of his awe as he conquered Colby's ass would turn her on until the day she died. The bond they'd strengthened overflowed her soul with happiness.

She slipped out the screen door, headed for the shadowy figure in the corner of the porch.

"Is your leg bothering you?" she whispered to the man in the moonlight.

"Nah. That's not it."

"Trouble sleeping?" She crossed to the spot where Silas leaned against the rail, staring out at the prairie and the mountains in the distance. The purple shadow glowed beneath the full moon.

Lucy wrapped her arms around his waist and snuggled into

his bare shoulders after kissing the Compass Ranch brand at the center of his tattoo. The heat pouring off of him made blankets unnecessary.

"Yeah. Colby had to run into town to bail out a couple of the hands. I planned to stay and hold you while you slept but I have a lot on my mind and..."

"What, Si?"

"Damn nightmares." He scrubbed his hand over his face. "I keep playing it over and over. Wondering. Could I have done something different? For Red."

"He chose his own path, Si." She stroked his chest while they talked. "You can't take the blame for him being there. It wasn't your fault."

"He'd already quit the rig that morning." Silas's confession crackled with guilt. "He didn't even work there anymore. He hung around to tell me he was leaving. He had a ticket out. A ticket home."

"Oh, Silas." Lucy nudged him toward the wicker loveseat. She propped him sideways on the cushion, his back resting against the arm so his leg extended the length of the bench. "That's awful. I'm so sorry."

"I'll live with it for the rest of my life." Her new lover drew her to him. She went willingly into his arms. She lay beside his brace—his other knee bent, his foot planted on the floor—and rested her head on his flat stomach.

"I only spoke to him once. That was enough to determine he cared for you very much, Si. He would have been glad *you* escaped. That *you* made it home."

"You're right, angel." He rested his palm in the dip of her waist, holding her close. "And that only makes it worse, doesn't it?"

"Not necessarily." She nibbled her lip as she chose her message carefully. "I think it means you owe him your best, though."

"I swear, Lucy, I'm going to make things right. I'm here for you, for Colby, for JD and Compass Ranch. I promise to do you proud. To keep you safe. To never disappoint you again. I'll do what's right, no matter how difficult it might be."

"And I'll be beside you every step. Colby too."

"I love you."

"Love you too."

She nuzzled his chest as they dozed together until the lights and purr of Colby's truck heading up the dirt road to their house extracted her from their hushed intimacy.

Lucy smiled as she imagined the three of them heading indoors to indulge their passion again or maybe staying right here and worshipping each other beneath the summer sky. She didn't expect the sudden tension morphing her pillow into a solid slab of flexed muscle.

"What the fuck happened to you?"

She inspected her husband when Silas's alarm infected her. Colby sported one hell of a shiner, a fat lip and a slice in his eyebrow that oozed blood. He spit over the railing, probably clearing the iron tang from his mouth.

"Nothing worth discussing." He grinned at Lucy then flexed his fingers into a loose fist. "I'm hoping you have some frozen peas stashed inside. I'm gonna need 'em."

She scooted off the loveseat and dashed into the kitchen. The rumbling of her men arguing, low and urgent, drifted through the open bathroom window as she gathered a couple other first aid supplies.

"It's not important. Some tool thought he could take out his ignorance on Billy. Made some asinine comment about the kid working for a homo. Billy fought back and the sheriff locked him up, but the dumb fuck wasn't ready to leave well enough alone. He must have been at The Soggy Boot. Saw me come for Billy then decided to go for another round."

"Son of a bitch!" Silas's curse cut through the night. "It's my fault this dickwad attacked you."

"You're so full of yourself." Colby attempted to take the sting out of the truth. "He was drunker than shit and looking for any excuse to start trouble."

"This jackass won't be the only one who has a problem with this…" Silas's voice trailed off.

"So I'll keep kicking asses and setting them straight. It's nobody's business who I fuck. Who I love."

"What will you do when someone attacks Lucy?" Silas's question faded then grew louder as though he paced with uneven hobbles. She hurried outside to calm him down. She could take care of herself, damn it.

"Silas Compton, stop this bullshit." She propped her hand on her hip. "You can't take responsibility for the whole universe."

"You two are my world. No one will hurt you because of me." He glared at her. "You should understand."

She threw the bag of peas at him, annoyed when he snatched it out of the air with ease and handed it to Colby. "It's not at all the same thing, Silas."

"It is." He adjusted his crutches then swung toward the stairs. "Colby, drive me into town. I'll confront these assholes myself. Then we'll talk. Maybe this isn't such a good idea after all."

"You swore you'd be here for us." She couldn't believe Silas would change his mind now. She'd never survive losing him.

"I swore to keep you safe."

Lucy watched until the taillights faded from sight before crumpling to the porch floor. Tears soaked her fingers as she covered her face and sobbed. He couldn't do this to them.

Not again.

Silas fumed the entire fifteen-minute trip into Compton Pass. Fury eradicated the opportunity to enjoy his first glimpse of the town he'd grown up in. Wrath blinded him to how it had evolved from a rural outpost into a bustling community, complete with an Internet café and an expanded school.

He refused to acknowledge Colby's attempts to woo him off the ledge. Fucked up leg or not, he planned to make a statement. A handful of titanium rods, screws and plates wouldn't stop him from protecting his family.

His lovers were not to be touched. Or there'd be hell to pay.

"Really, Si. This is ridiculous." Colby droned on above the country music spilling from the rowdy bar conveniently located behind the town's combo government building and two-celled jail as they swung into the gravel lot. "I don't need your sorry ass to fight my battles. Jones probably went home anyway."

"I'll check it out for myself." He slid from the bench seat of the pickup onto his good leg, ignoring how the jostling sent a tingle of pain up his spine.

"You're overdoing it today, Silas." Damn the observant foreman. "Let's go home. Lucy gives great massages."

"In a few." It had to be close to last call. Didn't a bunch of these cowboys have to be on the ranch in three or four hours? Hell, more than a couple probably started out the morning still tipsy or miserably hung-over.

He winced at the hypocritical disdain about to cause him to pass judgment on guys he'd never even met. Fuck. He'd lived through ten years of rough mornings and still managed to perform at the head of the pack. Wyoming could easily be someone else's Alaska.

Colby stepped in front of him as he limped toward the front door.

"Are you sure you're okay to go in there?" True concern radiated from his lover for the first time since he'd shown up at the house with his face somewhat worse for wear. "With all the alcohol? Shit, I can smell it from here. You said…"

Now that Colby mentioned it, so could Silas. The fumes curdled his stomach.

"I remember what I asked of you." He sighed. "I'm alright.

On that front anyway. Let me through, Colby."

"Fine."

Silas swung through the cracked door Colby held open as the other man mumbled beneath his breath.

"Stubborn. Egotistical. Overprotective..."

Silas headed straight toward the bar. Having left at eighteen, he'd never been inside The Soggy Boot but that didn't stop him. He'd familiarized himself with other less-than-fine establishments not so different than this since then. His eyes scanned the sparse crowd for the asshole who'd dared to threaten Colby, searching for a smirk or a confident leer he could wipe into the dirt.

Silas's stare made two circuits around the room before he quit. Only a smattering of half-passed-out men littered the place. None of them made good candidates for a bully. Shit, seemed as if the troublemaker had wised up and headed home after all. Damn.

"Didn't expect the pleasure of your company again tonight, foreman." The bartender dried glasses to be put up for the night. "Thought you'd be home milking those scratches so that sweet little wife of yours would fix you up right."

"Not my idea." Colby leaned a hip against the bar, looking more tempting than he had a right to. "You remember Silas?"

"How could I forget that ugly mug? How the hell have you been?"

Silas abandoned his single-minded perusal, disappointed his prey had escaped. It took a couple beats for him to shave years off the man in front of him in his mind. If he removed the masculine set of his jaw, some of the laugh lines around his mouth and a foot or two of his height...

"Donnie?"

Colby and the other man cracked up.

"Nobody's called me that since high school." He grimaced. "Except my ma."

They'd had some fun times with the adventurous kid. How many others had he almost forgotten?

"I assume you hauled Stan Jenkins in, foreman?"

"Stan?" Colby shook his head, a confused glint in his eyes. Silas couldn't stand to wonder another second.

"I need to talk to the dude who messed with Colby."

"Dude?" Don laughed again. "Tonight keeps getting better and better."

"What the fuck's that supposed to mean?"

"Didn't he tell you? Four hands decided to gang up on our boy here. No idea what they were thinking. Colby's never had a problem holding his own. He kicked their asses good and hard. Then fired them on top of it all. Morons." Don chuckled as he recalled the situation, not in the least concerned. "Had to cut one off after you left as he tried to drown his sorrows. The other three couldn't make their hands or mouths work well enough to even try. Almost felt sorry for the bastards. Almost."

Colby winced. "I got carried away."

"No one expected different. Everybody knows you don't talk shit about Lucy around you. Or this fucker for that matter." Don jerked his chin in Silas's direction. "They had it coming."

A sickness swamped Silas's gut. Had he underestimated his lover?

Colby stared at him, waiting for his reaction. Oh shit, he'd nearly fucked this up again. They had to cut him some slack, right? He didn't have a decade of experience in how to be part of a relationship.

"You're right. They did." Silas turned to leave, calling over his shoulder, "Good to see you again, Don. I think Vicky and JD are planning a barbeque for the weekend. Come on over if you're free."

He'd reached the door when Colby paused to ask, "What was that you were saying about Stan Jenkins?"

Don stepped from behind the bar to avoid shouting. He

lowered his voice until it wouldn't carry over the music blasting from the crappy speakers. "He said he was in the shitter when those four earned the smack down but he's a giant coward. I bet he hid in there on purpose. Afterward, he kept spouting off. The more he drank, the more he fired himself up. The fact no one else agreed pissed him off double."

The bartender scrubbed his hand through his hair then sighed hard. "I kicked him out after I heard him talking trash. About Lucy."

Don grimaced.

"We're rational men." Colby laid a hand on Don's shoulder then glared at Silas before adding, "Mostly. I won't let him punish the messenger. Spit it out."

"I told him he was no longer welcome here after I heard him say, 'If Colby ain't man enough for his wife, I'll give her a ride she won't soon forget. I'd have her screaming in no time.'"

"Motherfucker!" Silas smacked his crutch into the doorframe.

"I heard rumors he was the one who beat Beverly Morton last year, though the cops never did prove it. My waitresses refuse to serve him. He cornered Rae out in the parking lot one time. I don't care to think about what might have happened if I hadn't taken out the garbage right then. I don't like the bastard. I don't trust him. And I sure as shit didn't think you'd have appreciated the menace in his beady eyes as he insulted Lu. I thought maybe he'd tried something stupid."

"Fuck!" Colby slammed past him, out the door.

"Thanks, Don."

"I hope I'm wrong." The man wrung his dishtowel between his hands.

Silas cursed his jacked leg as he hobbled toward Colby. The man had already started the truck. Stray peas of gravel hit the side of the bar as he swung around in front of Si then slammed on the brakes. He leaned across the cab to push open the door. Silas tossed his crutches behind the seat, grabbed the oh-shit handle and clambered in. Not pretty but fast.

"Here. Call her." Colby tossed a cell phone into his lap.

Silas had the hunk of plastic halfway to his ear when it rang. He exchanged a look with Colby as the man took off at terrifying speeds given the road conditions and the obsidian darkness engulfing them as they left the radiance of the town behind.

Si wished he'd drive faster.

"What the hell are you boys doing out there?" JD's gruff reproach echoed loud enough for both of them to hear in the cab of the truck. "Do you know what time it is? Are you going to start acting like a bunch of dumbass teenagers 'cause you're all together again?"

"What do you mean?" Silas couldn't breathe past the constriction of his chest. "Because we went to The Boot? On a week night? Long story but Colby had to show some losers who's boss."

"Huh?" JD sounded like he might be running now. A car door slammed in the background. "You're not home? Neither of you?"

"No. We're heading back now though."

"Is Lucy with you?" his father shouted.

"No."

"God damn it!" JD cursed a blue streak. "My tires are flat, and I heard shots. Someone's unloading at your house. Woke me up the first time a few minutes ago. Heard two more rounds right before I dialed."

"We'll be there in five." At this rate they'd make it in half the time it'd taken to reach Compton Pass. Couldn't be soon enough. "We heard Stan Jenkins could be causing trouble."

"I should have fired that slimy jackass a long time ago. Never could catch him at anything I suspected," JD growled. "I'm gonna ride over. I'll come at the house from the back. Be careful. Both of you."

Chapter Eleven

"If he harms one hair on her head, I'll kill that bastard painful and slow."

"Drive, Colby." Silas scrubbed his face with his hands, a calm settling low in the pit of his stomach. "She's tough and she's smart. We're no use if we don't make it there in one piece. We have to trust her to take care of herself until then."

Colby took his eyes from the road for an alarming second to stare at him as though he'd grown seven heads. "Who the fuck are you? What did you do with Silas?"

"I may be slow but I'm learning." He grinned as he selected *Home* from Colby's cell phone directory.

Ring.

Ring.

Ring.

"Answer!" Okay, so he hadn't quite obtained mastery of Zen-like patience. Redial. Wait. Redial. When voicemail kicked on for the third time, he disconnected with a snarl.

Colby zoomed through the gate marking the edge of Compass Ranch. Another minute and they'd be home. "I don't think it's a good idea to bring you into this mess. You'll be a sitting duck, Si."

"Don't waste time trying to make me leave this truck before we're in the yard. I may be fucked up but I can still kick your ass."

"We'll see about that some other time." Thankfully, Colby didn't continue to argue.

He cut the lights when they neared. After they crested the hill, he killed the motor and put it in neutral. They rolled toward the house, their eyes adjusting to the blackness.

"Fuck! On the stairs." Silas pointed toward the figure creeping into the house. "Please tell me she has something to defend herself with."

Colby abandoned secrecy. He honked the horn and flashed his lights, doing anything possible to grant Lucy a heads up as they surged over the gap between them.

"We keep a shotgun loaded with rock-salt shells in the closet. I assume that's what JD heard before. But if she fired warning shots, I'm not sure how many cartridges she has left."

Silas opened the glove compartment and withdrew a revolver from the same spot his father had always stashed one. He checked to make sure it was ready to go then handed it to Colby as they screeched to a stop. "I'll be in behind you. As fast as I can."

Colby nodded then leapt from the truck, tearing up the stairs to the now open door. Before he'd finished taking the treads three at a time, a blast echoed from inside. Colby tripped. The sound shattering the night must have terrified him. He put one hand on the porch then kept running.

Silas cursed the entire journey into the house. He could hear shouting. All of it masculine. Where was Lucy? He slapped the light switch inside the kitchen, illuminating the chaos.

A man sprawled facedown on the kitchen floor. Colby kept him pinned there with a knee between his shoulder blades. The back of the trespasser's shirt and pants were tattered and spotted with blood. The wounds didn't keep him from hollering as though he were nearly torn in two, though. "Keep her away from me. She shot me in the ass."

"You're lucky I didn't shoot your nasty dick off after all the bragging you did. Maybe you can tell the guys in jail what a great lover you make. How you like to hurt your partner while you fuck. I'm sure you'll find someone willing to give you a taste of your own medicine." Lucy propped the shotgun against the kitchen table then flung herself into Silas's arms hard enough to knock him off balance.

"Shh." He cupped her head in his palm then tucked her against his chest. "You did fine. Better than. Brave. Smart. I'm proud of you, Lucy."

JD called out as he crossed through the living room, "It's me. Didn't see anyone out back. All clear."

"All clear," Silas repeated.

Colby cleaned the trash from their kitchen, accidentally kicking the asshole in the ribs as he escorted him outside to wait for the sheriff.

An hour later, Colby and Lucy signed affidavits swearing to the night's events on the hood of Compton Pass's single patrol car, which held Stan Jenkins in the backseat—sore but fine otherwise. Silas couldn't believe how old Sheriff Roberts, a friend of JD's, had gotten. Surely, the man should have retired by now. Guilt for denying both of them their rest warred with his impatience to have the matter resolved.

From the porch, his arms crossed over his chest, he thought of all he could do for Compass Ranch, his lovers and his family. Tonight had cemented his future.

Colby and Lucy held hands as they climbed to his perch. JD and the sheriff ducked into the patrol car with a pair of nods. He lifted one hand in a subtle wave as they carted Stan to jail.

On the horizon, the barest hint of sunrise lightened the sky.

"I should be tired, but I'm wide awake." Lucy sighed as she sank to the wicker loveseat beside him.

"Good. I need to talk to you two." Silas hated the dread creasing Colby's brow and the coldness freezing Lucy's pretty blue eyes into a decent imitation of an Alaskan glacier.

"I swear to God if you make one stupid comment, I'll go berserk." Lucy glared at him.

"What if I tell you both that I've been a complete moron?" He enjoyed the shock turning her pouty lips into a perfect circle.

"I'd have to agree." Colby winced as he tested the puffiness around his eye. "But for some stupid reason, we love you anyway."

"I'm sorry." He offered the only apology he could summon. How could he describe how much he regretted all the time he'd wasted by refusing to believe they were strong enough to handle their situation, the ups and downs, and protect themselves in the meantime? "So sorry. The perfection of the two of you together blinded me. I didn't dream big enough, that the circle could include all three of us and not break. I was terrified I'd destroy you both. All of us, really. I can't believe how insulting that was. Christ, I *am* a fucking moron."

He wished Colby could join them. The loveseat wasn't large enough. He bolted upright, balancing on his good leg, then scooped Lucy into his arms. Colby understood what he intended as though the man could read his heart and mind. He probably could.

After tonight, Silas swore he'd never doubt them again.

Before he could ask, Colby tugged the cushion from the furniture onto the decking. The other man took Lucy from him long enough to give Silas a hand down. Then he settled her beside Silas before joining them on the ground, one lover bracketing each side of his body.

They leaned in toward him.

"You're noble and proud, even if misguided sometimes." Lucy placed a tender kiss on his lips. He wrapped his arm around her thin waist and indulged in a taste of heaven.

"Too strong for your own good. To distance yourself so long and shoulder everyone else's burdens. You have to invite us in.

Allow us to help. Let us be there for you." Colby nudged his wife aside to stake his claim. "Shit, yeah. I love that."

Silas agreed. Rough skin abraded his face and the brute force of the man's tongue as it plundered his mouth fired him up.

Lucy returned, licking the intersection of their mouths until they joined in a three-way kiss that tasted like perfection. While they explored each other, someone slipped a hand beneath the waistband of Silas's shorts to encircle his cock. Before long another hand joined in.

Colby cupped Silas's balls in his calloused palm while Lucy stroked his shaft with her dainty fingers. He surrendered, granting them free rein. Whatever they wished for—whatever they craved—they could have from him. Now and forever.

The early morning air caressed his thighs when someone whisked his shorts off. Pressure built on his good thigh. Colby relinquished his hold on Silas's mouth to nestle between his legs instead.

"Oh, fuck." Silas gasped into Lucy's smile when Colby licked around his wife's fingers, stealing his first taste of erect cock.

"I was thinking more along the lines of suck. But I have no idea how to do this."

"What do you like?" Lucy coached her husband as though Silas weren't there. "Start with that."

She angled Silas's cock toward Colby's parted lips, encouraging him to experiment. The man reached his tongue out and licked the drop of pearly fluid from the tip. A simple act. One guaranteed to jumpstart Silas's libido.

"Get naked, Lu," he ordered, not entirely able to suppress his dominant tendencies. "Give me a taste of you while you teach him."

She stripped the jeans she'd thrown on in a flash when the sheriff arrived then knelt with one knee on either side of his head so she faced her husband, who had graduated to sucking on the tip of Silas's cock.

Si wrapped his hands around her hips then tugged her pussy to his face. He inhaled deeply, relishing the scent of his mate's arousal before he allowed himself to feast on the delicacy. She writhed in his hold, smearing her juices on his cheeks as he chased her clit until he latched onto the sensitive nub. He swirled his tongue around it, soothing her initial cries into moans.

When she'd calmed, she mentored her husband. She leaned forward, adjusting the angle of Colby's lips on Silas's cock so Silas glided to the back of the man's hot mouth. Fuck! Silas's hips jerked, forcing the head of his hard-on to slip into Colby's throat. When the man gagged, he backed off. Lucy soothed her husband while stroking Silas's cock.

After a few seconds, Colby reclaimed his position, swallowing Silas's full length with ease this time. He relaxed, massaging Silas's erection with involuntary muscles.

Silas renewed his attention to Lucy's pussy, lapping at the sweetness flowing more freely from her delicate channel. Every time Colby hit a particularly pleasurable spot on his cock, he rewarded Lucy's coaching. Soon, the man had honed in on what Silas preferred and drove him rapidly toward eruption.

Silas trembled beneath their combined assault then redoubled his oral play. Lucy laughed, then groaned. Colby abandoned Silas's cock for an instant to cheer him on. "Yeah, more. Make her come, Silas. She's gorgeous like this. Right on the edge."

He slid his hands from her hips to her breasts. At the same time he rolled her hard nipples in his fingers, he jabbed his tongue as deep as it would go in her tiny pussy. She bucked on his face, making him work to maintain contact throughout her explosive orgasm.

When she settled, he cleaned her with small licks of his relaxed tongue until she climbed to her feet.

"Going somewhere?" Colby asked when Silas could only

stare at the sight revealed to him. His powerful, respected best friend lounged between his legs, eagerly devouring Silas's cock.

Even his dreams hadn't seemed so erotic.

"Be right back, don't you worry." Lucy smacked her husband's ass—when had Colby shucked his clothes?—then sashayed inside, calling over her shoulder, "Make him good and ready, I want to ride him."

"Don't think that's a problem." Colby swallowed Silas's cock once more then chuckled, the vibrations nearly launching him into the stratosphere.

Lucy might have been gone hours, though it probably only seemed like it, leaving Silas stretched on a rack of pleasure. When she returned, she tapped Colby on the shoulder. "Turnabout is fair play, right, Silas?"

Before his mind could fully process her intent, Colby scaled Silas's supine body and presented his cock. Without thinking, Silas's mouth opened, inviting the man inside. The instant his lips encircled the shaft, a spurt of precome decorated his tongue. He swallowed, thrilling them both.

"That's right, Si." Lucy praised him. She straddled Silas's hips as she fit his cock to the mouth of her dripping pussy. "Take him deep like he did for you. From here, I have a nice view of his ass."

Silas groaned. His entire universe consisted of Colby, Lucy and the rapture they gifted him. Colby filled his mouth, giving him something to suck on, taste, explore with his tongue. Lucy used her wicked pussy to keep his cock happy. More than. God, he couldn't hold out long like this. Not with everything he'd ever hoped for in his reach.

"Suck him good, Silas, and I'll prepare him for you." She tempted Silas with dirty promises as she bounced on his cock. The stranglehold her inner muscles had on his erection couldn't fool him. She loved every instant as much as he did. "You'd like to fuck us both, back to back, wouldn't you?"

"Mmph." Colby's veined shaft muffled Silas's agreement.

The blunt crown grew more defined against his tongue. His lover would surrender soon. He'd make sure of it.

Silas imagined all the tricks Red had used on him during the long, cold nights. He wriggled his tongue, massaging the underside of Colby's cock. The pitch of his lover's groans escalated. The snick of the cap on the lube bottle, which Lucy must have retrieved from the bedside table, cut through the night.

Colby inserted his cock to the base between Silas's lips. The man's wife must be making good on her promises. Silas wished he could see her tiny fingers probing her husband's back passage, loosening him for Silas's invasion.

Their plan worked a little too well.

"I think he's ready, Silas." Lucy shivered. "I have almost my whole hand in him now."

Silas caught the tensing of Colby's sac on his chin but there was nothing he could do to halt the inevitable. Instead he tipped his head back, opening his throat to accept the giant load Colby pumped into him, spurt after spurt. He gulped, surprised to find he enjoyed the salty tang of the other man's ecstasy.

He gouged Colby's legs when Lucy followed suit, coming hard on his embedded cock. She rode him fast, grinding her slight weight on him with rock after rock. When Colby would have withdrawn, she perked up once more.

"No." A sharp slap rang through the early morning. "Don't move."

Silas froze as well.

Lucy laughed. "Not you. Keep sucking, Silas. Colby will get hard again, if you do it right. Just like me. If I keep fucking you, I'll be horny again in no time."

Silas gripped Colby's ass to pin his lover close then made it his personal mission to rejuvenate the man. He had an idea. A naughty, decadent, delicious idea.

Either he was a better cocksucker than he thought or

Colby had saved up a bunch of unfulfilled dreams of his own. In no more than a few minutes, the man sported a full hard-on once more. Impressive.

"Lu, I need him in my ass. I'll take care of you after, I swear, but I need..."

She swung her leg over Silas's hips, sliding off his length as she went.

"Ah!"

"Don't worry. Colby's going to finish you off, Si. You seemed to enjoy his ass before." The sparkle in her eye proved she'd enjoyed watching them fuck just as much.

Colby withdrew his cock from Silas's mouth then inched down his torso. Colby kept backing up until the stiff length of Silas's dick nestled between the cheeks of his ass.

Lucy fisted Silas's cock. "So thick. So huge."

She held him still for Colby, who descended, engulfing him in heat so much quicker than the gradual penetration he'd orchestrated earlier. Within moments, Colby squatted over him and began to fuck. Powerful thighs flexed to lift and lower the man. The motion caused his cock to bob and dance.

Lucy played with her pussy with one hand then took her husband's shaft in the other. Colby slammed his eyes closed when she began a skilled massage over the crown, slippery with Silas's spit and Colby's precome.

"You want it. Don't you, sweetheart?" Silas forced himself to segregate the section of his brain engulfed in fireworks to ensure Lucy's pleasure. As much as he'd love for the heat of Colby's come to spray over his chest, their woman had to have more.

"So bad." Lucy moaned. "When you're finished. I want him to fuck me. Hard. Fast."

"No." Silas grinned when they both threw him a curious look. "Not later. Now."

He put his hands beneath her arms then tugged her over

him. Colby clearly understood when her cute ass lined up with his cock. They partnered to position her with her back to Colby's front, straddling Silas.

The next time Colby lunged upward, his cock pierced his wife's wet opening.

"Oh, my God." She shuddered in their grip. "Do it again, Colby. Please. Please, fuck me."

Silas held her shoulders forward while Colby urged her to drop her hips

"Oh shit, yes. He's fucking me. Deeper. Everytime."

Silas pictured the head of Colby's cock tucked into her folds more thoroughly on every upstroke. Silas couldn't resist the temptation of Lucy's swaying breasts. He lunged up to capture her nipple in his mouth. He bit gently on the tip, causing her back to arch and Colby to burrow farther into her swollen tissue.

"Again!" she screamed.

Colby obliged, fucking them both in counterpoint.

Such divine rapture had to be fleeting.

A few more strokes and Colby's quivering thighs betrayed him.

Silas paused his attention to Lucy's tits to give her warning. "Your husband is about to come. Deep inside you, while holding me tight. Are you ready? Can you come with him? I'd die to hear you both. Loud. Strong. Do it. Give me your satisfaction."

Before he'd finished his request, Colby roared. He lost control, his evaporated timidity proving he forgot to be careful of Silas's thigh, as if Silas cared. Colby slammed his ass onto Silas's cock, grinding so the head nudged Colby's gland. At the same time, Colby contracted his arms, squeezing Lucy close, impaling her as fully as he could. She stopped breathing then screamed as she shattered, coming around her husband, on top of their lover.

Colby's ass hugged Silas's cock over and over as he emptied himself in his wife. The beauty of their unified completion forced Silas to join them. No way could he resist pure perfection.

He put one hand on Colby's thigh and the other over Lucy's heart as he poured himself into Colby's heated depths. He'd never come as hard or as long as he did in the throes of the orgasm assaulting him then. The bond between the three of them felt as tangible as the cushion beneath him.

For a moment he thought their devotion might be visible too.

And then he realized the sun rose behind his lovers, bathing them all in the light of a new day.

Epilogue

Silas shook his head when JD offered him a beer, snagging a Coke from the bucket of ice instead. “I’m good with this, thanks.”

He twisted the top off the bottle then sighed as he surveyed the crowd gathering to celebrate his homecoming. A bunch of the attendees joined them to support Colby and Lucy instead. They hardly knew Silas but the subtle congratulations proved all the friends his lovers had accumulated in the past decade could tell the pair had finally gotten what they really wanted.

The triad didn’t make a big production out of the fact that they intended to share more than burgers and potato salad at their simple barbeque. But Lucy in her gorgeous white summer dress, Colby sporting a perma-grin, and the pile of presents overflowing the table near the appetizers made it clear those who loved them all understood the significance of the day.

Understood and supported.

Silas couldn’t believe how different his life seemed now than a few short months ago. So many amazing changes almost obscured the pain—of his healing body, of losing Red, of dealing with his father, who still refused to visit a doctor.

If only his brothers were here, things would be as close to perfect as possible.

Vicky beamed at him as she approached. “It’s like old times, Silas.”

“I’m sorry.” He’d ached to apologize for years. Lucy looked

over at him and smiled, lending him her strength to continue. "If I hadn't gone, maybe none of the others would have followed. I see now how wrong I was. How much I wasted. I'm sorry."

"Shush." His mother hugged him, drying her eyes on his shirt. "Each of you had to choose your own way. I'm just thankful you found a path home."

"I'm thankful home was still waiting for me."

Colby had a group of kids laughing as he flipped burgers high into the air. Lucy zipped around, greeting guests and brightening the summer with her smile. Cindi chatted with Leah Hollister in the corner, and Don was welcomed with a round of slaps on the back from Jake along with a bunch of the other ranch hands.

The buzz of the party died down when a new arrival climbed from a rental car. Silas dropped his arm from his mother's shoulder, preparing for the thrilled shriek to follow.

Vicky didn't disappoint.

Her surprise didn't keep her frozen. Instead, she high-tailed it for the yard where she launched herself at her second oldest son. Seth caught their mother in mid-air, returning her hug with interest.

While everyone's attention focused on the reunion, JD glared in Silas's direction.

"Sorry," Silas mouthed.

His father closed his eyes for a moment then shook it off, as though agreeing to a truce. They'd enjoy the party. With half his sons on Compass Ranch, it was a rare day. A day to celebrate.

Tomorrow, they'd tackle the rest. Together.

Southern Comfort

Dedication

To our kid brothers, Tommy and Kolin. Thanks for teaching us what it means to be a good brother. For being protective and funny. For providing a shoulder to cry on and being a friend we can laugh with. This one's for you.

Prologue

Seth Compton let his horse run free across the dry earth, enjoying the cloud of dust stirring around them. He and his brothers raced over the mountain ridge, heading to their favorite camping spot. Summer was just kicking in, but given the heat and lack of rain, it promised to be a brutally dry one.

Though the heat and humidity were unusual for Wyoming, they certainly didn't bother him. He loved hard earth and the loud clomping of his horse's hooves as they beat out a tempo that proclaimed his freedom. He was connected to the land, to the animals, to the fresh mountain air and even the unusually brutal sun. All of it made him feel alive and he whooped, grinning at his brothers.

The ride to the campsite went a long way to easing the ache in his chest that had started at dinner, when his older brother, Silas, broke the news he was moving away. It had shocked Seth, stunned him. Silas was the most like their pop, JD, and he was the one brother Seth never thought would leave the ranch. He figured like every ancestor who'd come before them, Silas would lay down deep, solid roots in Compton Pass. He belonged to this place, to their home, and Seth simply couldn't imagine living here without him.

While Silas was made for Compass Ranch, Seth knew his greener pastures lay elsewhere. He longed to leave, to head south and work in Texas. While attending a livestock show with his pop a few months ago, he'd met Thomas Kirkland. Kirkland lived outside San Antonio and owned one of the biggest working ranches in the state. Seth had spent most of one afternoon picking Thomas's brain about the workings on a real Texas ranch. He must have impressed the man because Thomas had sent him a letter last week, inviting him to come down after graduation to work for him. Seth kept the offer a secret from his pop and brothers. He wasn't sure why, but the time to tell them his plans had never felt right.

The setting sun drew patterns on the ground, and Seth let the images wander through his mind. Some people looked for pictures in the clouds, but Seth found them on the earth. The shadows of the trees as they neared the mountain ridge looked like an army of soldiers, standing at attention, all waiting for his command. His destiny was at hand. He could feel it. One more year of damn high school and then he would be free.

He looked back at Silas once more, worried about the deep lines carved in his brother's face. Something had happened. Seth could sense it deep in his soul, but he knew his brother. Silas would never tell him why he was really leaving. Glancing forward, he watched the backs of the twins as they rode side by side, always together. Unlike most identical twins, there was no mistaking who was Sam and who was Sawyer. The two were as alike as mud and soap. Sawyer possessed a recklessness that didn't seem to reside in the refined Sam.

They hadn't discussed their plans for the evening, but the second Silas had made his announcement to the family, he and his brothers looked around the dining table and nodded. Seth saw Silas's pain and knew he'd support his brother no matter what he did. Hell, there was a selfish part of him that was actually glad his brother was leaving. It would pave the way for his departure next summer. Make it easier. Christ, his self-seeking thought made him sick.

Tonight was about Silas, about helping his brother. Besides, Seth felt a pain grip him low in his gut. When would the four of them all be together like this again? The idea cut through him like a knife and as he slowed his horse, a piece of his childhood died.

Tonight. Tonight would be their last time together and the heaviness that accompanied that realization threatened to stop him in his tracks.

Tonight wasn't their usual laid-back escape from chores and hard work and school. It wasn't a hunting trip or the beginning of a summer vacation or a winter retreat to test their wilderness survival skills.

Tonight wasn't about playing or bonding or just being guys. It was about saying goodbye to Silas, and in part, to his youth.

They slowed as they approached their destination and ducked beneath the shelter of the mountain cypresses. The uneven terrain forced them to walk their mounts. They knew better than to risk injuring their animals.

Seth shoved his concerns to the back of his mind. Hell, it was that or fall on his knees and beg his brother not to leave. He wasn't ready to be the oldest brother, to take on more responsibility, serve as a role model for the twins. Those traits had rested easily on Silas's shoulders and Seth suddenly realized there was a freedom in being the second oldest. He got away with more, didn't have to toe the straight and narrow line that Silas seemed to walk so easily.

They dismounted, and Seth helped Sawyer tie the horses to some low hanging branches. Sam gathered kindling for their bonfire, while Silas patched the pit they'd left from prior visits. Silas withdrew some hot dogs from his pack and grinned. They'd just eaten dinner, but he sure as hell wasn't going to turn down a dog cooked black from a campfire. Manna from heaven.

"Si, you're bleeding." Sawyer's comment distracted Seth from his stomach.

"It's nothing." Silas tried to hide his injury, but their youngest brother was relentless.

"It is something." Sawyer moved behind Silas to get a closer look. Sawyer's next comment clued Seth in to exactly what he was looking at. "It's too uniform to be a cut."

"Did you do it?" Seth tipped his hat away from his face and glared at his older brother. Damn him. They'd talked for years of getting tattoos when they were old enough. Swore they'd go together. When Silas didn't answer, he stomped over, determined to see his brother's betrayal for himself. "Holy shit. You did. You got a freaking tattoo. Without me? Without us? You asshole!"

Silas dodged Seth's half-hearted punch toward the sore spot between his shoulder blades. While he was pissed as shit, his heart couldn't let go of the idea that Silas was leaving in the morning. He couldn't let tonight end in a fight.

Silas shrugged. "I had a hard enough time convincing Snake to ink me. If I'd brought you guys with me he never would have caved. He only did it because I'm eighteen now."

Besides, if Silas had told Seth, they wouldn't have been able to stop Sam and Sawyer from tagging along too. Their kid brothers shadowed their every move. Sometimes it was flattering as hell, but most of the time, it was just fucking annoying.

"Well, I suppose that's true. Plus he's probably afraid JD'll kill him if he finds out," Sawyer said, ever the peacekeeper.

Seth rolled his eyes at his baby brother's words. Kid thought their pop walked on water. Of course, Seth had to admit, around here, the guy did. As head of Compass Ranch—the center of Compton Pass, Wyoming—JD Compton wielded a power most men could only dream of. However, while Seth's father's money opened doors, his personality made him a born leader. When JD spoke, people listened.

Silas nodded. "Yeah, that's why I took the bandages off. Didn't want him to notice."

Sawyer persisted. "But you gotta let us see it at least."

"Sure." Silas dropped a wedge of wood on the fire and stood. Seth moved to his brother's back, standing next to the twins, as Silas tugged his grey T-shirt over his head. He caught a slight hitch in his brother's actions and realized the tattoo must hurt like hell. None of them made a sound as they studied the artwork inked on his brother's back.

The sudden silence seemed to unnerve Silas, and he began to offer unneeded explanations. "It's swollen and stuff—"

"Whoa." Seth murmured, not needing any explanation.

"It's awesome." Sam laid his palm to the right of the emblem, careful not to touch the raw skin.

"Sweet," Sawyer agreed then added his hand, on the left side of Silas's back.

"Does it hurt?" Seth couldn't resist the urge to join in, touching the area below the design.

"So bad," Silas confirmed.

"I'm still doing it. Next year. The minute I turn eighteen." Seth had never spoken truer words. He wanted this pattern. Bad. It was perfect. "Exactly like this."

"Me too," Sam chimed in. "The compass design is fucking great. And the ranch brand is perfect. It matches the one we use."

"I didn't know Snake had this kind of shit in him. The shading is so cool. It looks 3D." Sawyer's hand shook on Silas's back. "I want one now. Like yours. But without the fancy N."

"You're only fifteen," Silas barked. "Wait a while and make sure it's what you really want."

"I know what I want."

"Things don't always happen like you expect, Sawyer." Silas sighed and Seth wondered what had altered in his brother's life. Then, he considered the adjustments facing him in the immediate future. The difference was, while Seth was a bit anxious about the move, he embraced the idea, excited by the prospect. Silas didn't seem to feel the same joy in venturing out of Compton Pass.

"Is that why you're leaving?" The high pitch of Sam's question told Seth his younger brothers were taking Silas's departure hard as well.

"Yeah." Seth knew that was the only answer his older brother would give them.

"Well, some people might flip flop around. Not me. Not going to change *my* mind." Sawyer's words were strong, self-assured. He'd always been the most determined to prove himself despite being the baby of the group. Maybe because of it. "I'm joining the Coast Guard. Gonna see the world."

"What!" Silas pivoted to stare at their kid brother, and Seth wondered at the vehemence in his tone. "You've been watching too many freaking commercials. Your place is here, on the ranch."

"No, it isn't," the teenager whispered.

Seth nodded in agreement. Sawyer was right to dream of the world beyond their property line. They'd lived like crown princes for all of their young lives, regarded with a fair bit of jealousy and even a bit of awe by their neighbors and the other kids in school. JD Compton was the uncrowned ruler of the area. In addition to owning a fair bit of the land in Compton Pass, the town was named for Seth's great-great grandfather and JD served as chairman on the town council. Very few decisions were made in this area that didn't have JD's seal of approval. Problem was, Seth knew there was a hell of a lot more to this world than Compass Ranch and he was aching to strike out and make a stand, build a life with his own hands, rather than riding in the shade provided by his father's very large shadow.

"You're not planning to stay?" Silas's forehead creased with disbelief. "None of you?"

The look of outright betrayal on his brother's face tweaked Seth's already stretched nerves. "Don't look at us like that! I figured you'd understand. I need to get the hell out of here. Find my own place. Same as you." His secret desire fell from his lips, and he was helpless to hold back. "Not Alaska though, I hate winter. You're crazy to take on all that snow. Somewhere warm.

Maybe I'll head down south." He withheld the information regarding Kirkland's invitation. He remembered Silas's tattoo and the image of his future became clear. "Yeah, that's what I'll do. A fancy S instead of an N on my compass, bro."

"What? No!" Silas threw his arms up in frustration. "It's not like that. I mean—"

"We understand, Si." Sam smiled and nodded. "I'd like to go to college. Earn a degree. Find a real job. Something where I don't have to dirty my hands to rake in cash. I'm going to have fancy clothes, a slick apartment and a kickass car. I'll party every night with the hottest girls in the city."

Seth grinned. He wasn't the only one with dreams bigger than Compton Pass. His brothers understood. They yearned for the same things.

Silas turned to Sawyer and Seth read the unspoken question, the lingering concern on his lips. Who would stay at Compass Ranch? A slight pang of guilt penetrated Seth's conscience, but he batted it away.

"Oh, no." Sawyer shook his head as he kicked a rock when Silas turned to him. "Don't give me that look. I told you, I'm *not* getting stuck here. Fuck that. You think someone should hang around, then stay put. It ain't too late to cancel your plane ticket."

"I-I can't," Silas said.

Seth understood his brother's feeling. Some undeniable lure was tearing them away from this place, something stronger than all of them.

"And neither can we." Seth hated the look of desolation on his older brother's face. He slugged Silas's shoulder, hoping to lighten the atmosphere. He didn't want Silas's last night to be weighted down with such heavy discussion. There was plenty of time to figure out what would come next. Seth still had a year until graduation, and the twins were only fifteen. Three years was a long time for a young man to change his mind. Maybe one or both of their little brothers would come to realize they didn't have to leave. Regardless of that, they didn't need to worry about any of that right now. He chuckled as he thought of a surefire way to make them all smile. "Come on, start the dogs. I'm starving. Jake slipped me a couple *Playboy*s for doing his chores last weekend so he could bang Missy Trelane."

"Nice! Me first." Sam squeaked a head start for Seth's backpack as Sawyer launched himself after his twin.

Seth laughed as he watched them wrestle and call each other names. *Yep*, he thought, *there's still plenty of time.*

Chapter One

Ten years later

Seth dismounted his horse, Charlton, and tried to slap some of the dust out of his jeans. Damn, it was hot. Weather forecasters proclaimed it the hottest June in Texas in the last fifty years, and he didn't doubt it was true. The air was so thick he'd need a chainsaw to cut through it. He couldn't believe he'd ever thought he wanted to live in a hotter climate. On more than one occasion lately, he found his mind drifting back to the Wyoming nights he'd spent sleeping on the screened-in back porch with his brothers.

On warm summer evenings, they'd take sleeping bags out of the shed and sack out on the porch floor, the mountain breeze blowing over them as they told ghost stories, trying to scare the bejeezus out of each other, laughing and talking until JD finally stomped out to yell at them to go to sleep. He'd been thinking about home and his brothers a lot and wondered when he'd become prone to homesickness. He pulled a handkerchief from his back pocket and tried to wipe the sweat out of his eyes.

"Hot enough for you?"

Seth looked up and saw Thomas Kirkland walking toward him from the other end of the large stable.

Seth nodded.

"Figure we could fry steak and eggs on the asphalt out there. Damn joy riders. You finish fixing that fence down on the south pasture?"

"Yep. CJ and Ronnie helped."

"I can pretty much guarantee they won't decide to sneak off in their daddy's farm truck with a six pack of Natty Light again anytime soon. Fool kids. They're lucky the only thing hurt was the fence. Could've broken their damn necks."

Seth chuckled. "Well, you gotta admit it's pretty hard to see if any damage was done to Carl's rusty piece of shit Ford. I can't believe the thing still starts, let alone runs."

Thomas agreed. "Think that's why CJ and Ronnie weren't hurt. The truck doesn't go much more than thirty miles an hour."

"Thought you'd like to know they were groaning about the belt Carl took to their hides while we were out there sweating our asses off mending the fence."

"Damn." Thomas shook his head. "I told him not to go too hard on them. Making them pay for the lumber and do the repairs was punishment enough for me."

"Yeah, well, given the fucking heat, I tend to think you're right. Besides, I'm not sure Carl hit to harm as much as to make his point. I think he hurt their pride more than their rear ends. Not fun to get your ass swatted at fourteen when you like to think you're a man and not a boy."

Thomas pushed his hat back on his head and ran his sleeve along his brow. "You've got a point there. Speaking of pride, Jody's back."

Seth tried to hide the combination of excitement and anxiousness his boss's announcement sparked. He'd been looking forward to her arrival for weeks. Hell, years. She'd graduated from college and was coming home for good. "Wonder why pride made you think of your girl?"

Thomas chuckled. "I'd like to say it's because she's my pride and joy, but I think we both know it's because that girl got in line twice the day they handed out that particular character trait."

"Three times," Seth joked. "Took her sweet time getting home, didn't she?"

"Yep. Don't know why the hell it took her a whole month to pack up her apartment. I told her I'd help her move back the weekend she graduated from college, but the damn girl insisted she had too much to do."

"Jody marches to her own beat, Thomas. You know that."

"Yeah, well. She pulled up in a U-Haul a half hour ago with ten times more shit than she left with and..."

Thomas faltered and Seth looked up, confused by the look on his boss's face. Thomas Kirkland was so much like his pop, JD, Seth swore they were separated at birth. Neither man was ever flustered, but right now, that was the only way Seth could think of to describe his boss.

"Well, Seth. She didn't just bring home a bunch of stuff. She brought home—"

A feminine voice hollering from the end of the stable cut Thomas short. "There you are. Daddy, what the hell? You know, hiding out in the stable isn't—oh."

Jody pulled up short as she approached and saw him standing there. "Hey, Seth. Thought you were out fixing a fence or something."

He removed his hat and ran his hand through his dark hair, the manners his mother had beat into his head coming to the forefront. Vicky's number one rule was always take your hat off in the presence of a lady. Problem was he was torn between calling Jody a lady and a hellion. She'd run riot over him for the past decade and half the time he didn't know which end was fucking up whenever she was around.

"Welcome home, Jody." He stepped forward and bent down to give her a hug. Her shoulder-length chestnut-brown hair smelled like honeysuckle. He had to force himself to keep the embrace quick and brotherly. His cock stirred, and he closed his eyes briefly, trying to ignore the usual arousal that accompanied her arrival. She was the boss's daughter and even at twenty-one, she was too damn young for him.

She'd been a tomboyish twelve-year-old when he first came to work on the ranch and the other hands had given him shit when it became obvious the young girl had a crush on him. Her infatuation hadn't abated until last Christmas, when he'd foolishly kissed her under the mistletoe and then shoved her away.

Since then, the easy camaraderie and innocent flirting they'd engaged in since her graduation from high school had evaporated. She'd only been home once since Christmas, but he could see in her face she was still angry with him. He was determined now that she was back to stay, he'd make things right again. He'd been thinking about her return a lot lately. Things were about to change between him and the little wildcat. He grinned at the thought.

"Thanks, Seth. Good to be back."

"Didn't get the impression you were staying," Thomas muttered.

"Daddy. Don't you think you were kind of rude to Paul?"

"Paul?" Seth asked.

"I mean we only just got here and told you our good news."

Thomas frowned. "Is that what we're calling it?"

Jody's eyes narrowed. "Yes, it is. Didn't you tell me you wanted me to find a nice man and settle down?"

"What the—" Seth crossed his arms over his chest, suddenly worried about the direction of this conversation. "You were pissed as shit when Thomas gave you that advice. Said women these days didn't need a man to be happy and you didn't plan to ever get hitched." The fight she and her father had had at the end of last summer was epic. Seth had tried to stay out of it, mind his own business, but when Jody and Thomas went toe to toe, it was hard not to hear. Neither of them understood the concept of *inside* voices.

Jody glanced at him and gave him a small smile that seemed too sad to be genuine. "Turns out I was wrong."

Seth fought to restrain a growl from escaping his chest. She'd brought home a man? Paul? Seth's fists clenched at the thought. "How so?"

Thomas shrugged, the helpless gesture at odds with his legendary ability to handle anything. Of course, now that Seth thought about it, Jody was the exception to her father's confident approach to life. Her mother had died when she was five, and Thomas had struggled to understand and raise his daughter since then.

Jody lifted her left hand, flashing a diamond the size of Dallas in his face. "I'm engaged."

"The hell you are." The words left Seth's mouth before he could catch them. While Thomas laughed at his reply, he could see he'd sent Jody's temper into orbit.

She retracted her hand and studied the ring, sarcasm dripping from her tone. "Really? I'm not engaged? Because I think this ring and the fact Paul got down on one knee and said, 'Will you marry me?' sort of proves that I am."

"Who the fuck is this Paul character?" Seth took two steps toward the main house, ready to confront the asshole who'd dared to propose without even bothering to meet her family first, but Jody stepped in front of him, stopping him.

"Back off, Seth. You know perfectly well who Paul is. He's been my best friend since freshmen year of college."

"*That* Paul? What the fuck? I thought he was gay. Hell, he spent his entire last visit here flirting with the ranch hands."

Jody closed her eyes and took a deep breath. But long before a ten count, she replied, through gritted teeth, "Obviously, he's not gay."

"Since when?"

"Since he fucking proposed to me. Why am I even having this conversation? This is none of your damn business."

He bent down until his face was mere inches from hers. "Is that right? Well, I beg to differ."

She leaned closer, and he could detect the slight scent of chocolate on her breath. Jody clearly hadn't lost her sweet tooth, though he was beginning to wonder where she'd misplaced her common sense. "You are not my boyfriend and you are not my brother. Hell, you're not a part of this freaking family at all. You are my father's foreman, which means my decision to get married is none of your damn business."

He struggled to keep his hands on his hips, rather than reach over and prove to Miss Jody Kirkland how very wrong she was. His fingers were itching to take her over his knee and spank some sense into her.

She'd made herself his business the very first day he'd come to work here and she'd climbed atop Coy, her father's newest addition to the stable. The far-from-tamed horse had taken exception to its rider and bolted across the yard, jumping a fence and sprinting across the lower pasture. Seth had chased her on Charlton for close to a mile before managing to catch up and pull the fool girl off the runaway roan.

He could still recall the way she'd trembled in his arms and looked at him like he'd hung the moon for rescuing her. By the time they'd returned to the stable, they were laughing like old friends and his position at the ranch had been solidified. As he looked into her blue eyes now, he missed the admiration and wished to hell he could get rid of the anger that had crept in instead.

"Jody," Thomas broke in. "You know full well I consider Seth a part of this family. If he takes exception to your asinine engagement, then perhaps you should listen to why."

Jody released a furious breath. "You can't object to a man who's been my friend for years."

Seth leaned back a bit. "Don't you think it's a little strange that one minute the guy's gay and the next he's not?"

"He never said he was gay."

"That's not something we needed to be told. It was kind of obvious. Is he bi?" Seth could understand bisexuality. He'd seen glimpses of it in his older brother, Silas, when they were growing up and he suspected now that his brother was back home in Wyoming, Silas would be acting on some of the feelings he had for his best friend, Colby.

Jody sighed loudly. “No. He’s in love with me. Just me.”

Seth knocked his hat against his jeans in frustration. “Never heard you talk about him like he was your boyfriend. You were home for Easter, Jody, and you didn’t say one word about dating him. When did this so-called love affair start?”

“It turned into something more than friendship recently.”

He tried to beat down the twinge of jealousy that accompanied the thought of her being *more than friends* with any other man. She was right. He had no claim staked on her. But it sure as hell felt like he did. “So why the rush? If you’ve only started dating, I don’t see why—”

“Because I want to. I don’t need any more reason than that.”

“Just like that?” Seth tried to understand what the hell was going on inside her pretty head. The only thing missing from her haughty proclamation was for her to stamp her foot on the ground like a three-year-old. She wasn’t like this. She’d never been a spoiled girl, never been prone to temper tantrums or selfish demands. She’d been a fun-loving tomboy who’d grown into his laughing, easygoing friend. This angry woman was a stranger to him, and he missed the real Jody.

“That’s right. And we’re not waiting. We came home to have the ceremony performed here.”

“When exactly?”

Thomas cleared his throat. Bewilderment crossed his boss’s face. He was sure the same confusion resided on his. There would be no help from that camp. “They plan to bring the justice of the peace out to make it official here at the ranch in two weeks.”

Hell to the no! Seth would see her married to some stranger only over his dead body. He started to say exactly the same thing, but the argument that came out was much different than what he'd intended. "What about love, Jody? Do you love him?"

His softly spoken question seemed to jar her a bit and for just a second, he saw the trace of his old friend before she disappeared again behind the indifferent, cold woman who'd replaced her.

"What kind of question is that?"

Thomas leaned against the horse stall and crossed his arms over his chest. "A pretty valid one, if you ask me."

Jody turned to look at her father and shook her head. "You two really are a matched set, you know that? Way to gang up on me."

"Answer me, Jody," Seth persisted. "Are you in love?"

She studied his face and a glimmer of pain shone in her eyes. Then she nodded, turned on her heel and walked out of the stable.

It wasn't until she disappeared around the corner that it began to sink in. Seth had missed his chance with her. He'd pushed her away for too long.

"You realize you made a mistake there, right?" Thomas asked.

Seth nodded sadly. Mistake was putting it lightly. He'd fucked up. Big time. "Yeah. I guess I did."

Thomas studied his face and then chuckled. "Think we're talking about two different things. Of course, maybe not. She may be in love, son, but she didn't say with who."

Chapter Two

Jody stormed back into the house, slamming the screen door behind her. “God damn, mother fucking, piece of arrogant shit asshole.”

“I take it you ran into Seth.” Paul’s sarcasm drifted to her from the dining room. She glanced in that direction and caught her best friend leaning against the doorframe.

She nodded, too furious to reply.

“Took the news of our engagement well, did he?”

She closed her eyes and mentally counted to ten. Seth Compton had some nerve attempting to lecture her about anything. Anything! He’d brushed her affections aside for over a decade and the minute she’d moved on and managed to say fuck him, he decided to act like he gave a shit. “He took it like the clueless caveman he is.”

“Tried to talk you out of marrying me?”

“As if he has the right to tell me what I can and can’t do. I offered him the position of boyfriend loads of times, and he rejected me. Now he can just take a giant leap and eat his fucking heart out.”

Paul laughed. “I love your locker room language. So colorful.” He took several steps toward her, stopping when he reached her. His hand drifted up to her cheek, and he brushed a stray hair away from her face. “I thought you said you were over him.”

“I am.”

Paul gave her a grin that said he wasn't fooled by her too-quick reply. "Jody, you can't kid a kidder."

She sighed. "I *want* to be over him."

"You realize that's not the same thing, right?"

She shrugged and turned away. "It's enough for me, for now."

"We don't have to go through with this. I can find someone else to—"

"No," she interjected. "I'm doing it. I want to marry you. Honest."

"But if Seth—"

She raised her hands, trying to halt his words. "He's a typical male. He wants what he can't have. If I'd shown up here available, acting the fool as always, following him around with my stupid heart on my sleeve, he'd still be dismissing me, offering up all those reasons why we can't be together. I'm sick of the game, Paul. I'm not playing it anymore."

"Fine. I get that. But that still doesn't mean you have to marry me. I'm not happy about you sacrificing your immediate future just to help me inherit my trust fund."

She leaned forward and kissed him on the cheek. "You're my best friend, and you need me. I'm marrying you."

"Well, isn't this sweet?" Seth's insulting tone set her teeth on edge again. She scowled as he opened the screen door and entered the house. "Been awhile, Paul."

Paul smiled and offered his hand. "Good to see you again, Seth. How are you doing?"

Jody resisted the urge to kick her best friend in the ass as he shook Seth's hand.

"Can't complain," Seth replied. "Besides sweating my ass off in this hellish heat, things are pretty much par for the course."

Paul laughed easily, the sound almost flirty, and Jody gritted her teeth as she watched her fiancé checking out Seth in his tight denim. Jesus. She took Paul's hand in hers in an attempt to distract him.

"Come on. I'll show you around the place. There've been a few changes since the last time you were here. Plus we need to pick somewhere for the ceremony. Still not sure if I want to set it up in the back or front yard." She started to yank Paul outside, but Seth stopped her with a hand on her shoulder. She sucked in a deep breath and tried to ignore the fact his touch made her so hot.

"Hold on a minute. Let me wash up and I'll join you."

She shrugged in an attempt to dislodge his hand. "Why?"

He grinned and she closed her eyes, unwilling to let his handsome face dazzle her. Fucking dimples got her every time. A quick glance at Paul nearly had her groaning aloud. Apparently, her fiancé was a sucker for dimples too.

"I thought it might be nice to get to know the guy you're marrying a little better, Jody. I mean he is going to be a part of the family very soon, and we've never had more than a couple chances to chat."

He stressed the word *family* throwing her father's words in the stable back in her face.

"We'd love to have you join us," Paul invited, his smile charming. She pinched his arm covertly and his grin faded quickly.

"Fine. We'll wait here. Don't take too long." She tried not to wince at her imperious tone. She hated sounding like such a bitch, but she couldn't seem to temper her bitterness around Seth. She was nursing a broken heart and doing a shitty job of it.

Seth headed down the hall to the bathroom. When she heard the door close, she turned to Paul. "Jesus Christ. What the hell are you doing?"

Paul tried to look sorry, but failed. "I forgot how good-looking Seth is."

She closed her eyes. "You cannot be serious. You're

attracted to Seth? My Seth?"

"Technically, he's not *your* Seth. You don't want him anymore, remember?"

She frowned. "You can't have him."

"Jody."

"Don't you *Jody* me. We're here to fool my family into thinking we're in love and we can't wait another minute to spend our lives together. That's the only way they'll allow me to go through with this. I explained that to you. That's hardly going to work if you start coming on to Seth."

Paul nodded. "You're right. I'm sorry. I'll behave."

Jody sighed. "This is still a good plan, Paul. The stipulation in your father's will was outright cruelty, and we won't let him win."

Paul kissed her on her cheek. "I love it when you're on a mission, but this isn't your wrong to right, Jody. There are lots of people in the world who think homosexuals are freaks of nature, and my father simply happened to fall into that lot. You have to be very sure you're willing to sacrifice a year of your life. That's a lot to give up to help me meet some silly stipulation in a will. Especially if you're doing it to spite Seth."

"I'm only twenty-one, Paul, and a year isn't that long. Besides, you don't have time to find anyone else. The will says you have to be married by the end of July to claim your trust fund. Are you forgetting about your plans for it? Think of all the good that cancer research facility could do."

Paul shrugged sadly. His mother had passed away from the disease when he was only ten. Sometimes Jody wondered how different his life would have been if she'd survived. His father, a cold bastard on good days, had treated him like a leper after discovering his only heir and namesake was gay. "I guess you're right."

"There's no doubt about it. You're going to earn your master's in architecture at Cornell and then you'll build the best damn cancer research facility in the world."

Paul laughed. "I do appreciate your confidence in me, sweetheart, but trust fund aside, all I'm saying is Seth isn't the only man out there. There are other fish in the sea. What if you run into your fish while you're stuck with me?"

Jody shook her head. "There aren't any other fish for me."

Paul reached for her hand. "Oh, Jody. That's not true."

Coming home and seeing Seth again was every bit as hard as she'd known it would be. She'd put off the return as long as she could simply because she kept waiting for some miracle to occur. Unfortunately, her feelings for Seth were stronger now than ever. She pushed the thought aside, tried to bring the remaining tattered shreds of her pride to the forefront. "I've been such an idiot, Paul. I can't keep playing this *Follow the Stud* game."

Paul laughed. "Is this some twisted version of *Follow the Leader*? Have you been holding out on me, Jody? Sounds exciting."

Jody chuckled and shrugged, appreciating her friend's attempts at alleviating her pain. "It's only fun when you catch the stud. Which every woman within a ten-mile radius of this ranch has done with the exception of me."

Paul glanced back down the hall where Seth had disappeared. "Seth doesn't strike me as the type to kiss and tell."

"Oh, *he* isn't, but some of the women have let details slip here and there. His reputation is actually sort of the stuff of legends."

Her friend's eyes widened. "Do tell."

She looked away, clearing her throat. "Apparently, Seth has a bit of a rough edge in the bedroom."

Paul groaned. "Sweetheart, as much as I'd love to hear the gory details, I'm sporting a hard-on just thinking about it. Since *your* Seth is off-limits to me, maybe you shouldn't tell me too much. The temptation would be terrible."

Jody sighed. "That's just it. I've known about his

preferences in the bedroom for years and I can't stop thinking about them. My body aches wishing he would—"

"Hogtie you to his bed and have his wicked way with you?"

A burst of laughter escaped her at Paul's attempt at a southern accent. "Ooo, nice use of the word *hogtie.* I'll make a cowboy out of you yet, city slicker. And to answer your question, yes. But Seth still looks at me like I'm some little girl he has to rescue."

Paul shook his head. "I always find that assessment of your relationship with him shocking. Clearly you should have invited him to visit you at the university. I've never met a fiercer woman. He should have been with us the night you pulverized Mark Robyns."

"He called you a fag."

Paul bent forward and kissed her on the end of the nose. "I *am* a fag, Jody."

"It was the *way* he said it. Like he had a mouth full of fuckin' manure."

Taking her hand and lifting it over her head, Paul spun her like they were dancing. It was a familiar move and one the two of them did often whenever something she said struck Paul as funny. Apparently he found her southern drawl and her penchant for bad words hilarious. "I love southern girls," he teased as they laughed.

"Am I interrupting something?"

Jody stopped pirouetting as Seth came back into the room. The lighthearted feeling Paul never failed to evoke in her disappeared as fast as pigs at slaughter time.

Paul turned and smiled. "Nope. Just dancing with my girl."

Seth studied her, his face a mixture of confusion and—she paused—jealousy? He'd never been possessive before, though God knew she'd tried to provoke that feeling in him. She propped her hands on her hips, defensively. "Do you have a problem with us dancing? It's not like we're fucking on the living room floor."

If she could have bitten her tongue off, she would have. His eyes darkened. If she still gave a shit what he thought, she would have banked her attitude, but for some reason, tweaking his temper made her smile. She'd spent a decade trying to stir some emotion in him. If anger was all she could rouse, so be it. Some petty, small part of her wanted him to hurt as much as she did. She wasn't proud of that fact, but it was there and she couldn't seem to stop it.

Paul put an arm around her shoulders and drew her close. His soft tone soothed her rankled feathers. "Be nice, Jody. He doesn't strike me as a man you want to piss off."

She flushed when it was clear Seth had heard her fiancé's warning. "You should listen to Paul. I'm not real fond of this sassy tone you've acquired since you've been away."

She rolled her eyes and untangled herself from Paul's grip. "Oh my. Seth's unhappy. I'll probably cry myself to sleep worrying about that. Come on, Paul. Tour time."

She hoped her snarkiness would deter Seth from coming, but as she crossed the yard toward the stable, she looked over her shoulder and discovered him right on their heels.

As she took Paul around the property, showing him all the buildings, introducing him to the new hands and letting him catch up with the guys he'd met on previous visits, Seth was there. He answered all of Paul's questions regarding the ranch in a cool, though friendly manner. Paul toned down the flirting with Seth, but when they ran into Chase, she knew they were in trouble.

Chase Webster was sex in cowboy boots, and she had it on good authority he didn't have a preference about who he slept with either. Male, female, one, two or even three lovers at a time, Chase could be counted on to be in the middle of the fun, stirring up the local gossips for days and making hearts race with just a wicked smile and quick nod. Unfortunately, Paul was far from immune to the handsome man's charm and the two of them engaged in a conversation that skirted the line between friendly conversation and foreplay. She looked around, trying to avoid catching Seth's eye. She didn't want to know what he was thinking.

Glancing back at Chase, she was reminded of last summer and a flush heated her face before she could stop it. She figured there must be a *Don't Do* list somewhere on the ranch with her name written across the top because Chase had never once offered her a night of raunchy fun, though she'd fought like the devil to get his attention in hopes of making Seth jealous.

Toward the end of last August, she'd decided to go for broke. She'd donned a too-tight tank top and her Daisy Duke's and headed to the stable in search of Chase. There was very little the man did that wasn't discussed at length by every person on the ranch and she'd felt certain if she could tempt the man to make out with her, Seth would hear of it. She hadn't made it two steps in the stable when she'd heard laughter coming from the tack room. Sneaking to the doorway, she'd listened to Chase and Seth laughing at her antics.

"She's relentless when she wants something," Chase had said.

"Jody's always been stubborn." She struggled to figure out if Seth sounded entertained or annoyed, but she couldn't tell. "Guess the fruit doesn't fall far from the tree."

They laughed.

"She leaves in a few days," Chase said.

Seth sighed loudly. "I know. Not much longer."

Was he sad she was leaving or glad? Jody inched closer, wishing she could see Seth's face.

"Bunch of us are goin' into Preston tonight. Hitting the strip club. You wanna come?"

Seth chuckled. "Yeah. I think I do. Lap dance might do just the trick."

Envy flowed through her, and Jody swallowed back tears of anger. Even a woman he had to pay for was preferable to Seth. He'd never choose her.

She'd run out of the stable, packed her things and returned to college three days early. She simply couldn't stand to wait in the wings while Seth found his pleasure with every woman in the county. She'd left without saying goodbye, a fact he'd taken her to task for the following week when she'd finally caved and answered one of his calls to her cell phone. Hearing his voice, listening to him tell her about home, had thawed the ice around her heart.

She glanced over at him, surprised to find his gaze on her as she reminisced. He jerked his head toward the barn entrance. "Hey, Chase, Paul, you guys mind hanging out here? I remembered something I have to show Jody in the barn. Won't take a minute."

Paul and Chase both nodded quickly before continuing their conversation. Jody had to kick some sense into her best friend. He wasn't taking this situation seriously enough at all. There was no way her father would consent to her entering a marriage of convenience, even for only a year. He had to think they were in love. Paul was seriously messing up the plan.

She followed Seth and took several deep breaths, trying to hold on to the memory of him cavorting with erotic dancers last summer. Anger would help her survive the next few minutes. "What do you want?"

He continued walking deeper into the barn and she glanced around, hoping to discover someone else around.

"There's no one here to save you."

She narrowed her eyes. "I wasn't aware I needed to be rescued."

Seth turned and crossed his muscular arms over his chest. She squeezed her legs together in hopes of cutting off the trickle escaping her pussy. Why did he have to make her so horny?

He grinned. "Oh, you definitely need protection."

His words rankled and reminded her of Christmas break. They'd met up under the mistletoe. In typical Seth fashion, he'd offered her a quick peck on the forehead. Still a bit miffed about the summer before, she'd taunted him, called him a monk and a coward and dared him to give her a real kiss.

For the first time in her life, he'd taken her up on it. His kiss proved to be her final undoing. His lips had burned an imprint on hers and there were times when she still thought she could feel the mark. "You said at Christmas the only protection I needed was from you, so maybe I should—"

She pivoted to leave, but hadn't taken two steps before Seth grabbed her. He turned her to face him, his eyes narrowed. "Quit screwing around."

Her temper broke. "I'm serious."

He snorted out a laugh. "Like hell."

She shook her head. "It's true. I'm moving on this time."

"What's that supposed to mean?"

"It means I'm done with the come-ons, the schemes to capture your attention. I've tried all I can think of. You made it abundantly clear at Christmas you aren't interested, so I'm bowing out of the race. You don't have to worry about my relentlessness anymore," she said, using the same description he'd uttered last summer. She'd made a vow that she would move on with her life, put Seth Compton in her past. It had been an easier thing to do at school. Distance helped her forget how strongly he affected her.

"It's not like your attention was exactly a hardship."

She sighed. "God, you sure acted like it. You've swatted me away like a gnat buzzing around your face for years. I. Get. It. I'll leave you alone."

"You've never bothered me, Jody."

"Yeah, right. I heard you talking to Chase right over there last summer." She pointed to the tack room. "Are we finished in here? I really need to find Paul."

"Paul's fine. Come here." He crooked a finger at her, and she fought the urge to follow him without question. "Is that why you bolted before the going-away picnic I'd planned?"

"What? No." Her gut cramped. He'd planned a picnic?

Seth closed his eyes before opening them again and giving her a look that practically demanded her acquiescence. "Damn stubborn fool."

His words infuriated her. "I'm hard-headed? Me?" She flung her hair over her shoulder. "Is this a cruel case of reverse psychology? I tell you I'm moving on and you think you can just point a finger and I'll come running. Fuck you!"

He reached for her before she could even think to run. "I'm damn sick and tired of your mouth. I'm trying to talk to you, but you're too busy biting my head off to listen." He tucked her close, his hands closed firmly against her upper arms, holding her captive. "You tell me to fuck myself one more time, and you're gonna find yourself with a mouthful of something big and hard to keep you quiet."

She laughed in his face. "You wish you had that much power over me. You ever try and I'll cut your dick off and shove it down your throat."

He pulled her closer and did the last thing she expected. He kissed her. She tried to shove away from him, tried to break free of his implacable hold, but he merely tightened his grip. When she started to angle her face away, he wrapped one arm around her waist, while the other pinned her head, keeping her lips glued to his.

Shock held her immobile for a moment as she tried to figure out what the fuck was happening. She'd begged for this for years to no avail.

Why now? The question burned in her brain.

She opened her mouth to tell him to stop, but his tongue seized control, robbing her ability to speak, to protest. When it became obvious she couldn't break free, she simply froze. Played dead.

She refused to kiss him back. Her mind screamed for her to stay strong. It took every ounce of strength in her body not to melt into his arms, not to soften her lips and sample more of the heaven he offered.

His grip lightened, and he retreated a mere fraction of an inch. “Kiss me,” he demanded.

She shook her head. “I can’t.” Her voice broke on the last word.

He studied her face. She dropped the barriers, allowing him to see her pain. He’d broken her young woman’s heart one time too many. She wasn’t coming back.

He looked toward the rear of the barn, then spoke softly. “Dammit. You make me forget myself, lose my resolve.”

“I’m not doing a thing. I’m home to plan my wedding and—”

Seth shook his head, stopped her words. “I don’t want to hear another peep about that.” He rubbed his hand over his face, and she wondered about the dark shadows under his eyes. He was different this time. She wasn’t sure what had changed, but it was clear something had.

“I didn’t bring you in here to fight...or to kiss you.” He pointed to a basket tucked into a corner. She could barely make out the image of three wriggling puppies.

She smiled, kneeling next to them. “Dusty’s litter?”

He nodded. “She had them last week. Knew you were coming home some time this week, so Thomas and I thought we’d surprise you.”

She reached down to stroke the soft fur of the little puppies, trying to forget how badly she was screwing everything up.

Seth crouched next to her. “I miss you.”

She looked at him, confused, until he continued. “I don’t know this new Jody. You’re mad at me all the time. I’m not saying I don’t deserve it, but—”

She started to speak, to refute his words with a lie, but he raised his hand to stop her.

“I understand why. I’d be a jackass not to get it. I’ve known about your crush on me forever.”

She winced at the word *crush.* It had been so much more than that to her. He'd been her first love. Hell, her only love.

"I haven't been careful with your feelings, Jody, even though I've always considered you mine to protect. How's that for irony?" He shrugged. "It's just you're so damn young."

"You're only six years older than me, Seth. That's not much of an excuse."

He shrugged. "It seemed like a hell of a lot when I was eighteen and you were twelve."

"Well, it was illegal at that point," she joked. They shared a chuckle before she sobered up.

He stared at the barn door, trying to find a way to explain. When he faced her again, his eyes were sadder than she'd ever seen them. "I know that. I guess it became a habit to convince myself your flirting was more infatuation than true attraction. I didn't take your feelings for me seriously and I was wrong. I think if I'd admitted they were genuine, I couldn't have forced myself to do the right thing."

She closed her eyes and suddenly regretted her past actions. When she wanted something, she went after it with a relentlessness that could be scary. She hadn't made things easy for Seth. "I sort of did the same thing to you. I'm sorry for that."

"What do you mean?"

"You must've shown me a million different ways that you weren't interested. I ignored you time and time again. My dad always says I'm too hard-headed for my own good and a bulldog to boot. I got it in my head that we were destined to be together and I held on to that idea, never thinking for a minute that you might not."

She blinked against the tears gathering in her eyes. She wasn't about to cry in front of him. She rose quickly.

"Jody," he stood and stopped her. "I've missed you these past few months."

After Christmas, she'd gone back to school and into a No Seth Zone. She'd severed the close friendship they'd always shared despite her—she paused, then forced herself to think about the word he'd used—*crush*, convinced it was the only way she could protect her heart and force herself to move on.

"I missed you too. I've been acting like such a bitch since I got home. What do you say we call a truce? Friends again?" She held out her hand, praying she could survive the next thirty seconds without breaking down.

He stared at her hand and for a moment, she thought he might reject her gesture. Then he reached out and wrapped his hand around it. He didn't shake it, as she intended. Instead, he merely held it, held her gaze with his. He nodded once, but she couldn't help but doubt his sincerity. He didn't agree at all.

Forcing a light smile, she edged away from Seth. "I need to find my fiancé. My life is good now, Seth, I swear. I hope you can accept that and be happy for me."

Turning, she left the barn, separating Paul from Chase before Seth could catch up with them. "I have a little bit of a headache," she said. "Mind if we finish the tour later?"

Paul gripped her hand and strode with her to the house. "Of course not. Are you sure you're okay?"

She nodded, resisting the urge to turn around. When they reached the front porch, the temptation grew too strong and she glanced over her shoulder. Seth stood outside the barn, staring at her. His hungry expression said it all. He wasn't accepting anything, and they definitely weren't friends anymore.

Chapter Three

Seth felt like a spider stalking his prey, waiting for the fly to land in his web. Jody had feigned a headache and hidden in her room last evening, refusing to come down for dinner. Paul had joined him and Thomas and the ranch hands for the meal, and Seth had to begrudgingly admit he liked the man. However, hell would freeze over before Paul stole Jody from him. There was something fishy about her so-called engagement, and he intended to find out exactly what it was.

He also planned to set Miss Kirkland straight on a few other things as well. He'd seriously fucked up, and he was determined to find a way to make things right again. She'd thought her attention to him was unwanted? She thought he wasn't attracted to her?

Jesus. He'd tossed and turned all night last night as he realized how badly he'd handled everything. When she'd been younger, it had been easy to dismiss her flirting as harmless. It wasn't until she came back home the summer between her freshman and sophomore years in college that things had gotten hard...literally. She'd stepped out of her daddy's pickup that summer in a sky blue, sleeveless blouse that showed too much cleavage and accentuated her pretty eyes far too well. Add to that her skintight jeans and his cock had inflated to dangerous proportions pretty fucking fast.

Jody might not have noticed his ogling, but Thomas had. Seth's boss had informed Seth in no uncertain terms that his little girl was going to finish her damn education and he'd forbidden any complications that might keep her from returning for the fall semester. Seth had agreed Jody needed to go to college, so he took the warning to heart and managed—just barely—to bank the fires that summer and the next.

Before she'd left Texas to attend Cornell, she'd experienced very little life outside the ranch. Seth encouraged her to enjoy the opportunity to see more of the world and to meet different people. Hell, he'd moved to Texas for the same damn reasons.

And now that you've broadened your horizons?

Seth found it more and more difficult to silence the part of him that longed for home.

He'd already stayed longer than he'd planned, living for Jody's infrequent visits. Jody sure as hell hadn't made it easy on him though. Seemed like the older she got, the more her clothes shrunk and he'd grown accustomed to spending his summers in a state of never-ending arousal.

Last summer had been the worst. Rather than following him around, she'd taken to hunting Chase. Seth had been hard-pressed not to beat the cocky cowboy into the ground. He'd issued the man weekly warnings to keep his hands off Jody and even casually made the suggestion that Thomas give the same admonition. He didn't relax his guard for one second during the three months she'd remained at home.

Then the fucking incident under the mistletoe happened, and he knew he had a problem. She'd dared him to give her a real kiss, and he'd caved. He'd been missing his family, the traditional Compton Christmas celebrations, and his brothers. Jody felt warm and soft and being with her felt too much like coming home. He took it too far, too fast and he'd been besieged with images of a naked Jody, tied to his bed as he fucked her. He wanted to claim her in a very primitive way, and he suddenly became aware of the real reason he'd never succumbed to his feelings for her.

He was a dominant male, and he'd fallen head over heels in

love with the least submissive woman he'd ever met. Jody's hands in his hair, the way she tried to control the kiss proved to him there was no way he could take her the way he truly wanted without scaring her away or having her pull a gun on him.

He'd broken the kiss and brushed her aside once more. He hadn't handled the situation well, but it had been hard to think with all the blood that usually flowed through his brain filling his cock. He'd struggled for a reason and ended up giving her some bullshit line about her being too young. When she'd tried to protest, he'd tacked on a ridiculous, hurtful comment about Jody not understanding exactly what she was asking for.

She hadn't bought it. Instead she'd insisted she was a woman, not a little girl. As if the curves filling his palms weren't proof enough of that. When he'd tried to explain she needed protection from him and his darker needs, the rose-colored glasses she'd always seen him through shattered. She'd laughed mirthlessly about him using the old *it's not you, it's me* line on her and stormed out of his life, furious and hurt.

Her anger had only amplified since then. After returning for her last semester at school, she'd severed the lines of communication, refusing his calls. With some distance, he was able to put his concerns into words that he'd written in at least a dozen emails. Emails she'd clearly never read. He crossed his arms and bided his time. She wasn't going to delete him from her life. At least, not without hearing what he had to say first.

"Bingo," he murmured, when Jody showed up in her jeans, intending to ride. He knew his girl, knew she liked to escape on horseback for hours on end when something was bothering her. Today, she wasn't escaping to anywhere until he came clean. She was out of college, so he didn't feel honor-bound to make sure she finished the degree her father insisted on. He also wasn't about to let her throw her life away, marrying a man she didn't love. Just a few moments in Paul and Jody's presence had proven to him that while they possessed a certain friendly fondness for each other, neither of them was in love. He wasn't sure what her scheme was in terms of this rushed wedding, but she could put the idea out of her head. Last night, he'd decided there was one only one man for her and it was him. He'd ease her into his needs...somehow.

"Mornin', sunshine." He stepped out of his hiding place when she reached for her saddle. "Need a hand?"

She glared at him. The shadows under her eyes proved she hadn't slept any better than him. She started to offer an angry retort, but seemed to recall her peace offering from the day before. She'd vowed they would be friends again. Jody never went back on her word, never broke a promise. It was that deep-seated honor that made him appreciate her all the more.

"I'm fine." She started to carry the saddle to her horse, but he stopped her, taking the heavy leather out of her hands. "I'm perfectly capable of saddling my own horse, Seth. I've been doing it since I was a kid."

"I know. I want to talk to you for a minute before you take off."

"We said all we needed to yesterday. Everything's cool. I promise."

He shook his head. "Nothing's cool, Jody. We're nowhere close to that." His body temperature had risen to unhealthy proportions the second she'd entered the stable in those tight Levi's. One touch from him would leave her with third degree burns. He was on fire for her.

He placed her saddle over the top railing of a stall and gestured to the tack room. "I need a few minutes."

He knew she wouldn't protest. Not when he added, "Just a friendly chat."

She stormed into the tack room. He glanced over his shoulder and confirmed the place was empty. He'd given every hand on the ranch a different duty this morning, all of them well away from the stable. He closed the door and locked them inside the quiet space.

"Is that necessary?" she asked.

"Maybe. How's your headache?"

She shrugged. "Better, I guess."

"You guess? You don't know?" He edged closer. She took two steps back before she could think better of it. Then, in typical Jody-style, she stopped and stood her ground. He took advantage of her stubbornness with glee. Reaching up, he placed his fingers on her temples, rubbing lightly.

Her hands came up to his wrists, intent on pulling his away, but he didn't budge.

"It's better," she said. "You don't have to do that."

He lowered his hands, but he didn't remove them from her face. Instead he cupped her cheeks, tipping her face up so she had no option but to look at him. "I think there are still some misunderstandings we need to clear up."

She tried harder to dislodge him. He held tight.

"Put your hands down," he demanded. She stopped fighting him, but her fingernails still gouged his wrists.

"By your sides, Jody. And leave them there."

"Who the hell do you think—"

He leaned down and gave her a quick kiss to silence her. When she started to speak again, he nipped at her lower lip.

"You ready to listen?"

Her eyes narrowed. "Oh my God. You have a death wish or something?"

He chuckled. She wouldn't bend her will to any man's. He dropped his hands and shook his head. "Nope. Just doing a little experiment. That was sort of a test."

"What kind? How to Piss Off a Woman 101?"

"You were wrong yesterday." His abrupt change of topic took her unaware, and she frowned.

"About what?"

"You said I wasn't interested in you. You think I don't want you."

She closed her eyes and tried to turn from him. "I'm not

talking about this any—"

"I do want you. So bad, it hurts."

Her eyes flew open. "What?"

"Jesus, Jody. All these years, I've been keeping my distance so I didn't give in to something neither one of us could handle."

"I don't understand."

He ran his hand along her cheek and enjoyed the slight shiver his touch provoked in her. The connection had always been there. He'd known it since the summer she'd turned eighteen. Their bodies responded to each other like opposing magnets, drawn to each other despite the innate differences that could tear them apart. "Gossip about my relationships has been flying around here over the years. What have you heard?"

She blushed, the reaction starting to prove another suspicion he had in regards to Jody.

"I've heard you like it rough."

"What does that mean to you?"

She struggled to maintain eye contact. She glanced toward the door, but he knew her pride wouldn't let her run. "I heard you like to tie women up."

"Is that all?"

She nodded. "I'm the boss's daughter. That fact pretty much guarantees folks clam up whenever I come around."

"I enjoy more than bondage, Jody. I like control in the bedroom. I expect absolute submission in my women."

She sucked in a breath and he tried to decide if her response was one of anger or surprise. "What are you saying? You want a sex slave or something?"

He grinned at her tone. Though the conversation clearly made her uncomfortable, she didn't back down from asking what she wanted to know. "I don't expect a woman to call me master or—"

She laughed. When he stopped and stared at her, she quieted. "Oh, you were serious. Shit," she muttered.

Now it was his turn to chuckle. "This is one of the reasons I never approached you. There isn't a submissive bone in your body, Jody."

"So I was right. You aren't attracted to me."

He shook his head. "You're not listening to me. I'm dying to fuck you unconscious, but I don't think you'd like the demands I'd put on you."

"You need the submission stuff?"

"It's hard to explain. It's a part of who I am. If you're asking if I could tuck it away, yeah, I could. I've spent more than a few nights with women who clearly weren't submissives, but I wasn't hoping for long-term relationships with them either. It would be like me asking you to give up riding when you're upset. You could do it, but you'd always miss it. It wouldn't be a fair request."

"Why didn't you share all of this a long time ago?"

He leaned against a nearby barrel. "What would you have said last summer if I'd told you all of this? Be honest."

She came toward him, claiming the barrel next to him. Quiet stretched for several minutes and when she spoke he could tell by her grimace her answer was bringing her no joy to admit. "I would have said it was okay. That I could give you what you need."

He reached down and grasped her hand. "You've tried to catch my attention for years. Doing some pretty out-of-character things in the attempt."

She nodded. "I guess I have."

"You climbed on that horse my first day here even though you knew it was dangerous. You've pranced around here in skimpy clothing, when you're more comfortable in your jeans. You came on to Chase last year with a vengeance, but I'm willing to bet you walked by guys like him at college every day and never gave them a second glance."

"Jesus. I knew I was pathetic, but hearing it all spelled out like that..."

He reached over and grasped her chin, applying light pressure until she faced him. "You aren't at all. You were being honest about your feelings for me. If anyone was pitiful, it was me. I made up a million lame excuses, lying to you at every turn, rather than admitting the truth."

"Which brings us right back to where we were yesterday. Friends."

He shook his head. "Nope. I can't turn this off, Jody." He leaned forward. "My dominance doesn't change a fucking thing."

"What do you mean?"

"I still want you."

"But you said—"

He pressed his cheek to her face, rubbing his rough skin against hers, trying to leave a mark. He was finished fighting it. They'd either move on or kill each other in the attempt. At this point, he didn't give a shit which way it ended—both would put him out of his misery once and for all.

"We're just gonna have to work through it." He punctuated his declaration with a kiss. He took her lips with everything he had, proving to her just how much he'd shielded from her. Jody didn't disappoint him. She wrapped her arms around his neck, opened her sweet lips and brought him in out of the cold. Their tongues tangled, and they shared the same air, the same space. Her fingers drifted to his hair, running through the thick, rough mass. He followed suit, taking a fistful of her soft, brown waves, tugging it with enough force to confirm the gossip about him liking it rough wasn't a rumor.

She groaned and followed suit, tugging his hair as well. He'd never been on the receiving end of such a touch and it certainly got his cock's attention. He was so hard, he winced at the tightness of his jeans.

He used his other hand to lift her T-shirt, stretching it over her bra. She was well-endowed, curvy, more than a handful. Christ, he couldn't wait to put his dick in the valley between her breasts. He'd cup himself in her smooth flesh, fuck her until he came, and paint her pretty pink nipples with his come.

She tried to retreat, but he refused to give up her lips. He'd ached to taste her for years and he was nowhere near satisfied.

She turned her head again. "I can't breathe."

"Yes, you can." He tweaked her nipple through her bra and she gasped. "See?" He angled her lips back to his before she could offer a smartass reply. Moving both hands to her breasts, he tugged the cups of her bra lower until her nipples appeared. Glancing down, he fought a wave of lightheadedness as he scored his first up-close and personal look at her. "Jesus. You're perfect," he whispered.

She rested her forehead against his and smiled. "Too big."

"Ain't no such thing." He bent to prove to her exactly how flawless he thought she was. Her hands flew to his hair once more, her back arching toward his mouth as he sucked hard on first one, and then the other tight nipple. As he applied pressure, he paid close attention to her body's other signals. He'd waited a lifetime to get her into his arms and he didn't plan to screw it up now. Sucking on one nipple, he reached over to pinch the other, relishing the image of her pressing her legs together. He was certain he could smell her sweet juice even through the denim of her jeans.

She liked a bit of pain with her pleasure. Suddenly, he started reevaluating his idea. She blossomed beneath his attentions, making him wonder if she might accept his dominance in the bedroom. Holy shit. Rising, he released her nipple with a soft pop. "Open your legs."

She hesitated for the barest moment and once again, faint unease about her level of innocence niggled at his conscience. Then her thighs parted. He stood between them, his lips returning to her breasts, sucking as she moaned and clung to his hair.

Distracting her with his mouth on her nipple, he unbuttoned her jeans and opened the zipper. Her knees tightened on his hips, and he suspected she would have closed them if his body hadn't blocked her. He paused and studied her half-closed eyes. Her face was flushed, her breathing labored. He knelt before her, leaning forward to place a kiss on her stomach. He grasped one of her hands and lightly ran his tongue along her wrist, her racing pulse confirming his suspicions once and for all. He closed his eyes and prayed for patience.

"Just my fingers," he whispered against her skin. She shivered. He focused on her and waited for the permission he needed to have before he would proceed. She held his gaze and nodded.

He tugged her jeans and panties to her ankles, the delicate scent of her arousal would have driven him to his knees if he hadn't already been kneeling. His mouth watered for a taste, but he had to go slow. As she watched, he dragged one fingertip from the top of her chest, between her breasts, and along her stomach. He didn't stop until his finger lingered barely above her clit.

Her hands had landed on his shoulders, and her grip tightened. Out of fear or anticipation, he couldn't tell. Forging on, he skimmed through the trimmed hair of her pussy until he found the little button he sought. She reared when he touched it. With his free hand, he pressed against her flat stomach, holding her in place. The shiny juices covering the tops of her thighs warned him it wouldn't take much to push her over the edge.

He rubbed her clit again, and she moaned aloud.

"Jody."

Her eyelids fluttered open, revealing her pretty blue eyes.

"I lied," he confessed. "Not only my fingers." He placed his lips around her clit and sucked on the tiny nub. He had to lean his forearm on her abdomen to pin her to the barrel as her hips fought desperately to squirm beneath his tongue.

"God, Seth."

He took her cry as permission to push her further. He ran his finger around the entrance to her body, slick with desire. Her hands returned to his hair, tugging harder than before.

"Please," she whispered.

He pushed one finger inside her far-too-tight sheath and the truth crashed down on him. Jody was a virgin. All bets were off. No man other than him would ever touch her, ever possess her. She was his, and he damn well planned to make sure she knew it.

He thrust harder when her cries grew louder, her thrashing wilder. She was riding the razor's edge of need. He prepared to relieve years of lust. He caught her gaze, savoring her passion-dazed eyes. "Come for me, Jody. Just for me."

He added another finger to the first as he sucked her clit into his mouth, harder than before. The avalanche of her orgasm rumbled through her body, and she cried out his name as she tumbled, trembling, clinging to him as if he were her only lifeline to earth.

His cock throbbed in his jeans, but he wasn't going to find satisfaction inside her body today. It was all too new. The realization of her innocence changed everything. When he took her for the first time, they would be in a bed, they would be totally naked and the ring on her finger would be his.

The thought of her fiancé sent a thread of insane jealously through him. "There's no way your precious Paul ever made you burn like that."

His statement reverberated in the room louder than cannon fire, and Jody reacted as powerfully as if he shot her.

"Oh my God." She wrenched from his hold, scurrying across the floor, fighting to drag her jeans over her hips as she moved away from him. He sat on his haunches, stunned by her response, his jaw hanging open as she yanked her bra up, tugged her shirt down.

"Paul," she whispered. "What have I done? I can't do this. I'm engaged."

"Jesus, Jody. That guy's wrong for you. You're making a mistake. Break it off."

"I can't," she insisted. "I promised him. He needs me."

"*I* need you."

She shook her head. "No. I can't be what you want. I've tried for years, and I've been miserable."

"You liked what I did to you." He took a step closer. When she threw her hands up, a look close to fear crossing her face, he stopped. "I'm not going to hurt you. I won't make you do anything you're not interested in. Trust me."

"You don't get it, do you? There's very little I wouldn't do for you. Even if..." She choked on the explanation, but he didn't need to hear it. He knew what she was thinking. If he asked her to play the part of his submissive, she would. Even though that role would never be a natural fit.

She ran a shaking hand through her hair. "This is over. I've spent the past few months forcing myself to move on. Fighting like the devil to put my silly dreams about you in the past. I've done that. You were right to deny us this. Now that you've shared your reasons, I understand. I need you to let me go."

"I can't."

She brushed a tear from her lashes, and it dawned on him he'd never seen her cry. All the years she'd flirted with him, she'd never used tears. And now he knew all his resistance would have faltered in the face of her crying. Standing helpless while she fought back the pain tore through his gut like a bullet. He'd give her anything to make the sadness disappear.

She walked past him, out the door, and he let her leave.

Chapter Four

"I think we should move the wedding date up." Jody entered the family room where Paul had set up his laptop, tinkering with one of his drafting programs. Their majors at Cornell couldn't have been more different. While she'd spent four years studying Agricultural Science, Paul had gotten his undergrad degree in architecture. If it hadn't been for the dance class they'd both signed up for, their paths never would have crossed on campus.

"Two weeks is soon enough to satisfy my dad's will." Paul responded, not looking up from his project.

"I know, but we're going to do it regardless, so why wait?"

Paul's gaze finally slid from the computer screen to her. She'd come directly from the stable, and she suddenly wished she'd detoured to her room until she'd wrestled her raging emotions under control. In typical fashion, Paul took one peek at her and saw far too much.

"Jody."

"Forget it." She started to back out of the room.

Paul halted her retreat with narrowed eyes. "What happened?"

"Nothing. It was a silly whim. Forget it."

He shook his head. "While the impulsive part certainly fits your personality, I don't believe that had anything to do with your suggestion. I'm guessing you ran into the hottest cowboy in Levi's this morning, right?"

"I don't know who you mean."

Paul wasn't her best friend for nothing. She had never managed to fool him yet. That fact didn't keep her from trying.

He laughed. "Sure you don't." Then he looked at her more closely. "Holy crap. What did Seth do? Your shirt's buttoned wrong."

She glanced down, then threw him a dirty look. "I'm wearing a T-shirt, asshat."

Paul laughed. "Gotcha. Now spill."

Dammit. She'd stormed into the house and into this room, determined to set her pretend marriage in motion so she wouldn't weaken, wouldn't succumb to Seth's advances. The idea that he really had wanted her all these years threw her for a loop. So did the realization that he intended to take control of her in the bedroom. Given the amazing orgasm he'd offered her with no more than his fingers and mouth, she could only imagine what he could do if she placed herself completely at his mercy. Once he tied her to his bed, what wicked things would he do to her? Her imagination ran wild with sinful possibilities.

She glared at Paul. "I'm not discussing it."

"Bullshit." Paul rose and took a seat on the couch, patting the cushion next to him. "Come here and give me all the nitty, gritty dirty details. Don't leave out a thing."

Jody sighed and sank onto the couch. "We're getting married, you know. You shouldn't be grinning while pumping me for information about my infidelities."

Paul laughed loudly. "An affair? Jesus. That's rich. It's a marriage of convenience, Jody. Christ, it's not possible to cheat in those."

"Of course, it is. I made you a promise, and I broke it."

Paul frowned. She wondered what she'd said to destroy his humor so quickly. "We've made no vows to each other. We're friends, sweetheart. Best friends. All I've ever hoped for is for you to be happy. You've been miserable over Seth this past semester, but if the status of your relationship with him has changed—"

"It hasn't." She cut him off. If he offered to let her out of their arrangement, she'd consider it. Temptation was not something she needed right now. Not when so much good could come of her giving up a year to Paul and so much damage could come of her giving herself to Seth.

He fell silent for a moment. "Are you sure?"

She nodded. "The wedding's still on. Nothing Seth can say or do..." Her insistence faltered as she considered what Seth had done. Heat crept to her cheeks.

Paul latched on to her hesitation in typical nosy-friend style. "What the hell did he do? I bet it was sexy as shit knowing that man. You've gotta give me something to live vicariously on. You've put me on a man diet with this *marrying for love* lie. Do you have any idea what kind of pain I'm in surrounded by all these muscular cowboys? That Chase is one fine specimen of a man and I'm positive he could do things..." He paused, allowing her to fill in the blanks.

"Jeez. We've been here twenty-four hours, Paul. Surely you can abstain a few days more. Actually, I would think you'd be thrilled by my suggestion to move the wedding up. I mean let's face it, the sooner we satisfy the marriage part of your father's will, the sooner you'll get your trust fund."

Paul shrugged. "I don't see how a couple of weeks is going to make much difference in the long run."

"It's not. That's why we should just go ahead and get it over with."

Paul winced slightly at her callous words and she hastily tried to apologize. He cut her off. "Your enthusiasm overwhelms me."

"Paul, I didn't mean that the way it sounded."

He nodded. "I know that. I also know something happened with Seth to prompt this sudden rush down the aisle. I'm starting to think I'd be smart to find someone else to help me satisfy the will. There are clearly unresolved feelings between you and Seth, and I don't think now is—"

"There are no unresolved feelings. In fact, we just had an epiphany."

Paul rose and leaned against the desk, gesturing with his hands. "Do tell."

Jody cleared her throat. While she and Paul were truly best friends and there was very little they didn't discuss openly, she wondered how to explain her new concerns in regards to Seth Compton. In the past, Paul had listened to her cry over the fact that Seth didn't want her. This morning, Seth had confessed he did. She should be over the moon. Instead, she was picturing exactly *how* Seth wanted her. The images flying through her head left her equal parts terrified and aroused. Not a good combination.

"Apparently Seth, um...wants more than, er—"

"More than the hogtying?"

She shrugged. "I think the words sex slave and master may have been used."

Jody fought back the urge to laugh and cry at the same time as Paul's face went pale. "Dear God," he said.

She put her hands up quickly. "No, it's not like that. I mean, that's sort of what he likes, but he knows I'm not the girl to give it to him."

Paul nodded slowly, and she watched him assimilate that idea. "And because you aren't a submissive, he doesn't want you?"

She rested her head back against the couch cushion and closed her eyes. "Oh no, he definitely wants me."

"I'm confused."

She chuckled and turned to look at Paul. "Join the club. Seth wants me, but he knows I can't give him what he needs."

"Why not?"

Jody sucked in a deep breath at her friend's question. The silence between them stretched on for several moments as Jody struggled to find an honest answer.

Paul saved her from having to respond. “Jody. If anything else should arise between you and Seth, I think you should go for it.”

She frowned. “I don’t understand what you’re saying.”

Paul walked toward her and grasped her hand. “You’ve been saving yourself for the guy forever. Since you seem to feel honor-bound to remain faithful during this marriage of ours, even though I don’t want or expect that, I think you should do it.”

Her body went still as she considered Paul’s suggestion. “You’re telling me to have sex with Seth?”

“I’m saying if he offers and you want to take him up on it, don’t let some silly promise you’ve made to me stand in the way.”

“I’m not going to sleep with Seth, and I’m not going to change my mind about this wedding.” She felt a certain sense of pride and accomplishment as her words were strong and confident.

Paul looked at her for a long time, but she didn’t crack. He sighed sadly. “Fine,” he said at last.

“Fine?”

He nodded. “We’ll move the wedding up. How soon were you thinking?”

She felt numb at his easy acquiescence and the realization that she would definitely be putting a period on any chance for a relationship with Seth if she married Paul, even out of convenience. “Day after tomorrow?” she asked, trying to figure out when she’d lost complete control of her life.

“Perfect. What do you say we go break the news to your dad? It’s bound to be a shock to the guy, so we might as well get it over with.”

She nodded woodenly, rising slowly and following her friend out of the room in search of her father. What the hell was she doing?

Paul's words kept playing over and over in her head.

Get it over with.

As they told her father their plans, they replayed, overshadowing her father's arguments that they wait.

Get it over with.

In two days, her plan to escape Seth once and for all would be complete and her heart would be shattered, broken beyond repair.

Get it over with.

"You got a minute?"

Jody looked up at the light knock on her door, nodding at her father as he stood in the doorframe. Dinner had been an awkward affair, the usually boisterous mealtime conversations muted. Her dad had not taken the news of her accelerated nuptials well, sitting at the head of the table with his eyebrows lowered, frowning at anyone who dared to laugh or even speak. If her heart hadn't been racing so, she would have laughed at the incredible speed her normally slow-eating best friend gobbled his dinner, excusing himself after only a few minutes.

"Yeah," she said. "What's up?"

Her dad walked in and she was surprised to see a large box in his hands. "I did a bit of digging around this afternoon and, well, I thought you might want this." He placed the box on the bed.

"What is it?"

"Your mother's wedding dress."

Jody's breath caught as she glanced at the box. She didn't want her father to see the tears that had suddenly sprung to her eyes. She was turning into a regular watering pot these days.

"Thanks," she said, the husky sound betraying the lump in her throat.

"Jody." Her father's voice demanded her attention and she gave it to him, hoping he couldn't see the fear, the pain, the confusion in her eyes. "You don't have to wear it if you don't want to. I just thought—"

"Daddy." She swallowed, trying to find the words to express how much his gesture meant to her. "Thank you."

She expected him to launch into more of his objections to the wedding. He'd worn her out this afternoon for nearly an hour as he tried to convince her not to move the wedding up. Hell, he'd spent three-quarters of that hour, trying to talk her out of marrying Paul altogether. She closed her eyes, wearily, not sure she could withstand another onslaught of protestations.

"Well. I'll leave you alone then."

She watched him walk out, torn between relief and the desire to call him back so she could cry in his protective arms. For several minutes, she simply stared at the box. Shaking off her melancholy, she lifted the lid and gasped. She'd seen pictures of her mother in her wedding dress, but the photographs had failed to capture the true delicate beauty of the silk. She tried to imagine all the feelings her mother must have felt as she wore the beautiful dress.

Reaching out, her hand closed in a fist, just before she touched it, a feeling of shame washing through her. Her mother and father had loved each other, fiercely, powerfully. She may have been young when her mother passed away, but she knew the truth of that love as surely as she knew her own name. She felt like she was dishonoring the dress, wearing it to a wedding, not born from love, but from necessity.

Slowly, she took the dress out of the box, walking to the full-length mirror that hung on the wall. Holding it in front of her, she allowed herself one tiny moment to pretend she wasn't wearing it for Paul, but for Seth. She closed her eyes and imagined the larger-than-life cowboy who'd captured her heart, standing at the end of the aisle. She pictured Seth's face, the dimples creasing his cheeks as he smiled at her walking toward him.

"Beautiful." The voice behind her fit the fantasy. She opened her eyes and found Seth's dark brown gaze soaking in the dress...and her.

"Seth," she whispered to his reflection in the mirror.

"Your father told me you're moving the wedding date up."

She nodded, unable to speak.

A flash of pain crossed his face before it was overshadowed by anger. "Don't marry him."

She smiled sadly. "I have to."

"Why?"

She lowered the dress and turned around to face him. "I promised."

Seth shook his head. "That's a shitty reason."

She walked away from him, carefully returning the dress to the box. "No, it's not." She replaced the lid and carried the whole thing over to her dresser before returning to sit on the edge of her bed.

Seth walked over, standing directly before her. Her gaze drifted to her bedroom door, and she wasn't surprised to see it closed. Knowing him, it was locked as well.

"You're not in love with him."

She tilted her head, realizing it was pointless to continue the deceit. "No. I'm not."

"But you're still going to marry him."

She nodded. "He needs me."

She'd promised Paul and she didn't break her promises. Ever. Given the facts that had come to light about Seth and his desires today, suddenly hiding in a loveless marriage for a year seemed preferable to losing herself to this cowboy who had far too much control over her sanity, her sense of self.

"I'm not giving up," he warned her as he bent closer.

"I wish you would."

His fingers tipped her chin up until her lips were just a breath away from his. "You can't marry him when you're in love with someone else."

"Someone else?" she asked.

"Yeah." She tried to move away, tried to escape, but he trapped her to the mattress, pushing her back in a move that couldn't be described as anything more than pure dominance. "Me."

His kiss proclaimed the truth of his statement and, though she struggled for release, he refused to relent, refused to let her hide from the truth.

His fingers worked at opening the button and zipper of her jeans and her traitorous hormones broke free. She pushed his hands away when he started to pull the tight pants down, shoving the jeans over her hips herself. He'd given her just a hint of what he had to offer and, wrong or not, she wanted it again. Wanted more.

Paul's comments flashed through her mind. She'd saved herself for Seth, for this. Would it be so bad to take a tiny taste?

The second the denim cleared her knees, he lifted his foot, pushing the denim and panties completely off in a move that was rough, hungry. She opened her legs, welcomed him between. The full weight of his body crushed her. He continued to kiss her as he rubbed his jeans-clad erection against her.

She wrapped her legs around his waist, wanting to direct more of the incredible sensations toward her clit, her wet opening.

He lifted himself up on one elbow, his lips still devouring hers as he ran his fingers along her slit. He pulled away briefly, his eyes narrowing. "Why the hell are you denying this? Your cunt is dripping and hotter than a Texas summer. Enough is enough, Jody. You're planning to marry someone else, while your body is on fire for me. Don't you think it's time you admit it?"

She feigned ignorance, while attempting to get her

breathing back under control. His fingers were wreaking havoc on her ability to think. "And what exactly is it you think I should be confessing?"

He grinned. "That you want me and only me."

She closed her mouth, afraid the words would slip out despite the common sense that said she had no business being here.

"Looks to me like you might need a little demonstration." He thrust two fingers into her pussy, and she gasped at the tight, delicious sensation of the rough way he was claiming her. Over and over, he pressed into her as her body began to tingle, sparkling with the bright light of her orgasm.

"You want me. Say it."

She shook her head, refusing. His thumb brushed her clit firmly and her hips began to move, seeking out the touch, looking for more. Seth bent his head and bit her nipple through her shirt. She gasped, her fingers gripping his shoulders tightly. He lifted his head. "Put your hands on the bed beside your head."

"I want to touch you," she admitted.

His gaze darkened, and she shuddered slightly at the pure dominance written there. He wasn't holding back, wasn't hiding his true spirit from her any longer. This was what she'd waited a lifetime for.

Seth, with the mask off.

Seth, willing to give her anything, everything.

"Put your hands on the bed," he repeated, his tone proving he wouldn't ask again.

She moved, letting her hands fall, palms up above her shoulders. The pose felt like surrender and for a moment, she wanted to balk, to move them back to his body.

His gaze stopped her. He devoured her, his eyes, his lips, his hands telling her how much he liked what he was seeing. His fingers began to stroke her faster, harder. "Come for me, sunshine. Let me see you explode." His words provoked the action, and she shuddered, crying out at the intensity as her hands closed into fists, but never left the mattress.

Seth didn't relent, didn't allow her surcease, as he continued to thrust harder, faster. She was on the verge of a second orgasm when he quickly pulled out.

"No," she said, anger permeating her dazed mind when he chuckled.

"I want everything from you," he warned, his dark, sensual tone sending another ripple of arousal through her.

When his finger returned, it wasn't to her pussy, but instead he pushed one wet digit into her ass. Her scream would have brought down the roof if he hadn't captured it with his own mouth, thrusting his tongue against hers as his finger plunged deeper into her ass. Her orgasm hit her like a freight train, and she clung to him as she quivered in the aftermath.

Seth's kisses didn't stop, but they grew softer. Soft enough that she managed to regain her scattered wits. She'd wanted a taste. Seth had given her a feast. She'd let things go way too far.

Furious with herself and with him for tempting her so, she turned her head, pulling her lips away from his. "Dammit," she cried. "You can't come in here and bully me like this."

He laughed. "I haven't even started to bully you yet."

An image of him tying her up, forcing her to one orgasm after another floated through her mind. "Shit," she muttered. "Get off of me." She tried to push him away, but moving her six foot two, nothing but pure muscle cowboy was a bit like trying to shove a skyscraper.

"Not yet. I have a question for you, and I want an answer."

She pursed her lips and waited, worried about what he might ask.

"Are you a virgin?"

Her heart lurched and she knew hell would freeze over before he got that answer. "None of your damn business."

He pressed her against the bed, but she refused to be cowed. "You keep saying that, but it is."

She shook her head. "No, it isn't. Go away."

Seth stared at her for a painfully, long minute, but she didn't budge. Finally, he spoke. "I don't need you to answer. I know the truth."

She sucked in a deep breath. She'd been riding a horse since the time she learned to walk. She was fairly certain any definite, hard proof of her virginity was long gone.

A brief glimpse of his earlier anger returned. "Why did you wait?"

She frowned. "What do you mean?"

"If you're gonna settle for a loveless marriage, why bother saving yourself at all?"

She didn't have an answer. She'd been a silly girl with more honor than sense. She'd waited because in her heart, Seth had been her future. It was an old-fashioned notion, but she'd clung to it thinking it would prove to Seth she was worthy of him and his love.

"It was a mistake," she said quietly.

"I see."

He rose from the bed. She sat up, wrapping the comforter around her waist. The movement wasn't based on shyness as much as a way to rebuild her defenses. "You won't tell my dad, will you? About Paul and I not being in love. I really think it would be easier for him if..."

Her words died at the pain flashing in Seth's eyes. Easy didn't seem to be an option anymore.

"You gonna tell me why you're marrying this guy? It doesn't make any sense."

She shrugged. "I have a good reason. Honest."

"But you're not going to tell me what it is."

She shook her head. It felt like it was going to explode. She was on the verge of tears, something she didn't want Seth to see. “Not tonight. Later. I promise.”

“No,” Seth replied. “I won’t tell Thomas. I’ve been keeping your secrets for nearly a decade. I don’t plan to break that tradition now.”

She smiled sadly as her mind drifted over all the confidences she’d shared with Seth through the years. The time she’d broken her mother’s favorite vase, Seth helped her glue it back together. The time she’d put a dent in her dad’s new truck, Seth found a mechanic to pound the ding out. The time she’d snuck out her junior year in high school to go to a party, Seth dragged her home, not betraying her to her father.

He’d been her friend, her protector and now he wanted to be her lover. The thought made her entire body ache. “Thanks.”

Walking toward the door, he opened it and turned to look at her. “This isn’t finished.”

When she was certain he was out of earshot, she whispered, “Yes, it is.”

Then, she gave in to her tears.

Chapter Five

"You planning on pulling your head out of your ass anytime soon, son, or are you just gonna stand around and let my little girl make the biggest mistake of her life?"

Seth looked up as Thomas climbed the stairs to the front porch of his foreman's cabin early the next morning. Seth placed his cup of coffee on the table next to him. It was his day off and he'd planned to spend it alone, trying to figure out where the hell he was supposed to go from here. Jody was driving him insane. He'd tossed and turned all night, waking up three times to jerk off to the image of her as she came in the tack room and again in her bedroom. She was gorgeous, sexy-as-hell and driving him out of his mind with desires he'd never experienced.

"Excuse me?" he said as Thomas rested against the porch railing, crossing his ankles as well as his arms.

His boss had never given him any indication that he'd welcome Seth approaching Jody romantically. The only words Thomas had issued the past four years had been more along the lines of warnings for Seth to keep his damn hands to himself.

"I believe I made myself clear."

"What would you have me do, Thomas? Jody's more headstrong than Hugh Natter's bull. Trying to get that girl to change her mind on anything is like trying to dig a hole the size of the Grand Canyon with a teaspoon."

Thomas silently studied him for so long, Seth had to fight the urge not to squirm. "Never pegged you for a quitter. You gonna let that Paul character take your woman?"

Seth narrowed his eyes. "You wanna let me know exactly when Jody became *my* woman. Last time I glanced her way you threatened to apply the bander you use on the bulls to castrate me. That's sort of a far cry from calling me *son*, wouldn't you say?"

"I wanted Jody to go off to college, to get her degree. She's a smart girl and leaving this place to continue her education was good for her. You know it, and I know it. She left here a willful, opinionated, inexperienced girl. Now, four years later, she's come back to us an intelligent, mature woman. I knew you'd be a big obstacle in her way if you decided to pay that girl any attention and I knew it would be a mistake for her to stay here. She needed to see a bit more of the world, meet people who weren't ranchers, experience a bit of culture."

Seth nodded, begrudgingly. The time away from home had done wonders for Jody. "You're right."

Thomas took his admission with a smugness that made Seth want to roll his eyes. "Now she's graduated with honors and with a knowledge of Ag Science that makes her the perfect life partner for a rancher."

"Last time I looked, I was a foreman."

Thomas uncrossed his arms, rubbing his chin as he sighed. "That could change pretty damn quick with ring and a few words spoken before a Justice of the Peace."

Seth was pretty sure throwing a punch at his boss would get his ass canned quick, but he rose anyway, his fists clenched. Thomas's words were an affront to his morals and an insult to his daughter. "If you think I'd marry Jody to inherit this goddamn ranch, then you don't know me at all. How dare you haggle with your daughter's life? I don't give a fuck who you are, if you think you can sell Jody off—"

Thomas chuckled and put his hands up. "Just checking,

Seth. Wanted to make sure your intentions were true."

Seth tried to hold on to his irritation, but he couldn't blame Thomas for double-checking. "Had your fun?"

Jody was set to inherit a shit-load of money from her old man one day and there weren't too many cowboys in the state who didn't know it. Difference was his family was pretty well off too and he learned a long time ago, money didn't make you happy.

Thomas's grin slowly faded. "You gotta stop her, Seth."

Seth thought of the previous night. Of how she'd come apart in his arms and how she still pushed him away. Jody had pride by the bushel and overcoming the mistakes he'd made in the past as well as asking her to go back on the promise she'd made to Paul was proving tougher than he thought.

"How?" he asked, silently praying Thomas had an answer. God knew he was running out of ideas.

"Be creative."

Seth shook his head. "Shit. That's the only advice you have? Be creative? What the fuck does that mean?"

Thomas rubbed his jaw and Seth figured he and his boss were mirror reflections of frustration. "Hell if I know. Only thing I do know is you love her and she loves you. It's time to make the insanity stop."

Thomas turned, stepped off the porch and walked away.

Insanity, Seth thought. Yep. He had that in abundance.

It was late afternoon when Seth heard footsteps on his porch. He glanced up to find Jody peering through the screened door.

"Knock knock," she said, when she spotted him.

"Come on in." He'd been in the process of making a late lunch. He gestured at the sandwich fixins in front of him. "Hungry? I make a mean ham on rye."

She shook her head. "No, thanks. I already ate. I wanted to

talk to you about tomorrow."

Her wedding day. He gritted his teeth. "Unless you're here to tell me you've called the wedding off, I don't want to talk about it."

She sighed, but wasn't deterred. "I'm not calling it off, Seth, but—" she hesitated and he wondered what she was going to say. "I wanted to say some things to you beforehand."

He crossed his arms, certain he wasn't going to like what she was about to say. His stance seemed to slow her momentum for a minute and she took a deep breath.

"I appreciate what you said, what you did yesterday morning in the tack room."

He scowled. "I fucking buried my face in your sweet cunt and set you off like a firecracker and you *appreciate* it."

She took a step closer. "Don't be crude," she snapped. "That's not what I'm talking about."

He cursed under his breath.

"For years, I've walked around here feeling like I wasn't good enough for you. I've spent most of my adult life trying to catch your attention and feeling like I was falling short because of some weakness, some inadequacy—"

"God dammit, Jody. I told you. None of that's true."

She smiled. "I know that...now. I never understood why you rebuffed me, but now that I do, I get it. You were right to fight this." She waved her hand between them and it took all the strength in Seth's body not to grab that hand, pull her toward him and prove to her how wrong she was.

She walked over to his kitchen table and claimed one of the chairs, sinking down heavily. "I can't be what you want. I can't give in to your needs without betraying who I am."

He stepped closer, taking the seat next to her. "I don't want to change you, Jody. My reasons were right at the time. You were too young, too inexperienced. Time has changed that. You've grown up and matured. You're more than strong enough to handle me now."

She laughed sadly. "No. I think we both know exactly how inexperienced I still am."

"I'm not talking about sexual experience. When you were younger, you worked your ass off trying to be the woman you thought I wanted, rather than the woman you were, the woman I adored. You know who you are now. I'm not looking to change that."

She looked down at her hands and he could see she was considering his words. She raised her gaze to his once more, her face sadder than he'd ever seen it. "I know you don't want to change it. Problem is I'm not sure you could help it."

He shook his head, but his cell phone rang, cutting off any reply she might make. He was going to ignore it, but glancing at the caller ID, he saw his father's number. His brother, Silas, had returned home after receiving some pretty serious injuries during an oil rig explosion in Alaska and he'd asked JD to call him as soon as Silas was settled in back in Wyoming.

"I have to take this," he said, opening the phone.

She nodded and started to leave, but he grasped her hand with his free one, shaking his head and indicating he wanted her to stay.

He spoke briefly to his father. The conversation was short. It was obvious from JD's comments his bedridden brother was already bored with the role of invalid. Hearing about Silas's gruff complaining went a long way toward setting Seth's mind at ease.

He'd wanted to return home immediately after finding out about Silas's accident, but his mother had convinced him to give Silas some time to recuperate and adjust to being back home. He'd suspected his mother had been trying to keep him away because it was worse than they were letting on. Talking to JD set those fears to rest. Clearly, there was another reason his mother wanted him to postpone a trip home. When JD mentioned the good care Silas's best friends, Lucy and Colby, had been giving him, the light bulb went on in Seth's brain and he grinned. Silas really was home.

"How are you doing?" he asked his dad, concerned by the weariness he detected in his old man's voice. It couldn't have been easy on his parents when they'd learned of the accident that nearly killed their oldest son.

"Hanging in there," JD said. As usual, trying to get too much out of his father about himself was impossible.

True to form, JD changed the subject quickly. "Your brothers are setting up one of those video chat things on the computer. Silas said you should check your email for the day and time, make sure it works for you."

Seth and his brothers had lived apart for nearly a decade. In order to keep in touch, his younger brother Sam had started setting up conference chats for them. Seth looked forward to the chats. He enjoyed seeing his brothers' faces and hearing their voices. "I'll be sure to check my email."

He said his goodbyes and hung up. He looked at Jody as he considered all the near misses in his life lately. He'd almost lost Silas, and now he was in danger of losing her. The idea made him even more determined to win her heart.

Jody looked at him. "Your father?"

He nodded.

"Is Silas okay? He was hurt in Alaska, right?"

When he gave her a surprised look, she explained. "Dad told me about it last week when I called to tell him I was coming home."

Ordinarily, he would have called to talk to her about it, but since she'd started avoiding his calls after Christmas, he hadn't bothered dialing her number. He'd missed telling her about the day-to-day stuff. "Apparently he's bitching about being stuck in bed, so I'd say he's good. Gotta say getting the call about that explosion—" His words drifted off as he recalled the night JD had called to tell him about Silas.

Jody smiled and when she squeezed his hand, he realized

he'd never released it. "I can't even imagine how scary that must have been. I know how close you and your brothers are."

He wanted to pull her to him, wrap himself up in her embrace. He hadn't known how much his brother's injury had been bothering him until he heard JD's voice. It would be so easy to fall into her arms, to let her comfort him.

"I miss them. Miss home sometimes."

"Do you ever think of going back to Wyoming?"

Her question triggered the secret desire he'd been harboring lately. He nodded. "Yeah. I do. When I was young, all I could think about was getting the hell out of Compton Pass on the fastest plane I could find."

"And now?"

"Now I'm wondering why I ever left."

If he expected her to be surprised by his comments, he would have been disappointed. "I've always been jealous of your stories about growing up."

He grinned. "Really?"

"I'm an only child and the daughter of the boss. Spent a lot of my childhood alone with my horse. I used to imagine what it would be like to be a part of a big, loving family. To have brothers or sisters to fight with, play with."

"Most of the time it was a pain in the ass," he joked, though her comments sent a jolt of homesickness through him.

She laughed. "I don't believe that for one minute."

They fell silent and for a moment, Seth was reminded of the way things were before he'd fucked up at Christmas. Then he remembered her wedding tomorrow and a wave of desperation rose.

"Jody," he started, but she raised her hand, cutting off his reply. It was obvious her thoughts had drifted in the same direction.

"Please, Seth. Please try to understand that I've made my decision. I'm marrying Paul because I genuinely believe it's the best thing for me."

"I'll never understand or believe that."

She released his hand and stood. "Then I guess there's nothing left to do, but say goodbye."

He chuckled, the sound turning to a laugh when confusion colored her pretty face. "Ah, sweetheart. That was a nice, but weak attempt. I'm not finished yet. You go ahead and fool yourself into thinking you're gettin' hitched. I'm here to tell you it's never going to happen."

Her eyes narrowed and his vivacious Jody reemerged ready for a fight.

She leaned toward him. "Get ready to be disappointed, Compton. I'm a big girl and perfectly capable of charting my course all by myself. I'm marrying Paul tomorrow and there's absolutely nothing you can do about it."

She turned and stomped toward the front door of his cabin. He waited until her hand reached out to open the screen before speaking. "See you soon," he said, taking care to lace his voice with just enough threat and promise.

She parted her lips to speak, then changed her mind. Scowling, she stormed out, slamming the screen door behind her as the seed of a plan sprouted in Seth's mind.

"You have a minute?"

Seth looked up and tried to suppress a groan as Paul climbed the three steps to his front porch. His cabin had turned into Grand Central Station today. He'd just poured what he intended to be the first of many whiskeys tonight. He nodded and gestured to the empty rocking chair beside him. "Sure." His tone didn't sound particularly inviting, a fact that clearly wasn't lost on Jody's fiancé as Paul hesitated briefly before finally taking the proffered seat. "What's on your mind?"

"I was wondering if I could ask a favor."

Seth's grip on his tumbler tightened. If the man asked him

to stand up for him in his wedding to Jody, he'd be hard-pressed not to punch the guy's lights out. He was still doing his damnedest to figure out how to stop the ceremony. Thomas's and Jody's words kept drifting through his mind. He couldn't see himself storming into the church as the minister asked for objections, shouting his protest like some romantic jackass from the movies, but he certainly wouldn't rule the idea out.

"What kind of favor?"

"I suppose you know Jody is out tonight with some of the hands. Her twisted version of a bachelorette party." Paul's light laughter proved he found Jody's exploits entertaining, another begrudging point Seth had to give in the man's favor. It appeared Jody's fiancé wouldn't try to change her, wouldn't try to curb her impulsiveness and joy for life.

"I know about the party." The ranch hands had thrown the celebration together on a whim when they'd heard about her rushed nuptials. He'd had to fight the urge to threaten every last one of them if they let anything happen to her tonight. He'd also been a bit annoyed about being left off the guest list, but given the fact he'd been snapping off anyone's head who came within five feet of him, he couldn't blame the hands for wanting a break from him.

"Well, um. I was wondering if you'd ever seen Jody drink."

Seth frowned, wondering where the hell Paul was going with this conversation. "No. She only turned twenty-one in May. I assumed she did her partying at college because she's never had anything here."

"I never saw Jody have a drink until her birthday. She was always happy to be the designated driver, claiming she didn't like the smell of liquor. For her twenty-first birthday party, a bunch of our gang got together and took her out. She had two shots of tequila, and I suddenly understood why she didn't drink."

Seth leaned forward, curious. "Mean drunk?" he said, the idea sort of funny to him. He could see his feisty gal getting into a fight after a few.

"No, something a bit more disturbing."

Seth didn't like Paul's serious face. "What happens to her?"

"She loses all her inhibitions."

"What?"

Paul nodded. "I've never seen anything like it. Jody's always the life of the party, don't get me wrong. She's a fun girl with a great sense of humor, but she's always in control of herself. She says she doesn't need to drink because she can have just as much fun without alcohol."

"What did she do on her birthday?" Seth couldn't imagine Jody not being in complete control. She was too much like him in that regard.

"Like I said, we bought a couple of rounds, next thing I know she's up on stage, singing with the band that was performing that night." Paul chuckled. "She's actually a pretty good singer. Thing is it's like it wasn't her I was watching. She's singing, dancing in this very provocative, sexy way. At the end of the number, she started making out with the guitar player on stage. Needless to say, I pulled her out of there. She didn't remember doing any of it the next morning and swore off alcohol after that."

Thank God Jody had been with friends. He didn't like to consider what would have happened if Paul hadn't been there. He was glad to hear she had enough sense to know to stay away from the stuff. "Surely she wouldn't drink tonight."

Paul shrugged. "I would hope not, but Jody hasn't really been acting like herself lately. I'm not sure what she'd do. I was sort of hoping you'd go crash the party, keep an eye on her. I'd go, but as the groom, I'm pretty sure I'd get booted out quick."

Seth ground his teeth at Paul's reference to himself as groom. It took every ounce of willpower not to inform the man in no uncertain terms he'd never have Jody as his wife. Instead, he said, "I think they were headed to Philly's. I'll hop in my truck and go check things out."

Paul rose, his grin wide, as he reached out to shake his hand. "I'd appreciate it, Seth."

As Paul walked back to the main house, Seth entered his cabin, pulling off his ripped T-shirt and reaching for a clean cotton shirt. He considered Paul's words. The ceremony was scheduled for tomorrow afternoon, so his time had definitely run out. Opening his closet, he bent down to pick up his cowboy boots and his gaze landed on his hunting rifle tucked against the back wall.

A grin crossed his face as the plan he'd considered earlier came back to him. He'd dismissed it as too much, too over the top, but now...

Reaching into the back pocket of his jeans, he pulled out his cell phone and called Thomas.

"Yallo," his boss drawled and Seth could picture the man kicked back in his recliner, beer in hand, watching a repeat of some golden oldie sitcom on TV.

"*MASH* or *The Andy Griffith Show* tonight?" Seth asked.

"Neither one. Found a *Matlock* marathon. Why are you calling me? Thought you'd be finding a way to stop this asinine wedding Jody's got her mind set on."

"Got a plan, but I need to use the hunting cabin down in Walker's Ridge."

"You're not gonna woo my girl with a hunting excursion."

Seth grinned. "No, but the cabin is secluded. Thought it might be a nice place to do a little private seduction, especially if the lady in question kicks up a bit of a fuss at the beginning."

Thomas chuckled. "I like your style. The place is yours. You still got your key?"

"Yeah, I got it. I'm also gonna need the next couple days off."

"Think a couple will be enough? Jody's pretty headstrong, you know. Got that particular character trait from her mother."

Seth snorted, knowing good and well where Jody got her

stubbornness. "Why don't we say a couple to start with and I'll call you if it looks like my campaign might take a little longer?"

"Deal," Thomas said. "I'll hold down the fort here with Paul. Come up with some reason for her disappearance."

"Good. Think I could raid your kitchen before I leave? Pack up a few days' worth of food. I don't have much here in my cabin, and I don't have time to hit a store."

"Not a problem. I'll get the cook to start putting the stuff together for you. She'll have some extra time now that she doesn't have to prepare food for the party after the ceremony. Gonna be tough to have to postpone the wedding," his boss added with a chuckle that told Seth he was looking forward to making those calls.

"Thanks."

"Oh, and Seth?"

"Yeah?"

Seth could hear Thomas's soft laughter through the phone. "Way to be creative, son."

Chapter Six

Seth walked into Philly's and immediately tried to process what he was seeing. Jody was wearing tight jeans, cowboy boots and a low-cut T-shirt that barely contained her breasts. She was also dancing on a pool table to "Redneck Woman". She was gyrating, lip-synching to the song and moving like the most seductive cowgirl he'd ever seen. He would have bet his family's ranch every guy in the place was sporting a hard-on watching her. His cock filled instantly at the image, then his anger kicked in as he watched his ranch hands surrounding the table, cheering her on.

Obviously, Paul hadn't exaggerated about her alcohol issue. His temper rose to think none of the men she'd grown up with could recognize the fact she was out of control. He pushed his way toward the table, patrons giving him dirty looks until they saw his face, and then stepping out of his way. A couple of cowboys tried to shove back and he clenched his fists, ready to pound them into dust.

"You don't wanna go there," he warned one asshole who looked like he was itching for a brawl. The man told him to fuck off, but moved aside.

Chase grinned when he saw him as Seth finally managed to get to the table.

"Hey boss. You got here just in time for the fun."

Seth scowled, and Chase's grin faltered. "How much has she had to drink?"

Chase shrugged. "Not that much actually. She's a pretty cheap drunk."

Chase's words were the straw that broke the camel's back. Seth curled up his hand and threw the fist before he could think about it. Chase staggered back, his hand flying to his jaw. "What the fuck was that for?"

"You think this is funny?" Seth yelled, pointing to Jody, who was oblivious to anything going on in the bar. A guy Seth didn't know hopped up on the table and started dirty dancing with Jody, his hands roaming over her body in a way that made Seth see red. She started dancing with the stranger, stealing the cowboy's hat and putting it on her head.

Chase looked chagrined when it was apparent things had spiraled out of control. "Sorry, boss," he murmured, but Seth didn't acknowledge his words.

He reached up and attempted to grasp Jody's waist to pull her off the table. Her new dance partner took offense and put himself between Seth and Jody. The move was a mistake.

Seth hopped up on the table. The patrons of the bar started to cheer, making crude comments about a cowgirl sandwich, encouraging Seth and the other cowboy to do a little double-teaming.

Seth's temper exploded as the other man grabbed Jody and tried to kiss her. Seth reached over and shoved Jody behind him.

"What the fuck, man?" the cowboy bellowed.

Seth was furious, but more than ready to take on every prick in the joint if they tried to touch his woman. "If you're smart, you'll go back to your table. If not, stand there another three seconds and see if I don't beat the fucking shit out of you."

The man wanted to argue, Seth could see it.

"Is she your wife or something?" the cowboy asked, apparently trying to decide how far he wanted to push things.

"Or something."

Jody was still dancing behind him, much to the amusement of the drunks in the room. She pressed her chest against Seth's back as she moved. If he hadn't been so pissed off, her motions would have sent his libido into orbit.

"Not now, Jody." Seth pushed her hands away from his waist without turning his back on the man in front of him.

The cowboy took a last look at his face and threw his hands up. "It's cool. No fight here. Just having fun." He hopped off the pool table and headed in the other direction.

Seth twisted in time to see Jody had gotten down and was doing another shot of tequila.

"Jesus." He jumped to the floor and knocked the glass away from her lips.

Some of the liquor spilled on her shirt. "Hey, what the hell?" She looked up and blinked rapidly. "Seth? You made me spill my drink. What are you doing here?"

He pulled the other cowboy's hat off her head and handed it to Chase. "Party's over, Jody."

She glanced around, confused. "Already? We just got here."

"I think you've had enough fun for one night."

She leaned closer, running her hand along his chest. "I haven't had any fun yet. Maybe you could help me with that." She began to rub her body sinuously against his once again.

He seized her hips and pushed her away, praying his rising erection wasn't visible through his jeans. "God dammit. We're getting out of here. Now!"

The ranch hands were hovering too closely, listening to every word. The gossips were going to have a field day with this. Seth Compton pulling a drunk Jody Kirkland out of her own bachelorette party.

Paul hadn't exaggerated about the alcohol. If he weren't so worried, he would be slightly amused. There was no way she would voluntarily come on to him like this. She was disoriented, confused...sexy as shit.

She reached around his hip and grabbed his left cheek. “I love your ass,” she said, squeezing it as some of the hands laughed.

He stifled their humor with a dark look that promised they’d pay for anything they did now in the hot Texas sun tomorrow.

She started to unbutton his shirt, and he gripped her wrists as the ladies around them started to whistle.

One woman yelled for Jody to keep going. Jody grinned, pushing her hips against his as he restrained a groan. She was just asking for it.

Another man moved closer as Seth managed to thrust her back again.

“If you don’t wanna piece of that, I’ll have some,” the stranger said.

Jody laughed and started to move toward the other man.

“Oh no, you don’t,” Seth said, holding her in place.

Unlike the other men, this cowboy didn’t like being deprived and he moved closer. “Come on over here, darlin’. I’ll show you how a real man does it.”

Seth turned toward the stranger, sizing up the threat as he forced Jody behind him. The cowboy was about an inch or two shorter, but his aggressive stance and the scar on his right cheek seemed to bespeak he had plenty of experience with bar room brawls.

“She’s spoken for,” Seth said, his voice filled with menace.

“Doesn’t look like that to me,” the cowboy said, as a few of the man’s friends rose and walked over. The four of them made an intimidating front, but Seth would die before these assholes laid a hand on Jody.

From the corner of his eye, he saw Chase and the other ranch hands stand, placing themselves firmly behind Seth.

Great. Jody had set events in motion and Seth wasn’t sure how he was going to escape the evening without nursing some wounds from a full-scale battle. He didn't know who threw the first punch, but one minute they were in the face-off from hell, and the next, furniture was breaking as fists and beer bottles flew. Seth took a hard left to the jaw, which he returned with interest. He managed to land three or four more good swings, all while trying to keep an eye on Jody.

Damn woman had joined the fight. He turned just in time to see her kick the cowboy who'd started the whole thing in the nuts. The man crumpled to the floor, and Seth used his distraction to drag Jody away. Tucking her close to his side, he shoved and punched at least a half dozen other men as he made his way to the door.

"Come on." He pushed her through the front exit of the bar, the sound of glass breaking and people yelling, dimming as the door shut behind them. If he'd expected her to kick up a fuss, he would have been disappointed. She followed him like a docile puppy on a leash, a sure sign the alcohol was fucking with her head.

As they reached the truck, he opened the passenger door and helped her inside. When he reached over her to snap the buckle of the seatbelt, her arms latched around his neck.

"Hey, good lookin'," she drawled, leaning closer and rubbing her cheek against his.

Despite the fact he knew she was drunk, his cock stiffened up like a fireplace poker. "Behave, Jody."

Her tongue darted out, teasing his earlobe. "I don't wanna behave. I wanna be bad. So bad."

He gritted his teeth and pulled away. "Dammit, woman. Now is not the time."

She reached down and cupped her breasts, pushing them up. "I want you to suck on my nipples again, like you did in the tack room." Her eyes drifted closed as her fingers played with herself. Seth stood spellbound, watching her for a full thirty seconds before his brain reengaged.

"Jesus." Crossing in front of the truck, he drank in huge

gulps of air, trying to cool his overheated body. She was drunk. He couldn't touch her tonight because she didn't understand what she was asking for and she was *really* asking for it.

He climbed into the driver's seat, surprised to find Jody had unhooked her seatbelt and was waiting for him in the middle of the cab.

Seth narrowed his eyes. "Get back in your seat, darlin'."

She shook her head and leaned closer, dragging her hand along his chest. "I wanna suck your cock."

"Fuck." He gripped her hand firmly, removing it from his chest. "Jody. You're getting married tomorrow, remember?" He didn't mention the fact he was currently setting a plan into motion that would prevent her walk down the aisle. Unfortunately, it was the only thing he could think of that might possibly stop her. He was desperate.

"That's okay. Paul said I could fuck you if I wanted to."

He frowned, certain he'd heard her wrong. "What?"

She started to unbutton his pants, but he halted her, holding her hand firmly in his.

"Paul pointed out that I'd saved myself for you and since our marriage is one of convenience, he doesn't mind if I have a little taste before we say our vows."

He tried to focus on her words, but the second she said *taste*, his mind started conjuring images of everything he wanted to give her a taste of. "I'm begging you. Get back in your seat and stop talking."

She laughed lightly, the sound entirely too sexy. "I've never even seen you naked." She reached down and rubbed his cock through his jeans.

He groaned, covering her hand with his to still it. He leaned closer to her, relishing the fact that she didn't draw away. He'd grown accustomed to the leeriness in her eyes whenever he got too close. While he knew it was the tequila taking away her inhibitions, he savored the tiny bit of closeness the situation afforded him. "You're gonna get up close and personal with my cock real soon, Jody. Trust me. You just don't start something you can't finish."

She raised her chin. Even under the influence, she was indomitable. "Who says I can't finish?"

He raised her hand to his lips and kissed her knuckles. "I do. When I take you the first time, you're gonna be stone sober and begging for it. Now get back over in your seat like a good girl or I'll punish you."

She narrowed her eyes, and he smiled. Life with her would be one sweet battle after another. She opened her mouth to speak. He reached up and gripped her head, pulled her close and silenced her with a quick, hard kiss.

With his hand in her hair, he held her in place as he spoke. "Drunk or not, there's nothing I'd like more than to spank your ass after that little bar brawl you just instigated. You decide, Jody. Move over into the passenger seat and put the seatbelt back on or keep playing this game and see if I don't pull down your pants and bare your ass to God and everybody right now."

Despite the alcohol in her system, his words penetrated. She shifted back to the passenger's seat and buckled up. He started the truck and began to drive. For nearly twenty minutes she was quiet, looking out the passenger's side window, and Seth wondered if she'd passed out.

"Why did you come get me?" Her question broke the silence, and her voice sounded tired. He suspected she wouldn't remain awake much longer.

"You needed me."

She looked at him and even with a glance he could read the sadness in her eyes. "I've needed you forever. You've never come before."

His heart broke at her admission. She never would have spoken such thoughts if she weren't tipsy. He'd obviously hurt her more than he'd realized by rebuffing her all these years. He'd make it up to her. Somehow, he'd show her what she really meant to him.

He reached over and grasped her hand. "I always wanted to come. You just weren't ready."

She frowned. "And now I am?"

He nodded. "Yes."

"You're wrong." She didn't speak again and when he looked over, her eyes had drifted shut. He silently said a prayer of thanks. It would be much easier to do what needed to be done with an unconscious Jody. When she woke up tomorrow, she was going to be hungover and pissed off.

He grinned when he imagined the coming skirmish. She'd fight him tooth and nail. Odd part was he was looking forward to it. Now that he had her—with her father's blessing, no less—he planned to pull out all the stops. He was going to seduce sweet Jody right off her cute little size six feet.

He drove to Thomas's hunting cabin and parked the truck in front. He carried her inside, pulled down the sheets and laid her on the bed before sitting on the mattress at her side. She slept peacefully. He studied her face. The anxiety and worried lines that had covered her face since she'd returned home disappeared in sleep. She looked happy, beautiful. He intended to make sure she always looked that way.

He savored the image while he could. The only look he'd see on her face tomorrow would be fury. Slowly he undressed her. She'd be mad as hell when she woke up, but she wouldn't be getting married tomorrow. That was for damn sure. Once she was naked, he pulled the covers over her body. Lifting her arms above her head, he used a couple of the ties he'd packed to bind her arms together to the headboard. Then he undressed, walked to the opposite side of the bed and crawled in.

He lay for several moments with a smile on his face. Tonight was Jody's first night in his bed. He hoped there would be a lifetime more. He chuckled softly as he looked at her. God willing, maybe after tonight, he wouldn't have to tie her up to keep her there.

"What the hell?" Jody jerked awake when she realized she couldn't lower her arms.

"Mornin', sunshine."

She was startled by the deep voice and looked to her left. She was in bed with Seth. And he was shirtless. Shit. She struggled to remember the previous evening, but everything was blank. She tried to move and couldn't.

He chuckled, and she fought the urge to kick him in a place sure to wipe his smug smile away for a good long time. She started to do just that, but he dodged the blow too quickly. Grasping both her ankles before she could predict his actions, he managed to tie her legs to the footboard.

She worked hard to take a calming breath, but her heart was racing and her mind was whirling. "Why am I tied to this bed?"

"That's sort of a long story," he teased.

"Give me the SparkNotes version. Oh, and untie me while you're at it. I don't have time for your games."

"You have all the time in the world."

His words had her seeing red. "In case you forgot, dumbass, it's my wedding day. I'm not in the mood for this."

Seth's face darkened slightly. "This isn't a game, Jody. Make no mistake about that."

His gaze drifted down her chest and she realized that in her struggles, the blanket had gone south. "Fuck. I'm naked."

He nodded, his gaze not leaving her bare breasts. "Yep," he drawled.

Oh yeah. She was definitely hurting him. She wiggled again. He had her tied like a calf in a rodeo. This was not good.

"Why am I naked?" She racked her brain trying to remember what happened last night. She could recall going into Philly's and the guys buying a round. "Fuck. Tequila."

He nodded, though he didn't seem amused. "You're not a good drunk."

She tried not to groan. That wasn't exactly news. Usually she put a wide berth between her and the stuff, but last night, she'd been overwrought, frustrated, determined to erase Seth Compton from her mind for a few hours.

Well, that worked.

What the hell had she done? She looked at Seth. The sheet covered him from the waist down, but she'd seen his boxers when he tied her up. Regardless of that, an uneasy fear took root. She wanted to push it aside because the thought of it killed her, but she couldn't dismiss it. Had she given Seth her virginity? How could she not remember something so special? "Did we have sex?"

He scowled. "What kind of asshole do you think I am? Do I look like the kind of guy who'd bring a drunk girl home and fuck her?"

She raised an eyebrow. "Well, I'm naked, and we're in bed together. So why don't *you* tell me what kind of asshole you are?"

Seth moved closer, and she tried to still the racing of her heart. Regardless of her confusion, lying in bed with him was a dream come true and she was having a hard time keeping her libido under control.

"Not that kind. Although," he paused, giving her plenty of time to consider what he'd say next, "maybe I am an asshole. I did kidnap you, undress you and tie you to my bed."

"Kidnap?" she asked with a laugh she hoped wouldn't betray her sudden nervousness. "Don't joke."

She let her gaze travel around the room, expecting to find herself in Seth's foreman's cabin. One quick look told her that assumption was wrong. "Where are we?"

"Walker's Ridge."

"My dad's hunting cabin? How the hell did we get here?" The cabin was over an hour away from Philly's.

"I drove us."

"Why?"

Seth moved even closer, his hands engulfing her waist. Only the sheet separated them.

"You know why."

She licked her lips.

"You're mine and I think it's high time I proved that to you," he whispered, just before his lips took hers. His kiss let her know exactly how captive she was. He forced her lips apart, his tongue rubbing against hers. She wanted to resist him, but nothing on earth could stop her from responding. She moved closer, cursing the ties binding her to the bed. If she could get free, she could fight this sexy assault.

"Untie me," she whispered against his lips.

He reached up and freed her from her constraints. She started to rise, but his hands moved to her shoulders, massaging the kinks left behind by the bondage and she moaned at the glorious feeling. She was stiff, and he was hitting all the right spots.

He kissed her again. Before she could think better of it, she ran her hands through his hair, her breath catching when his bare chest rubbed against her naked breasts. Her nipples were tight, sensitive. This really wasn't good. He pulled her closer and her brain kicked in.

The asshole had kidnapped her. Snatched her right out of her own bachelorette party. Oh hell no. She shoved him away and sat up, pulling the sheets to cover herself.

"How dare you," she yelled.

Seth rolled over onto his back and gave her a rueful grin. "That didn't take long."

She bent down and untied her feet. "Take me home."

"No."

Her temper snapped. "When my father realizes I'm missing, he'll hunt you down like the lowdown skunk you are and shoot you."

"Thomas knows we're here."

His words took her aback, then fired her up even hotter. "Of course, he does. The two of you probably had a real good time figuring out how you could screw up my wedding day. This won't work, you know. You can't keep me here forever."

Seth shrugged. "I'll only keep you here long enough to make you see sense."

"Ha! That's rich. You kidnapped me, Compton. There's someone lacking sense around here, but it sure isn't me. Where are my clothes?"

Seth sat up, leaning against the headboard. She tried to ignore the slight tenting beneath his boxers.

She glanced up to find Seth grinning, and she knew she was blushing. "Wanna peek?"

She scowled. Arrogant, cocky cowboy. "You've seen one, you've seen them all."

Now it was his turn to frown. "And just whose cock have you been looking at?"

She shrugged, loving the zing of her lie. "I may be a virgin, Seth, but I'm hardly an innocent."

He moved forward, and she struggled to hold her ground. She'd returned home with her future set. She'd promised to marry Paul, to help him achieve his dream of building the cancer research facility. Giving up a year of her life to make that a reality seemed a small price to pay.

What she hadn't counted on was Seth. She'd spent months trying to move on. She wasn't going to backpedal now. She needed to find some way to convince him to let her go.

"Well," he purred, his nose brushing against her cheek, his hot breath warming her face...and a lot of other parts of her body. "Since you're so experienced, maybe I shouldn't worry about taking things slow. You offered to suck my cock last night. Being a gentleman, I refused."

Heat rushed to her cheeks. Good God. She'd obviously put

on quite a show. "If you were a gentleman, you'd stop playing this stupid game and give me my clothes."

He gripped her arms and before she could react, he pulled her down on the bed, covering her with his body. "I told you before. This isn't a game."

He kissed her, his hands grasping her face, holding her still for his assault. The kiss was too hot, too deep. She closed her eyes, letting the emotions it evoked wash through her. She'd lied about being experienced. Like a fool, she'd saved herself for him. Spent years turning down dates and eschewing relationships out of respect for what she thought was true love. She'd been an idiot.

If it hadn't been for Paul, she would have rectified that oversight on her twenty-first birthday. She'd gone out intent on experiencing the life she'd been denied while deluding herself into thinking Seth was the only man she ever wanted to be with. Paul had pulled her out of the bar before she could add yet another mistake to the list she'd tallied up over the years...all because she'd fallen in love with Seth Compton when she was twelve years old.

He moved back, though their lips were just a hairsbreadth away. "Let me show you what you'll be missing if you choose Paul."

His words splashed over her like ice-cold water as everything crashed down on her. Paul. The trust fund. The will. The wedding she was about to miss.

She pressed against his shoulders, and he moved back. She crawled out of the bed, embarrassed by her nudity. She should be moving beyond the stage where she was modest in front of him, but it was too new, too unfamiliar. She looked around and spotted his T-shirt hanging on the back of a chair. God only knew where he'd hidden her clothing. Grabbing it, she drew the soft cotton over her head as he moved to the side of the mattress, facing her. "I have to get out of here."

"Dammit, Jody. Do we really need to go over this again? I

told you why I couldn't let things between us go too far."

"You're right. We're beating a dead horse," she said, tugging the T-shirt down, wishing it covered more. As it was, it only hit her about mid-thigh. "And you know what, hotshot, those reasons haven't changed. I'm not gonna bend over and be a good little submissive for you. I'm not gonna play some weak, helpless woman in this macho kidnapper scenario you're working on. What I am going to do is get dressed, go home and marry a man who's never pretended to be anything other than who he really is."

Her comments had struck a chord, but by the set of Seth's jaw he wasn't giving up yet. His stubbornness in the face of hers was more proof that a relationship between them would never work. Instead of compromising, they'd continue to butt heads until one of them had brain damage.

"You know what," she started. "You were wrong to wait for me to grow up. You should've snatched me up when I was young and stupid and willing to do anything for you. You let the hourglass run out."

He shook his head. "You don't get it, Jody. I didn't want the young girl with stars in her eyes. I wanted the woman I knew you could be. The woman you are now. I don't want a doormat. I want an equal. I want you."

She laughed, though the sound didn't portray happiness. "Oh the irony. You didn't want me when I wanted you. Now when you do want me, I've moved on. Life's a bitch."

Her words were harsh, sarcastic and full of shit.

"I don't believe you don't want me."

She shrugged. "I don't really care what you believe." She glanced around. She needed to get the hell out of this room, away from him before all the months she'd spent hardening her heart collapsed around her. "I need to go to the bathroom."

He narrowed his eyes suspiciously, then took in her appearance. Obviously, he decided in her current get-up she wasn't a flight risk. "Go ahead. I'll make us some breakfast."

She nodded once, then turned to cross the room. As she passed the kitchen counter, she spotted the keys to his truck. She could feel his gaze burning into her back as she walked away. When she got to the counter, she pretended to step on something.

"Shit," she said, bending down to brush away the make-believe annoyance while laying her other hand over the keys.

"What's wrong?"

"Nothing," she grumbled. "Just stepped on a pebble or something. This damn cabin could use a good cleaning." She closed her hands around the keys and continued toward the bathroom. Once inside, she locked the door and rushed over to the window.

She grinned as she slowly raised the glass. Maybe she'd send someone to pick Seth up in a day or two. After her wedding ceremony.

Climbing through, she landed softly on the grass outside the window, grateful the cabin was only one story. Quickly, she dashed around the corner toward the truck. She didn't have much time.

She pulled up short when she saw Seth leaning against the hood, wearing nothing but a pair of Levi's and a big smile.

"Goin' somewhere?" he asked.

She sighed, feigning surrender. "Guess not," she said. "Here." She tossed the keys at him, aiming for his face. She didn't wait to see if he caught them.

Instead, she turned quickly and took off in the opposite direction. She'd always been a fast runner. If she could just make it to the road, maybe she'd get lucky and someone would be driving by. She could hear Seth behind her, but she couldn't risk turning to look. Her heart was racing and God help her, she was actually becoming aroused. Apparently, this kidnapping thing was starting to get to her, pushing some previously unexplored buttons.

A hard hand grabbed her T-shirt, drawing her back. She

stumbled and started to fall. She threw her hands up to save herself from the hard ground, but at the last minute, Seth twisted her, taking the impact as she fell against his chest.

"Ouch," she said, perfectly aware their tumble had probably hurt him worse than her.

He grimaced. "Yeah, ouch."

She pushed up onto her elbows. "You okay?"

He lay still for a moment, and she wondered if he was taking inventory before answering her. "I'm fine, but sweetheart—"

His odd tone alerted her to the fact she was straddling his waist with her very bare ass. She could feel his erection pushing against his jeans.

"Shit." She started to stand, but Seth clasped his hands around her hips and held her in place. "Seth. Let me up."

"I wanna see something first."

Before she could reply, he tumbled her to her back, covering her with his bulky muscles. "What the hell?"

His fingers drifted down her stomach before touching her clit. She gasped, unable to speak as he touched her.

"You're soaking wet."

She tried to suck in breath, but her arousal was seriously cutting off the flow of air to her lungs.

"You like being chased, captured," he murmured against her cheek. He dipped a finger inside and she closed her eyes, trying not to acknowledge how very close she was to coming. "You liked being tied up, too, didn't you?"

She refused to answer. Shit, she couldn't answer. Every brain cell in her body was focused on the finger he was moving in and out of her pussy. Before she could consider her action, she thrust toward his hand on one retreat, her inner muscles clenching in an attempt to hold him, keep him.

"Please," she whispered, breathlessly. His touch was too light, not enough. Nowhere near enough.

Unfortunately he didn't grin or gloat or brag. If he'd done any of that, she'd have found the strength to shove him away. Instead, he added another finger to the dance and increased the speed.

She gasped when his thumb began to rub her clit in time with the pounding of his fingers. With each thrust, he moved faster, went deeper. Stars began to float behind her closed eyes and her treasonous body surrendered to his touch.

He leaned closer, placing a soft kiss on her cheek before whispering in her ear. "Come for me, Jody."

His words pulled the trigger and she cried out, her inner muscles flexing almost painfully against his fingers. For a split second, a weak moment, she wished it was his cock inside her as he milked every bit of pleasure from her. His thumb stimulated her clit, pushing hard against the sensitive nub. Every time she felt herself coming down, he found another way to prolong the beautiful agony, until at last she grasped his wrist and begged for mercy.

For several minutes, neither of them moved. Jody wondered if Seth was afraid to break the spell he'd placed on her. She wished he would. Prayed he'd say something to remind her of her anger. Right now, she was wavering and she wasn't sure how much of his seduction she could resist.

And she had to resist him.

God. She had to.

Chapter Seven

Jody struggled with the ties as Seth fiddled with his laptop in the corner. After returning to the cabin, he'd promptly led her back to the bed, stripped off her T-shirt, and tied her up again, saying he needed to do something and he couldn't worry about her trying to escape. She'd tried to convince him she wouldn't go anywhere, but he didn't buy the lie. Dammit.

She heard voices coming from the computer, and she listened as Seth replied. After a few moments, it became clear he was talking to his brothers via a web link. She tried to block out their conversation, using Seth's distraction to work herself free from the ties binding her to the bed. Lucky for her, Seth wouldn't do anything to hurt her, so he hadn't tied them as tightly as she suspected he really could have.

Her ears perked up when she heard one of Seth's brothers talking about racy letters from a woman named Lucy. Typical men.

She tried to bite her tongue, but failed. "Tell your brothers it's not nice to kiss and tell. Well, I suppose this Lucy did, but sharing a note with a lover is different than tossing those fantasies to a pack of rabid, ungrateful, fickle cowboys."

"Who the hell was that?" a voice said from the computer.

Jody got excited. His brothers could hear her. "Only the cowgirl your fucking asshole brother is keeping prisoner in this godforsaken shack. Will someone please call 911?"

Seth grinned as he glanced over his shoulder at her. "Don't

make me gag you, darlin'."

Another voice came from the computer speakers. "Holy shit. What is that in the background? Do I see pretty ankles tied to the end of your bed, Seth?"

"I'm Jody Kirkland. My dad is your brother's boss. He'll probably also be the man to murder this piece of shit, arrogant, limp dick when he finds out what he's up to." She knew her threat wasn't true, but his brothers didn't.

"I'll give you arrogant, but I'm guessing Seth's anything but a limp dick right now, honey."

Jody rolled her eyes at the comment. Great. So much for the cavalry coming to save her. Seth's brothers were as cocky as him.

"Argh! You're all alike. I can't believe there are really *four* of you. Thank God you spread yourselves out. No state should have to house that many Compton Brothers. Especially if you're all as dense as Seth."

"I like this girl," another voice chimed in.

"So you're calling the police?" She thrashed her legs hoping it might strike some chivalrous bone in one of the men.

"I don't think my mom would appreciate Seth missing out on the next ten Christmases because he's in jail. Sorry, honey. I bet he could help you make the most of the situation."

"You're all bastards. Every one of you. Asshats!"

Seth shook his head and his exasperated groan spoke volumes. "Jody. Give me two minutes. Then we'll talk, okay?"

She bit her tongue, only because it was clear none of Seth's brothers intended to help her. She'd be better off focusing her attention on getting free of the ties while he was distracted. She twisted her wrists one last time in total desperation and to her amazement, one of her hands slid free. Reaching over, she quickly untied her other hand.

A glance to her left proved Seth was still talking to his brothers. She bent to untie her ankles when she heard,

"...instead of playing with the sexy woman tied to his bed, about to escape."

Great. They could see her. She tried to move faster, but one of the knots was too tight. She sprung up quickly as soon as it slipped loose.

"What!" Seth spun in his chair. When he spotted her, he rose, snagged a blanket off the foot of his bed and wrapped it around her. "What the hell do you think you're doing?"

"Leaving, moron." She thrashed in his embrace, frustrated. She'd had a taste of freedom and the idea of losing it so quickly wasn't sitting well with her.

She could hear his brothers laughing at their struggles, and she fought back a scream of fury.

One of them said, "Okay, as fun as this is, I have to be on deck in five minutes. Someone better fill me in later."

"No, there will be no filling in." Seth tossed her on the bed and marched to the camera, blocking it with his palm. "I have to go. Si, we'll talk more. Soon."

She rose, trying to shove off the blanket he'd tangled around her and her feet had no more than hit the floor before he was back on her again.

"Goddammit," she yelled, stomping on his foot as hard as she could.

He wrestled her back onto the bed, but made no move to bind her again. His chest covered her back as she was pushed facedown into the mattress.

"Two days," he said, panting slightly.

She stopped moving. "What?"

"Give me two days. If you still wanna leave, still wanna marry your gay boyfriend, I'll walk you down the damn aisle myself. Just give me two days to show you what you'll be giving up."

She lay motionless, considering his words. "Two days and then you'll take me home?"

He nodded, though she wasn't sure she could trust him to keep his word.

"And what'll happen during the next two days to change my mind?"

"You know what's gonna happen, Jody."

He lifted up enough that he could flip her over onto her back. She was trapped beneath him, his strong legs straddling her thighs. His erection was evident through his jeans. She felt certain it couldn't possibly be as large as it looked. Suddenly saving herself for Seth didn't seem like such a wise decision. He'd rip her in two.

Apparently he noticed her distress. He bent down to kiss her. "We'll go slow."

She accepted his light kisses before pulling away an inch or two. "I'm not sure slow is gonna help."

He grinned. "Have to say I haven't touched a virgin in years. Not since I was a young, stupid guy in high school, strutting around like God's gift to women."

"I see nothing's changed."

He laughed. "Everything's changed."

He was right. It had. "Seth."

"Shhh. Trust me?"

She nodded. She trusted him with her life. She had ever since the first day she met him and he pulled her off the runaway horse. He'd been the center of her universe for a decade.

He leaned down and kissed her. For all his talk about dominance, his kiss betrayed his softer side. It was gentle, tender, perfect. His hand stroked along her neck, down her side to her leg and back up again, settling on her breast. He cupped her flesh, then bent his head to capture her nipple between his lips. He wasn't trying to claim her or mark her as his.

It felt as if he was cherishing her, loving her. Her eyes closed—a defense mechanism, pure and simple—but there was no blocking out the feeling. She'd lost her heart to Seth Compton when she was only a child, and she'd spent the last few months of her life trying to deny it. Suddenly she was faced with the irrevocable truth.

"Look at me," he whispered.

She opened her eyes, saw his beloved face and couldn't hold back the tear that slid down her cheek.

Seth caught the drop on his finger, his gaze carefully studying her expression, making sure she was okay.

She was fine. Just caught in the most perfect moment of her life.

She smiled. "I don't know why I'm crying. I'm not sad or scared."

He kissed her again, then pressed his forehead to hers. "I know why. I love you, Jody."

She sucked in a shaky breath. "I love you too."

He rose slowly, his eyes drinking in every inch of her naked body as his hands began to unzip his jeans. Her lips parted, sucking in some much needed air. She felt dizzy, hot, lightheaded.

He shrugged his jeans over his hips as she watched, spellbound. His cock was bigger than it had appeared beneath the tight denim.

"Shit," she murmured, and he laughed as he climbed back onto the bed, caging her beneath him. She wondered if there could be a more wonderful feeling in the world.

He kissed her again, long, slow, wet kisses that left her feeling drunk and ready for more. His hands caressed her as his lips worshiped her. She was on fire, every inch of her skin sensitive to his stroking fingers.

Her legs parted, seemingly of their own volition, and she wrapped her ankles around his strong thighs. She wasn't sure when he'd reached for the condom, but she opened her eyes when she heard the crinkling of the wrapper. She wished...

"You aren't on birth control, are you?"

She shook her head. There'd never been any need.

He put the condom on as she watched. "We'll correct that oversight after you choose me."

She giggled. "Cocky bastard."

He shrugged good-naturedly, then all thoughts of the future were wiped away by the present. He placed the head of his cock at her wet entrance.

"Breathe, Jody."

She expelled loudly, immediately gasping for more.

"Okay?" he asked with a crooked grin.

"Terrified, excited, nervous, happy."

He pushed in a fraction of an inch. His wide head stretched her. It was uncomfortable, but not painful. He bent down to kiss her again, and for several moments, she lost herself to his lips as they caressed hers. When she came up for air, she realized he was deeper. She'd never felt so full, so utterly possessed.

"Keep your eyes on me," he said.

She fell headfirst into his hungry gaze. "Seth," she whispered, unable to put into words exactly what this moment meant to her.

Each shallow retreat was followed by a deeper thrust. She wanted to look away, hide from the intensity, the beauty, but he wouldn't let her escape. She sensed he was gauging her reactions, her pain.

"Can you take more?" he asked as he forged even farther inside.

"God," she cried, her fingers digging into his upper arms. "There's more?"

He laughed lightly. "Just a little bit. Hold on to me."

She tightened her grip and held her breath, never letting her gaze waver. He pulled out until just the head of his cock was lodged in her pussy, then he moved back in, not stopping until he was completely buried. She shuddered at the unbearably beautiful combination of pain and bliss.

Seth kissed her gently, giving her time to adjust to his invasion.

"Guess that's the end of the virginity thing," she joked when his lips drifted lower to kiss her neck.

He chuckled. "Yep."

She rolled her eyes. "You don't have to sound so smug about it."

Her taunt sent him into a fit of laughter. "You're perfect," he said. "Now hush. I need—" He didn't finish his thoughts with words, rather he let his body express exactly what he required. The gentleness of his actions as he'd initiated her body to the act of sex evaporated as his movements quickened, his thrusts becoming harder, deeper.

He reached down to rub her clit, and she cried at the mini-sparks his touch spurred in her body. She started to anticipate his downward motions, her hips rising to welcome him.

"Can't wait much longer," he said, each word broken up with a harsh gasp. "Come, Jody. Come for me."

He pushed on her clit more firmly, and she cried out as her orgasm crashed around her like waves in the ocean. She felt herself being pulled under, the tide dragging her along in a whirlwind of ecstasy. She vaguely recalled hearing his own climax, his words a continuous string of romantic curses.

Shit, I love you.

So fucking gorgeous.

God damn, I need you.

For several moments, they lay still, their bodies pressed together. Then he gave her a quick kiss and pulled out. She winced before she could shield her reactions.

He frowned. "Don't move," he said as he stood up.

"Where are you going?"

He gestured to his deflating cock. "Need to get rid of the

condom and clean up."

She watched him walk to the bathroom, helpless to contain her smile. She'd had sex. She'd done it. With Seth. And it had totally been worth the wait.

She briefly considered Paul. She glanced at the clock on the bedside table. If she were back at the ranch, she'd be walking down the aisle. Marching firmly and resolutely toward the wrong man.

Spending a year in marriage to him had seemed a small price to pay at the beginning. Now, as she considered twelve months away from Seth, it seemed like an eternity.

Seth reemerged from the bathroom with a washcloth. Rather than climbing back into bed, he perched beside her on her side of the mattress.

"Open your legs," he said as she blushed. He grinned. "I've already seen it, Jody.

She rolled her eyes. "I know. I'm just not, I can't be so—" She waved her hands around as he pushed her knees apart, using the warm cloth to gently wash away the evidence of their lovemaking.

"You never have to be embarrassed with me," he said. "You're beautiful. Every part of you." He finished his ministrations and placed the cloth on the nightstand. "Sore?"

She shook her head. He narrowed his eyes, proving she hadn't fooled him.

"Maybe a little. Not enough that I don't want to do it again." She ran her hand along his upper thigh, seductively.

He laughed, grasping her hand and kissing it. "That's my girl." He rose and crossed the foot of the bed, climbing in next to her. "Later."

Always her protector, she knew he'd keep her safe, even from herself and her desires. She curled up in his embrace, wondering if she'd ever been in a nicer place in her life. She lightly stroked his chest, his breath warm and steady against the top of her head.

"Stay with me for two days."

He pressed his suit and she realized she'd never responded to his request. She nodded her assent. "Okay."

"Promise me." He knew her too well, knew she would never break a promise.

"I promise."

God help her. Two days wouldn't be long enough.

Chapter Eight

Seth opened his eyes, surprised to see the sun was setting. He hadn't intended to fall asleep, thinking he'd only rest for a little while.

However, Jody had rocked his world. He lay on his stomach, grinning like a fool. Glancing over, he noticed the bed was empty.

"Fuck." He sat up, cursing himself for letting down his guard. He'd asked her for two days, and she'd promised. She'd never broken a promise in her life and now...

"What's wrong?" Jody's head popped up from behind the island that separated the bedroom from the kitchen. The cabin was small. One large room contained the sleeping, eating and living areas, the bathroom the only separate space.

He tried to hide the fact he thought she'd gone, but she grinned and he knew she wasn't going to let his mistake go without ridicule.

"You thought I left."

He shook his head, tried to deny the truth. "No, I didn't."

"You were regretting not tying me up again, weren't you?"

He rose from the bed, not bothering to hide his nakedness. Her gaze drifted to his cock. He was hard as a rock and ready for round two. His conscience told him he should go easy on her, but he wasn't sure he was a good enough man to pull it off. Then she licked her lips and he knew he wasn't good enough.

"What are you doing?" he asked.

"I'm going to whip up some grilled ham and cheese sandwiches. I was looking for a pan, not plotting my grand escape."

He laughed. "You promised to stay, Jody."

She pointed the spatula in her hand at him. "That's right, I did. You should know I don't make vows lightly."

Her words reminded him of another promise she'd made.

"What's the deal between you and Paul?" The idea of her marrying a man she clearly wasn't in love with had been driving him crazy since she'd returned home. She kept saying Paul needed her, but there was clearly some piece to the puzzle he was missing, something she wasn't telling him.

She sighed, carrying the pan over to the stove. For a second, he thought she was going to ignore his question. Finally, she spoke. "My mom died of breast cancer."

He nodded, confused. "I know."

"Paul's mother did too. Did you know that?"

He shook his head.

"I think that's why he and I are such good friends. We have a lot in common. We sort of see things the same way."

He frowned. Was she marrying Paul because of some common bond over their mothers? "Seems like a poor reason to marry someone."

She smiled sadly. "It's more than that. We have a shared goal for the future."

"What sort of goal?"

Jody turned on the burner, placing the sandwiches in the pan. Her words were coming slowly and Seth began to think that whatever was driving her to marry Paul wasn't going to be that easy to overcome. "Paul's studying to be an architect. He's incredibly talented. He's going to build a cancer treatment facility with some trust fund money he's about to come into."

Seth rubbed his jaw, trying to figure out what the hell she

was talking about. How was this connected to her wedding? "That's real nice of him."

She smiled. "He has to be legally married by his next birthday in order to get the money."

Suddenly a light came on and Seth began to understand. Her words triggered his temper. "You're marrying him so he can get some trust fund?"

She sighed and crossed her arms. He tried to ignore the fact the pose accentuated her breasts and made him hungry for a taste. She was dressed in his T-shirt and nothing else. "Do you know how much good can come from the research that would happen in Paul's facility?"

He ran a frustrated hand through his hair. "My issue isn't with Paul's plans for the money. It's an admirable thing to do. I just don't understand why you have to sacrifice your future, spend your life in a loveless marriage so some building can be built."

"It wouldn't be my whole life. Just a year."

He paused. "What?"

"According to Paul's lawyer, if he were legally married for a year, the stipulation in the will would be met. If he fails to get married, the money goes to a distant cousin."

"Maybe the cousin would agree to give the money—"

"The cousin's an addict. He'd blow every penny of the inheritance, filling his veins with drugs."

"Oh."

Suddenly her vehemence about following through with this wedding made sense. He wasn't fighting another man for her heart. He was fighting against her dead mother. He sighed. It was a competition he couldn't hope to win. Jody would gladly sacrifice a year if she thought it meant other young girls' mothers could be saved. Fuck. Even he could understand now. That didn't mean he agreed though.

"Surely there's some other way."

She shook her head. "Time's not exactly on his side. He has to be married before his next birthday, which is just a few weeks away."

Seth crossed the room and sat down. He leaned back in the chair, desperately seeking for an answer. "Seems like an odd stipulation for a will."

Jody shrugged, flipping the sandwiches. "Not if you consider the fact Paul's father was the world's biggest homophobe."

He sat up, his suspicions confirmed. "So Paul *is* gay."

She nodded. "The will was a punishment. Plain and simple."

"Pardon me for saying so, but Paul's father was a prick."

She smiled. "Amen."

They were quiet for a few minutes as Jody finished the sandwiches, putting them on plates and adding a handful of potato chips. She came over to the table and placed a plate in front of him. He had an ache in his gut that wouldn't go away until he asked the question he already knew the answer to. "You won't go back on your promise, will you?"

She sat down across from him, but she didn't answer. Her face said it all.

"I'm going to change your mind," he said, unwilling to consider spending five minutes without her, let alone a year. He had her here and he was going to make sure that by the time these two days were up, there was nowhere else on earth she wanted to be. There had to be an answer to Paul's dilemma that didn't include Jody. When they returned to the ranch, he'd demand to see the will. He'd fax a copy to his dad's lawyer. There had to be a loophole, an out.

She shrugged, a noncommittal gesture that tweaked his temper. Reaching over, he pulled her chair toward his.

"Hey," she said.

"Open your legs. Wrap your ankles around the front legs of

your chair to keep them apart."

She hesitated.

"Do it now, Jody."

He hadn't bothered to dress and suddenly, he didn't like the fact that her body was hidden beneath his large T-shirt. He pulled the thin material over her head before she could stop him. She wasn't wearing panties. Her hands moved to cover herself, but he gripped them, applying the slightest bit of pressure when she tried to pull them free.

"Don't."

Her breathing was ragged, and he could sense her rising arousal. She definitely liked it when he took control.

He looked down at her legs which were still tightly closed. He took a deep breath and started counting to ten in his head. If she hadn't moved them by the time he reached the end, she was going to be introduced to the concept of punishment.

He hadn't made it to five when her knees parted, her ankles looping over the legs of the chair. He looked up and smiled. She narrowed her eyes, and he knew she wanted to make a smartass comment. Amazingly, she refrained.

He pointed to her sandwich. "Better eat before that gets cold."

She'd just taken her first bite when he reached over and pushed a finger into her pussy. She was wet and hot and more than ready for him.

She gasped.

"Chew," he said, when her eyes drifted closed. She obeyed, putting the sandwich back on the plate.

He thrust first one, then two fingers inside her, maintaining a steady, deep pace. Her hips began to move in time.

"Keep eating."

She shook her head, and he sensed she was close to coming. He withdrew his fingers.

"Seth," she protested.

"Pick up your sandwich and keep eating. You aren't allowed to come until your plate is clear."

"That's impossible."

He chuckled. "No, it's not. Eat."

He waited until she took another bite before replacing his fingers in her pussy. She managed to choke down two more bites, though he sensed she was struggling to hold off her orgasm. She'd just popped a chip in her mouth when he started stroking her clit with his thumb.

"Fuck," she muttered, her hand flying up to cover her mouth. Ever the Southern lady, she managed to chew with her mouth closed. Her pussy muscles clenched, and he stopped moving.

"I have to come, Seth. Now." Her tone was a perfect mix of pleading and demanding.

He looked at her plate. "You know what you have to do."

She hastily shoved a large mouthful of the sandwich in her mouth as he added a third finger to the first two. Her hands grasped the sides of her chair and tightened into a white-knuckle grip.

"Your orgasms belong to me," he whispered, leaning closer when he felt her fighting her body's natural impulses.

She shook her head. "My body belongs to me. And only me."

He removed his fingers. "Is that right?"

She moaned, trembling at the loss. "Dammit, Seth. Finish what you started."

He stood up and walked to the bed. Reaching beneath it, he pulled out an overnight bag. When he'd picked up the groceries from the ranch house last night, he'd gone to Jody's room to pack some extra clothes for her. The devil in him had prompted him to rifle through her nightstand drawer.

He opened the bag, pulled out the treasure he'd found and turned back toward her.

Her eyes narrowed. “Where did you find that?”

“Where do think?”

She rose, angrily. “Did you go through my drawers?”

He grinned. “I thought you might like some clean clothes. Have to admit I didn’t expect to find this.” He waved the vibrator he’d found in front of her. “Bit disappointed to see it’s still in its wrapper.”

She shrugged. “It was a gift.”

He walked closer to her. “From who?”

She smiled smugly, clearly happy to have gotten his goat. Damn woman would always keep him hopping. “My fiancé.”

Seth frowned. “Just how good a friend is Paul?”

She laughed, good-naturedly, and let the joke go. “He gave it to me the night he proposed. Said he’d always make sure his wife was well provided for. He was kidding, of course. I thought it was a pretty funny gag at the time.”

He was glad she had a friend like Paul in her life. He’d worried about her going off to college so far from home. Paul had filled a void and kept her safe. He admitted to himself he owed the guy a great deal of gratitude for that.

“Doesn’t explain why you never tried it.”

She rolled her eyes. “He only gave it to me a couple of weeks ago. I’ve been packing up to come home. Time hasn’t exactly been on my side.”

“Well, now it is.”

“What do you mean?”

“Go lay on the bed. I think you and I need to have a little heart to heart about who owns this body of yours.”

She walked to the bed, but she wasn’t cowed. “You can talk until the cows come home, but that’s not gonna change the fact that my body and my orgasms belong to me.”

He tried to stifle his smile. This was going to be fun. She crawled onto the bed, taking care to make sure he got a very good look at her bare ass before she rolled over onto her back.

She beckoned him with a finger and he struggled to look stern. She was topping from the bottom. Obviously it was time to take off the kid gloves and teach Ms. Kirkland a little lesson in submission.

Walking to the kitchen sink, he opened the package containing the vibrator and washed it. He took his time. Through the reflection in the kitchen window, he could see Jody squirming on the bed. She'd been close to coming on the chair. It wouldn't take much to push her over the edge. He'd have to tread that razor's edge lightly. Before she came, she'd know without a doubt that her body belonged to him. He aimed to wrap her up so tightly in lust and desire that she'd never consider marrying another man, promise or not.

He walked to the foot of the bed. Jody lounged, trying to give the appearance of nonchalance, though he detected the slight tremor in her hands and her accelerated breathing.

"Open your legs," he said softly.

For a moment, he thought she might refuse. Then she gave him a smile sexier than silk sheets and spread herself open for his perusal.

He could see she was wet even from several feet away. She wanted this, wanted him. "Touch yourself. Get yourself hot, but don't come."

She bit her lower lip and again he sensed her nervousness, her desire to withdraw. However, his girl was nothing if not resilient. Her fingers drifted down her bare stomach slowly before lightly rubbing her clit.

He watched quietly for several moments as she toyed with the firm nub, her fingers moving faster before dipping inside her pussy. He let her stroke herself several times, enjoying the flush covering her body, her breasts. She was hot. Hell, he'd say she was on fire.

"Stop," he demanded.

Her fingers paused, still buried deep within her cunt. Her breathing was labored.

"Seth," she whispered. "I need you."

He grinned, climbing onto the mattress. He knelt between her parted legs. "Taste yourself."

She licked her lips nervously, slowly dragging her fingers out of her pussy.

He leaned closer as her fingers moved toward her mouth. "Rub your juices on your lips. Pretend it's lip gloss."

She grinned and rolled her eyes, but she obeyed.

"Now lick your fingers."

She stuck two digits in her mouth, sucking on them in such a provocative way his vision went black for a second.

"You're going to do that to my cock very soon," he whispered.

She glanced down at his erection letting him know she was more than ready for that reality.

He grasped her wrist, pulling her fingers out of her mouth with a light pop. He needed to get back on track or he'd be the one begging for release, not her. He lifted his right hand and showed her the vibrator.

Without speaking, he put the toy at the opening to her body and pushed it inside slowly, but steadily. He kept his eyes on her face, watching for any discomfort. He wasn't forgetting the fact that she'd been a virgin a few hours earlier. Once the toy was fully enveloped in her hot flesh, he flipped the switch on the bottom on low speed.

She jolted as it started vibrating.

"God," she said on a breathless sigh.

"You like that?"

She nodded, her eyes drifting closed.

He bent down, lifting one of her breasts in his palm and directing her nipple to his mouth. He didn't hold back, didn't refrain from taking her exactly the way he'd always dreamed of. He sucked on the turgid tip roughly, giving it the occasional bite. She groaned, writhing on the mattress.

"Please," she whispered.

"You need more?"

She nodded, without opening her eyes. He reached down and increased the vibrator's speed. She cried out loudly, her hips gyrating wildly, as he turned his attention to her other breast.

When he sensed she was getting close to coming, he quickly turned off the vibrator.

She trembled, her eyes flying open. "What the hell?"

"Who owns your orgasms?" he asked, repeating his question.

Her teeth clenched and she refused to answer.

He smiled. "Stubborn girl."

Leaning forward, he placed soft kisses on her throat until he felt her pulse calm. Once her impending need to climax passed, he turned the vibrator on once more. Bypassing the lower speeds, he cranked the toy up to its highest setting. Her head flew back against the pillow, her hips thrusting uncontrollably.

He gripped her hips tightly, holding her still as he moved downward until he could suck her clit into his mouth. Her legs started to clench around his head and he pushed her knees farther apart, giving him more access to her sweet arousal. Nipping her tight bud, her cries grew louder, more frantic.

When her orgasm seemed imminent, he pulled the vibrator out completely.

"God dammit," she screamed.

"Who owns this pretty body?"

She shuddered and wrapped her arms around her waist. He wondered if the movement was for self-defense or comfort.

"You," she whispered.

He smiled. "Say it again."

She blew out a frustrated breath. "You. You own my body. I'm yours, Seth. I've always been yours."

He tried to recall if he'd ever heard a more beautiful sentiment. No force on earth could have stopped him from kissing her at that moment. He moved over her body and placed his lips on hers. He could taste the tang of her arousal there and it drove his higher. Dragging his tongue along her soft lips, he tried to show her how much her words meant to him.

Rising at last, he quickly donned a condom and pushed inside her, memorizing the beautiful expression on her face as he took possession of the precious gift she'd given him. Slowly, he moved inside, the two of them finding their rhythm, their cadence. Neither of them rushed to find their release. Instead they let the power of the moment close around them and when they reached the peak, they dove into the light together.

Chapter Nine

Jody smiled when she noticed Seth's gaze on her face. She'd been lying on her side since waking up, studying the tattoo on his back, as he slept peacefully on his stomach.

"Like what you see?" he asked, giving her a shit-eating grin.

"You know I do." She reached out and ran her finger over the tattoo that had fascinated her for years. She'd caught more than a few glimpses of it, mainly in the summer when Seth pulled off his T-shirt on the piping-hot days.

He closed his eyes and sighed contentedly as she outlined the dark shape, following each intricate line. "That feels nice," he mumbled after a minute or so.

"A compass?"

His eyelids rose slowly. "Mmm hmm. I grew up on Compass Ranch. You knew that. My brothers and I all got the same tattoo."

She nodded. "The brand in the middle? That's the one you use on the ranch?"

"Yep."

She touched the bottom of the tattoo and paused. "The S on the compass is bigger than the other direction marks."

He turned onto his side, facing her. Reaching out, he pulled her closer until they were chest to chest, nose to nose. He wasn't the only one suddenly wide awake. His hard cock pressed against her stomach, and she felt her pussy clench with need and desire.

"I got the tattoo right before I left home. I was young, cocky, wild and ready to see the world. In my mind, all my dreams were gonna come true in Texas."

She wrapped her arm around his waist, loving the closeness between them. For years, she'd wondered what it would be like to share a bed with Seth. Dreamed of engaging in pillow talk.

"Did they come true?" she asked.

"You're in my bed, aren't you?"

Her heart lurched at his sweet words.

"Sweet talker," she said, struggling to get the light-hearted words out. This moment, hell, the past twenty-four hours, had sent her world spinning. She was dizzy and giddy and happier than she thought possible.

He leaned closer and kissed the tip of her nose. "How about a shower?"

"Together?"

He laughed. "I have one more day with you, darlin'. You're gonna be hard-pressed to keep me more than an inch away from you."

She pushed closer. "I don't remember complainin'."

He gave her a hard, quick kiss, before rising and climbing out of the bed.

She started to pull on a T-shirt, modesty still winning out despite the fact Seth had probably seen more of her naked body than she had. He'd studied every nook and cranny of her throughout the night, the light of the moon casting a romantic hue on the bed as he made love to her time and time again.

"No clothes," he said, taking the T-shirt out of her hands. "It's a quick trip."

She felt herself flush, but willed her embarrassment away, taking his proffered hand as he led her to the bathroom.

Bending down, he turned on the hot water and she

watched the small room quickly fill with steam. Together, they stepped into the stream and she sighed blissfully as the heat hit her stiff muscles.

"Sore?" he asked.

She shook her head once, but stopped when he narrowed his eyes. "Maybe. A little. You've been giving me quite a workout."

He grinned. "I haven't even started yet."

She glanced down at his erection as a naughty idea came to her. "Makes two of us."

Before he could consider her comment, she knelt before him and gripped his cock tightly in her hand.

Seth hissed with surprise, but he didn't move away. Instead, his hands grasped her head, pushing until she was looking up at his face. She immediately saw the dominant man she'd met yesterday reemerge. His face was set, determined, and hungry.

"Are you sure?" he asked.

She wasn't sure what he was asking, but she knew without a shadow of a doubt she wanted this next experience, this new adventure. She nodded.

"Have you ever given a blow job before?"

She shook her head. She'd saved herself for him. Always. For him.

His gaze darkened with lust. "I'm going to teach you what I like."

She tightened her grip, cupping his balls with her free hand to let him know she was ready for anything.

His fingers gripped her wet hair almost painfully. She groaned and felt a gush of arousal between her legs.

"I won't," he paused, swallowing heavily. "I can't make this easy for you, Jody. I want this too fucking much."

She didn't reply with words. Instead, she bent forward and sucked the head of his cock into her mouth.

The fingers in her hair began to direct her motions and she let him draw her along, let the heady excitement of his control drive this game. Thrusting into her mouth, he gradually went deeper until he brushed the back of her throat. She started to gag and tried to retreat, but he held her in place.

"Look at me." His voice was commanding, and her pussy fluttered at the sound. She raised her eyes to his face, his cock buried deep in her mouth.

"I'm going to fuck your mouth. I want to take you hard, fast."

Her breathing accelerated and she sucked as much air as she could through her nose, trying to will her heart to stop racing. She was scared, excited, horny as hell.

She grasped his hips, digging her fingers into his muscular ass to let him know she was ready.

It was his turn to groan. Using his hands to hold her in place, he took her mouth in earnest, giving her everything he'd warned her about, everything he'd promised. It took several tries before she was able to swallow his head, but she soon caught the rhythm. Seth pumped into her mouth, his fingers tangling in her hair almost painfully. Jody pressed her legs together, dying for some relief of her own. She kept one hand wrapped around the base of his cock, while the other massaged his balls.

Seth murmured dirty, sexy words as he took her and she closed her eyes, envisioning the erotic pictures he drew in her mind. When she sensed he was getting close, she released his balls and moved her fingers farther back, exploring the crack between his legs.

When she pressed a finger against his anus, Seth jerked.

"Fuck," he cried.

Refusing to relent, she pushed the tip of her index finger inside the tight hole while Seth's thrusts grew more frantic, less controlled.

"God dammit, Jody. I can't—" His words gave way to the

explosion racking his body, and she felt the first spurt of his come splash into her mouth. She swallowed as jet after jet erupted. When every drop had been spent, he reached underneath her arms and lifted her. She stood, thrilled when his lips claimed hers. His heated, passionate kisses told her without words how well she'd done.

She wrapped her arms around his neck and returned his kiss. Finally, he moved away, resting his forehead against hers.

"I love you," he whispered.

She smiled, grateful for the spray of the shower as it masked the tears forming in her eyes. Surely it wasn't possible for someone to feel this complete. Then she considered her promise to Paul.

For the first time in her life, she suspected she was about to go back on her word.

Seth released a long breath and started to stretch. His eyes flew open when he realized he couldn't move. It was mid-afternoon, the bright sunlight streaming into the room from the window momentarily blinding him. Blinking rapidly, he tried to figure out what the hell was going on.

Wiggling his wrists, he looked up to find his hands bound tightly to the bed. A quick flex of his legs proved the same held true of his feet. He was flat on his back and trussed up tighter than a package in Santa's sack.

"Hiya." Jody's soft voice drifted over him and he glanced to his left, surprised to see her sitting in the chair by the desk, watching him.

He narrowed his eyes. She was still naked, a state he knew she struggled with despite everything they'd done to and with each other in the past two days.

"Having fun?" he asked when he spotted the self-satisfied grin on her face.

She giggled softly and nodded. "Oh hell, yeah."

"Untie me," he said, trying to keep the menace from his voice. She was tugging on the tiger's tail and she didn't seem to realize it.

When she rose and crossed the room, the mischievous look in her eyes told him she knew exactly what she was doing.

"Jody," he added warningly.

"Shhh," she said, leaning forward and placing her finger against his lips. "There's a little question I've been pondering and I think this is the best way to get my answer."

His jaw clenched and he tugged against the ties holding him to the bed. He'd never been the captive, always the captor. He wasn't sure he liked this turn of events. "Sweetheart, if you have a question, all you have to do is ask. You don't need to go to such lengths. Now untie me."

She shook her head. "No. I don't think you'll give me the right answer...without persuasion."

He pulled harder against his bindings and she laughed.

"Seth. I was raised in the South. My little league wasn't soccer or tee ball. It was rodeo and my club was 4-H. You're not gettin' loose 'til I say so."

He threw her the dark look that never failed to strike fear in the ranch hands. "Jody. Stop fucking around and untie me. Do it now and your punishment won't be too bad. Keep up this game and I'm gonna make you pay."

She rolled her eyes and he frowned. Foolish girl didn't have an ounce of fear in her. If anything, she seemed amused by his anger.

Seth restrained a growl and tugged once more, wondering how much strength it would take to break the headboard.

That thought was washed away when Jody climbed onto the bed, throwing one leg over his body, straddling his hips. Despite his annoyance at being rendered helpless, his cock responded to the wet heat of her pussy, resting just a couple inches away.

"Don't you wanna know what my question is?" she asked.

He sucked in a deep breath and decided to humor her for the moment. "What do you wanna know?"

She ran her hand along his chest, then pinched his nipple roughly. "We determined that you control my orgasms, that my body belongs to you. I was wondering who owned yours?"

She punctuated her question by leaning forward to bite his shoulder. She'd certainly taken to the concept of rough play. Problem was she was turning the tables on him. He was amazed by how much that fact didn't bother him. She was sexy as shit and he couldn't wait to see what she'd do next.

Rather than capitulate, he decided to provoke her. "My body's mine, darlin'. Always has been. Always will be." It was a lie. He'd belonged to Jody Kirkland for years. He may have slaked his needs with other women in the past, waiting for Jody to grow up, but that didn't change the truth. He was hers and he would be until the day he died.

Her eyebrows lowered, her face betraying her impatience just as he'd known it would. He gave her a cocky, unconcerned grin that irritated her even more.

"Wrong answer."

She dragged her fingernails down his chest slowly as he watched. His wildcat was marking her territory. His cock thickened more. Jesus. She was spectacular.

"Careful, Jody. Everything you do now is adding to the tally. There's going to be a reckoning. Bear that in mind."

She tilted her head haughtily. "Maybe you should focus on the question at hand. I didn't like your first answer. Care to reconsider?"

She lifted up onto her knees, moving slightly. When she lowered to his body again, she took care to cover his erection with her pussy. She held his cock in place against his body, surrounding it with her wet warmth. He swallowed heavily when she began to move her hips very slowly so that her cunt rubbed his cock in a way that was too good, but not near enough.

"That's a real nice massage, babe," he taunted. "Untie me and I'll show you what that cock can really do for you."

She smiled, but didn't stop her tantalizingly slow strokes. "Give me what I want and I'll be more than happy to untie you."

He feigned stupidity. "What is it you want again?"

Reaching behind her, she cupped his balls with one hand. He gasped when she began to squeeze them tightly.

"Careful, angel. You don't wanna damage the crown jewels there."

She laughed lightly and released him. "You liked it when I played with your ass in the shower earlier."

He'd been shocked by her touch and surprised by how much he liked it. He'd never let a woman touch him there before. Hell, he'd never let a woman take control like this either. Jody had a lot to learn about submissiveness.

"Maybe I should get my vibrator," she said.

He shook his head. "Don't even think about it. I'd hate to break your daddy's bed, but if you try to stick anything up my ass besides that little finger of yours, we're gonna have some mass destruction."

She bent down and kissed him. "We'll work up to it."

He nipped her lower lip before she could sit up again. "No. We won't."

Running her hands along his chest, she moved until they rested on his stomach. As he watched, she lifted one to her own pussy.

"What are you doing?" he asked, lacing his question with warning.

"Playing."

He lifted his hips as much as his bindings would allow. "These ties don't change anything, Jody. Your orgasms are mine. You can play all you want as long as you remember you need permission to come."

She lowered her eyes, acknowledging his comment. Her finger stroked her clit slowly at first, building in speed and strength until she was panting. Her hips were moving as her arousal rose. He felt the juices from her cunt sliding along his hard-on and he swallowed hard, fighting to maintain control.

Just when he thought she was about to break his rule, she stopped, pulling her hand away.

"You want me."

Her words weren't a question. Given the size of his cock and his own labored breathing, he'd say his desires were a foregone conclusion.

"You're mine," she whispered. As she spoke, she rose slightly, placing the head of his cock at the entrance to her pussy. "Say it."

He closed his eyes as she pressed down, taking the head of him inside. "I'm yours, Jody. Only yours."

She didn't move again, and he opened his eyes to look at her. She was smiling. It was the most beautiful sight he'd ever seen. "And I'm yours."

She pushed down, taking him to the hilt. He gritted his teeth against the incredible sensation. Her inner muscles clenched against his sensitive flesh as she rose and fell, the motions shallow at first. Slowly, the strength of her thrusts grew until she was riding him with abandon. Creating a memory he felt certain he'd carry with him 'til the day he died.

"Cup your breasts," he said, as he watched her move.

She reached up to push the creamy white globes together and his hips jerked against her harder. Over and over, she moved, but it still wasn't enough. He needed more, needed it all.

Finally, he cried out. "God dammit, Jody. Untie me."

She seemed to sense his deeper, darker needs. She stopped moving, still holding him tightly within her body. Turning at the waist, she looked like a bit of a contortionist as she worked loose the knots at his ankles. Once his legs were free, she bent over his chest, reaching up to free his hands. They kissed as she untied him.

The second his independence was gained, he rolled, shoving her roughly beneath him. He pushed in twice before his brain engaged and he realized why she felt so fucking good. He wasn't wearing a condom. As much as he wanted to say to hell with it, he knew Jody still had a decision to make.

She chastised him when he pulled out. "No," she cried.

"Shh. Condom."

She blinked several times, and he knew her omission hadn't been intentional. She'd forgotten as well.

"Shit," she whispered. "Sorry."

He grinned. "You're going on the pill. Soon. That felt too fucking amazing."

She rolled her eyes good-naturedly as he reached for a condom. The brief respite gave him time to regain his wits. As he covered himself, he swatted her left thigh. "Roll over. Get on your hands and knees. I want to take you from behind."

She turned quickly. The moment her ass was displayed before him, he lifted his hand and smacked it.

"Hey," she said, trying to move away. He'd expected her attempted escape and was prepared. Grasping her waist with his left hand, he gathered up a large handful of her long tresses with his right.

He pulled her upright by her hair, sensing her growing excitement. She loved his rough touch. Once he had her back to his chest, he leaned forward until his lips touched the shell of her ear. "I warned you. You played with fire and now you're going to feel the burn."

Her body trembled and he fought to maintain control. "Put your head on the bed, but keep that pretty ass up."

She complied and he immediately placed three smacks on her ass. He paused, praying the soft moan she gave was one of enjoyment. Dipping his fingers into her pussy provided the proof. She was drenched. He dragged his fingers out slowly, then gave her several more hard swats. Her ass flushed. Finally, his patience in tatters, he gave in to his own needs.

Placing his cock at her opening, he reached around her, cupped her breasts and lifted her upper body up against his. She was trembling and on the edge.

"You want to come?" he asked.

"Yes."

"I'm going to fuck you hard. So hard, you'll never forget who you belong to."

She turned to look at him, her mouth opening to speak.

He silenced her with a kiss. "And I'm going to prove that I'm yours. Only yours."

She smiled, and he moved her until she was once again on her hands and knees.

"Hold on," was the only warning he gave as he pushed in to the hilt. He didn't pause or give her time to adjust. He couldn't. At this moment, he needed to fuck her or die.

He pounded into her without respite, without mercy and she responded to his hard blows, moving into them, silently begging for more. His fingers clenched against her waist, and he suspected she'd have bruises there tomorrow. He wanted to feel guilty about that fact, but he couldn't. Shit, he knew the sight of them would only make him want to claim her again. He'd never felt this overpowering need to possess.

She screamed as she came, the sound long and loud and glorious. It was too much. He followed her. His climax so strong, his eyes rolled back in his head. As the last drop of come was squeezed out by her clenching pussy, he froze for an instant. He hovered over her, trying to prolong the moment as long as he could.

She moved first, collapsing onto her stomach with a soft groan. He lay next to her, gathering her close, pulling her back to his chest. He cradled her in his arms and felt sleep begin to claim them again.

"You're mine," she whispered, long after he thought she'd drifted off.

He placed a soft kiss on the back of her head. "Always."

Chapter Ten

A buzzing noise woke Seth up. Glancing around the dark cabin, it took him a few seconds to figure out that the sound was coming from his cell phone on the nightstand. A glance at the clock showed it was only nine in the evening. He and Jody had spent a couple of long, active days. No doubt it had caught up with them.

Consulting the caller ID, he was surprised to see Silas's number. He sat up as he answered the phone.

"Si?"

"Hey. Tie your girl up right this time. Gotta distract you from your life of crime for one minute."

Seth chuckled at his brother's joke as he stood and turned to look at his sleeping hostage. "Not sure it classifies as that anymore. Hard to kidnap the willing."

Silas grunted. "I don't know which Compton ancestor is responsible for passing us the get-lucky gene but I do appreciate it."

Seth grabbed his jeans from the floor when Jody turned. She remained asleep, and he decided to continue this call on the porch. He didn't want to disturb her. Grinning, he considered how worn out she probably was.

Si didn't speak. He waited with more patience than he was generally known for. Had the blast altered him? Or...

"Is something wrong?" Seth asked as he trapped the phone between his shoulder and ear, while he tugged on his jeans.

"Yeah. I'm afraid there is."

Afraid? Si didn't get scared by shit. Not even the crazy jobs he'd worked, which would have frightened the piss out of any sane man, had fazed his brother.

Seth walked outside and took a seat on the front porch step. No doubt, he was about to swallow a dose of bad news. "What is it?"

"It's JD, Seth. He's sick."

"Sick how?"

"Hell if I know, but something ain't right. Stubborn bastard won't see a doctor."

"Like you would if it were you? Hell, you practically got your leg blown off and you fought the hospital staff until they shipped you halfway across the continent just to get rid of your ornery ass. Didn't bother to call your brothers for help either, did you?" Seth shook off the lingering sting.

"Fuck. Don't you think I've taken enough shit from Colby and Lucy? Focus. We're not talking about me. JD's favoring his side and his coloring is off. Kinda like his perma-tan faded into a weird orange since the last time I saw him." His brother cursed softly. "Caught him hacking up blood too."

"Jesus. Get him to the damn doctor."

"I tried arguing with him. You know how much good that does."

"Yeah, works about as well as it does on you. Two peas, both of you."

"I even threatened to sic mom on him." Silas groaned. "He promised to kick my ass, and he meant it too. The only time I've ever seen him really look worried. Look, it's not like I can throw him over my shoulder and hobble to the doctor on these goddamn crutches."

Seth ran a hand through his hair, his mind trying to process the idea of his larger-than-life father falling sick. He'd never had a cold that Seth could remember, never mind something...so severe. "I'll come home."

"I know you have shit hitting the fan down there..." Silas released a loud sigh.

"Yeah. And you wouldn't ask if you didn't have to." Seth dropped his face into his hand. "Thanks for calling when you needed someone this time. I'm not a kid anymore. I'll figure it out."

"Sooner would be better."

"Yeah," Seth said. "I'm getting that."

"Call me when your flight is booked. I can't drive and Colby's gotta hang around here for some welcome home thing Mom's planning for tomorrow afternoon, but I can send one of the hands to the airport."

"No worries. I'll rent a car. Be there as soon as I can."

"Thanks, Seth."

As Seth closed the cell phone, he sat on the step, letting the silence envelop him. JD was sick. He was going home. Part of him wanted to wake Jody, wanted to soak up all the comfort he knew he could find in her arms.

The two days was over. She'd been true to her word and tomorrow he'd have to set her free to make her decision. He wished he knew for sure she'd choose him, but unless he could find a loophole in the will, she'd feel honor-bound to abide by the promise she'd made to Paul. Besides, how could he ask her not to marry the man when it was clear there was so much good that could come from it?

He thought about Silas's description of JD's illness. What if his father had cancer? What if Paul's research facility found the cure that could save JD? He rubbed his eyes wearily. When had his simple ranch life become so complicated?

He rose tiredly and returned to the cabin. Finding a piece of paper and a pencil, he sat at the kitchen table to leave Jody a note. He needed to get home to his family, and she needed time to think. As much as it killed him to do so, he had to let her go, give her space to decide her own future. He wrote the words written on his heart and prayed they would be enough to convince her to give them a chance.

Propping the note up on the kitchen table, he quietly packed up his stuff and loaded it in the truck. Returning to the cabin, he stood by the bed to take one long, last look at the woman who held his heart in her hand. He'd let her sleep. One last, peaceful night of sweet dreams. Tomorrow would be here too soon.

Locking the door behind him, he climbed into the truck, unaware of the slight breeze from the open window that blew his note off the table and under the couch.

Jody climbed into the truck, riding back to the ranch house in silence. She'd been surprised to discover herself alone when she'd woken up. She'd dressed, searching inside and out for a sign of Seth, but there'd been nothing. All his things were gone, as well as the truck. He'd left her without a word. She hadn't had more than a few minutes to process that horrible realization when a horn honked outside.

Smiling, thinking he'd returned, she'd rushed to the door only to find Scotty, one of the ranch hands waiting to take her home. A few quick questions proved that her escort didn't know anything more than Seth had asked him to pick her up.

As the Texas landscape passed by her at fifty miles an hour, she wondered about Seth's sudden desertion. The closer she got to home, the more obvious the answer became. She'd run him off with her power play. She'd tied him to the bed intending to show him that she was strong enough to be his woman.

Foolishly, she'd fallen asleep before telling him she'd made her choice. She wanted Seth Compton. Wanted to spend a lifetime with him. However, after one silly, impetuous action, she'd driven him away. He'd tweaked her pride the first day they'd spent together, insisting that he owned her orgasms and body. While she certainly didn't mind commending those things to his oh-so-capable hands, she wanted an equal share. She wanted him—all of him, body and soul.

When did it go wrong? When they'd drifted off to sleep, she'd been so sure of their love. Their happiness. Why did he leave?

Sadness gave way to confusion and as they turned onto the lane that led to her home, confusion gave way to rage and hurt.

The truck pulled up in front of the ranch house and Jody wearily rubbed her hand over her face, frustration and fury whirling inside her.

"Jody," her father said, coming out on the front porch as she emerged from the truck.

She had to bite back her anger. Her father had given Seth his blessing. Let the man kidnap her away from her home, miss her wedding. And for what? So he could simply abandon her when things didn't work out.

She glanced over her shoulder toward the foreman's cabin. Seth's truck wasn't there. She needed to find Paul. To explain why she'd missed the wedding and ask for his advice. She could use a friend right now.

Then, she was going to find Seth and demand answers. If the jerk thought he could leave her without a hi or bye, he had another think coming. She'd show him.

"Where's Paul?" she asked brusquely as she passed her father without accepting his proffered hug and walked into the house.

"Well," Thomas rubbed the back of his neck. "I don't really know."

Jody whirled on her father, her fury flying out. "What do you mean you don't know? You sent him away, didn't you? It wasn't enough that Seth had to fuck up my wedding plans, you decided to add your own piece to the pie by forcing him to leave."

"Whoa, whoa, whoa," Thomas said, raising his hands in surrender. "Nobody sent anybody away. Paul vanished the morning of your wedding day. I went to tell him you were missing, only to find him gone. Chase is AWOL too. Haven't seen hide or hair of either of them in two days."

"He's missing?" Jody felt the fight leave her. She was drained, tired, bewildered and depressed.

Thomas nodded. "Yeah. What happened with Seth, honey?"

She shrugged, wishing she knew. "I guess it didn't work out."

Her father frowned. "I don't believe that."

"He's gone. He left me in the cabin alone without a word."

Thomas put his hands on his hips. "He left without explaining why?"

Jody looked at her father and suddenly she realized he'd talked to Seth since last night. She nodded, unable to hide the pain any longer. "He was just gone. What did he tell you? Where is he now?"

"He's flying to Wyoming." Her dad consulted his watch. "In fact, his flight is probably just taking off."

"He's going home?"

Thomas nodded. "There was an illness in the family. He was needed back there."

Jody worried for a moment that something had happened to Silas. She'd thought Seth's brother was on the mend, but maybe he'd suffered a relapse. Even so, that didn't explain why he left her without a word. "Did he leave a message for me? Maybe a note?"

Thomas shook his head slowly. "I assumed you knew he was leaving."

"He didn't tell me anything. Just slunk away like a thief in the night." She sounded like a bitter, angry woman, but she couldn't rein in her resentment and pain.

"It was a misunderstanding. It had to be."

Jody shook her head, but her father wouldn't listen. "He'll land in a few hours. Get some rest. Calm down, then call him.

Talk to him. I'm telling you right now, there's gotta be a logical explanation."

There was no way she could tell her father about the truth behind Seth's desertion. There could be no other answer. She'd come on too strong, pushed him away. She couldn't be the woman he wanted. He wanted a good, little submissive and she'd failed the test. "No," she said at last. "He made his decision. He's gone."

Her father's temper snapped. "God dammit, girl. For once, can't you swallow some of that damn pride? Call Seth."

She narrowed her eyes and leaned closer. "All I've done is swallow my pride where Seth is concerned. If one more mouthful goes down, I'll choke. Seth Compton is history. And I'm going to bed."

Thomas fell silent, his shoulders sagging. She turned toward the front door, rather than have to see his concern and the worried lines on his face.

Jody climbed the stairs to her bedroom, slowly. Realization dawned hard. She'd lost Seth and in the process, she'd lost herself. Closing her door and locking it, she crossed the room and collapsed on her bed, giving in to the tears she'd held at bay since waking up.

Seth climbed out of the rental car he'd picked up at the airport. After Silas's call, he'd returned to his cabin, packed his bags, and booked a flight on the first plane headed to Wyoming. He landed in Casper and drove the two hours to Compton Pass in record time. Throughout the trip, he thought about Jody. The way she looked when he'd left her.

He prayed he'd made the right decision. He'd asked her for two days and dear God had she given it to him. He'd spent the best forty-eight hours of his life lying in her arms. The time had only solidified his belief that she was the only woman in the world for him.

Silas's call had put a period on that. The idea that JD could be sick—hell—that he could be dying cut through Seth's gut like a machete. His father was indomitable, larger than life. He'd grown up knowing there wasn't a force on earth that could take down his rugged father.

He looked across the yard at the crowd of people. He'd shown up just in time for a party he vaguely recalled Silas telling him about. It was in full-force. He hadn't made it two steps from the car when his mother's excited yell reached his ears seconds before she engulfed him in a long, hard hug.

He smiled. He was home.

"Hi, Mom." He smiled down at her.

"Two of my boys home," she said, her hand resting lightly on his cheek. "And it's not even my birthday."

Silas hobbled up behind Vicky. Seth tried to keep his face implacable, though it was hard to see his sturdy brother looking so broken as he crossed the yard on crutches.

"What a surprise," Silas said. His tone clued him in that, while Silas had called him home, his parents weren't expecting him. Obviously JD was still pretending all was well.

"I wanted to come home when I first heard about your accident. Mom told me to give you time to settle back in." It wasn't a lie and it helped smooth over his unexpected arrival.

"Seth?"

He turned to see JD standing behind him and he felt like the breath had been knocked out of him. Silas was right. It was bad. His father's skin tone was off and there were distinct lines around his eyes and mouth that bespoke pain.

"Hey, JD," he said. He embraced his father, the hug lasting a shade longer than their usual greeting. Seth didn't want to pull away and he sensed JD didn't either. This wasn't going to be easy.

He let his mother drag him around, introducing him to new arrivals to the ranch and neighborhood, while forcing him to reacquaint himself with countless others.

His heart wasn't into the party. His mind wrestled between two worries, Jody and JD. While it felt good to be home, he knew Compass Ranch was in for some big changes. And without Jody, he wasn't sure he was ready for them.

Chapter Eleven

Jody sat in the living room, staring at the television, not caring that it wasn't even on, when she heard a commotion in the front foyer. She'd hidden in her room for four days, struggling to pull the pieces of her shattered heart back together. Her father had tried to console her, tried to convince her to call Seth, but she wouldn't play the fool for him again. Never again.

Glancing up, she was surprised to find Paul in the doorway. "Hey," she said with a forced smile.

Paul's genuine grin faded as he looked at her. "What the hell happened?"

She chuckled at his question, the sound quickly turning to a sob. Paul was across the room in an instant, sitting on the couch and pulling her into his comforting embrace. "I screwed up everything," she said, between gasping cries.

"I don't believe that."

"It's true. I pushed him away."

"Seth?" Paul shook his head. "No way. You couldn't push that guy away from you with a two-ton truck."

She looked up at her beloved friend's face and realized she needed to get out of Texas, away from this place where she was surrounded by memories of Seth. "Let's run away. Go to Vegas right now. We can elope."

"Jody. No."

"Paul, please. It's the answer to both of our problems. I can't stay here." She started to rise. "We can pack up and be on the next flight to Nevada before the sun sets."

Paul tugged on her hand and pulled her back to the couch. "I can't. Hell, even if I could, I would never do that to you. Running away isn't the answer."

"Why can't you? We're running out of time. Your father's will—"

"Has been satisfied," Paul interrupted. "I've met the stipulation. You're free of your promise."

She tried to process his words, understand what they meant. "How?"

Paul smiled, the happiness he obviously felt, busting at the seams. "I found the loophole. The will only said I had to get married. It didn't say my spouse had to be a woman."

The pieces fell together and suddenly Jody understood Paul's absence. "You eloped."

He nodded.

"With Chase?"

He laughed and nodded again. "Oh my God, Jody. He's perfect. Sexy and fun and amazing."

"You're in love with him." She'd never seen her best friend fall for anyone. To see him in such high spirits made her happy and miserable at the same time. Did Paul think she wouldn't keep her promise? If Seth hadn't abandoned her, would she have followed through? No. She wouldn't have. She'd made that decision in the hunting cabin. Even so, she hated that her friend had reason to doubt her. "Did you think I wouldn't marry you?"

Paul gave her a rueful grin. "I was afraid you *would* marry me. Terrified you'd sacrifice your future to keep a promise to me. I want you to be happy. You're my best friend, Jody. I love you. You're never gonna be happy without Seth."

"Great. Nice to know what my future holds. Eternal

misery."

Paul frowned. "Where's Seth?"

Jody blinked hard, brushing away her tears. She couldn't believe she had anything left inside her to cry. "Wyoming."

"Why?"

She shrugged, unable to find the words to explain.

"Maybe you should start at the beginning," Paul prompted.

"He kidnapped me from my bachelorette party and took me to my dad's hunting cabin."

Paul smiled. "Holy shit, that's romantic."

Jody laughed and rolled her eyes. "Yeah. I guess it was. We, um, well, we had sex."

"I figured as much. And?"

"And it was amazing. Earth-shattering. Perfect."

Paul nodded slowly. "I'm not hearing the catch yet."

Jody rose, pacing around the room, wondering how she could explain. Hell, she wasn't even sure she understood. "He left because of me. I think I came on a bit too strong."

"Define *too strong.*"

Jody leaned against the living room wall and took a deep breath. "I tied him to the bed. Made a few demands."

Paul burst into laughter.

She crossed her arms over her chest, her anger building. "Glad you find this so amusing."

"No," he said, sobering up. "It's not funny. It's a misunderstanding."

She rolled her eyes and slammed her hand against the wall at her back. "Why does everyone keep saying that? He's not here. He left without a word, without a note right after I tied him to the bed. I told you what he wanted, Paul."

"A sex slave?"

She shook her head. "A submissive woman."

"Did you let him take control of you in bed, Jody?"

She started to point out the fact that she'd tied him up again, but Paul stopped her with a wave of his hand. "Besides your one so-called lapse in judgment, did you submit?"

She considered her actions, the way Seth had controlled her orgasms, pulled her hair, spanked her. At the time, it had all seemed sexy, hot as hell, but now she realized she *had* submitted to him. She'd handed her body over to Seth because she trusted him and knew he'd never hurt her. "Yes. I did."

"And you're convinced his departure isn't a misunderstanding."

She nodded sadly. It was no mistake.

"Well, then. He's a fucking asshole," Paul said, rising, his voice laced with fury.

His words sparked the anger that had been buried deep beneath her pain. "Yeah," she agreed. "He's a prick."

Paul walked over to her, pointing his finger at her face. "That jerk owes you. You've spent years saving yourself for him. Does he seriously think he can abduct you from your own bachelorette party, steal your virginity and then saunter off into the night without a goddamn word?"

"You're right!" Her fury exploded and she suddenly felt stronger than she had in days.

"He owes you, Jody. He owes you an explanation and a fucking apology."

Paul's anger and uncharacteristic use of foul language spurred her on and suddenly her path was clear.

"Oh hell yeah, he does. That's it. I'm going to Wyoming."

"Good," Paul said loudly. "You go north and you demand he give you the respect you're owed. Don't take no for an answer."

"You don't have to worry about that," she said, walking toward the hallway. Seth had promised to always be hers. An idea flashed and she decided to give Seth a lesson in what exactly that word meant to her. "That asshole is going to get his. Mark my words."

Thomas and Chase were standing in the foyer watching Jody stomp up the stairs when Paul came out of the living room.

"Where's she going?" Thomas asked.

Paul grinned. "To Wyoming."

Thomas ran a hand through his hair and shook his head. "How the hell did you convince her to do that? I've been trying to get through to that stubborn girl for days."

Paul leaned his elbow on the banister. "What reason did you give her to go to Seth?"

"I told her she needed to swallow her pride and let the man explain to her why he had to leave."

Paul rolled his eyes as Chase laughed.

"Amateur," Paul teased. "The best way to get Jody to act is to stoke her anger, get her fired up. She's madder than a wet hen, and I have a feeling that emotion isn't gonna simmer down until she's standing in front of Seth."

Thomas swore under his breath. "Shit."

Chase crossed the room and put his arm around Paul's shoulders. "Sounds like Seth better have a damn good reason for leaving her or he could get hurt."

Paul chuckled. "As mad as she is, he might want to protect all the protruding parts of his body."

"Or just the important one," Chase joked.

They all glanced toward the top of the stairs and Thomas cursed again. "Christ. The poor guy won't know what hit him by the time she's done."

Seth sat in the waiting room of the doctor's office with Silas and JD on his fourth day home. They'd run a gazillion tests on the poor guy two days before. The doctor had called the ranch earlier and asked them to come in. Seth knew it was bad news. Doctors had no compunction about telling someone they were fine over the phone. Face to face meetings weren't good.

They'd been cooling their heels for nearly an hour. The nurse had come in twice to apologize. Apparently there'd been some small emergency. JD offered to come back tomorrow, but the nurse refused to let him leave. None of them had said anything in the last thirty minutes and Seth felt like he was about to come out of his skin, his mind whirling over his father's health and Jody.

She hadn't called since he left her in the cabin. He'd tossed and turned every night, worrying about what her silence meant. In his note, he'd promised to give her time to make her decision. He'd also vowed to stand by her decision. Problem was he didn't know how much time she needed and he'd thought she'd call to tell him one way or the other. Between worrying about her and JD, he was living with a perpetual headache.

"Mr. Compton," the nurse said, opening a door between the waiting area and the examining rooms. "The doctor will see you now."

JD rose slowly, Silas and Seth following suit.

"You boys don't—"

"Save your breath, JD," Silas interrupted. "We're comin' back with you."

JD nodded, muttering, "Headstrong, stubborn, pigheaded."

"Fruit doesn't fall far from the tree," Seth joked, wishing these next few minutes were already over. His stomach was in knots.

They walked into the doctor's office and Seth was surprised to see a young man sitting behind the desk.

"Where Doc Cahill?" JD asked.

"This isn't his area of expertise. He referred your case to me," the young doctor said. "Mr. Compton, I'm Dr. Philips."

"You can call me JD. These are my sons, Seth and Silas."

The doctor shook their hands and then gestured that they all take a seat. "I'm an oncologist, Mr. Compton."

The word *oncologist* hit Seth like a punch to the chest.

“Yeah. I figured that much,” JD said.

Dr. Philips walked behind his desk and resumed his seat. He picked up a medical chart and opened it. “You have stage three pancreatic cancer.”

Seth looked at Silas. One look at his brother’s face told him he understood exactly what those words meant.

Dying. Their father was dying.

“How long do I have?”

JD’s question told them all he knew the prognosis as well.

“Mr. Compton, there are—”

“Dammit, man, if you can say cancer, you can say JD. Something tells me you and I are gonna be spending a bit of time together these next few months. Let’s do it on a first name basis. I’m JD.”

Seth almost felt sorry for the young doctor. It was clear he was new to this practice. Treating JD would certainly be an initiation by fire.

“My name’s Ron. Ron Philips.”

“Well, Ron. It’s nice to meet you. Now, I’m sure you’ve got a whole spiel ready to lay out for me and I know my sons are gonna want to hear it. Before you do that, let me tell you a few things. I’m not doing radiation and I’m not doing chemo.”

“JD,” Silas interjected.

“No, son,” JD said. “I’m not going to spend what time I have left sitting in a hospital.” He turned back to the doctor. “There’s no cure for what I’ve got, right?”

Dr. Philips shook his head. “There are things we can do to try to prolong your life, but no, ultimately this type of cancer is fatal.”

JD nodded. “Thanks for your candor, Ron.”

“God dammit, JD,” Seth exploded. His world was falling apart. “Can we just ask a few questions, maybe get some options before you dismiss everything out of hand?”

JD put his hand on his shoulder, and Seth swallowed hard against the lump in his throat. He refused to break down, refused to cry, even though every part of him wanted to yell at the top of his lungs about the injustice, the unfairness of this situation. "Seth, it's gonna be okay. Hell, I'm nearly seventy. Had a good long haul with a pretty gal and four boys a man can be proud to call son. Can't ask for more than that."

Seth sat stiffly, fighting desperately to hold it together.

"Now, you boys go ahead ask Ron your questions."

Silas leaned forward, his face creased with pain, though Seth wasn't sure if it was his leg or his heart that was bothering him more. "Mom's gonna wanna know how long." The words sounded like they were being ripped from his brother's chest and Seth felt a new ache as he considered Vicky. Losing JD would kill her.

Ron cleared his throat and Seth found a new respect for the young man. It couldn't be easy working day in and day out with patients who were facing death. "Maybe a year. More likely less than that. Five to eight months is probably a better estimate."

"Five months. Jesus," Seth whispered, unable to hold the words in.

"Well, hell," JD said, rubbing his chin. "That doesn't give us much time. I was hoping to get you more settled at the ranch, Silas. I know you've still got about a year of physical therapy ahead of you for your leg and—"

"I'm moving home," Seth said, cutting off his father's words.

JD turned to him, frowning. "I can't ask you to leave Texas."

"You didn't ask." Seth crossed his arms over his chest and dared his father to contradict him.

JD chuckled. "Like looking in a mirror sometimes. Nothing I can say will change your mind, will it?"

Seth shook his head. JD reached out and put his hand on Seth's shoulder. Seth was surprised by the strength in his grasp. He'd bet his whole life savings that JD would make it an entire year.

"It'll be good to have you home again. Thank you," JD said softly. The words were his undoing. Seth nodded and rose quickly. He had to get out of the room, out of the stifling air before he lost it.

He looked at Silas and figured the desperation in his face must've showed.

"Why don't you go get the truck?" his brother said. "Me and JD can finish up here. We'll meet you out front."

Seth nodded stiffly and headed for the door. He felt like a jackass for leaving, but too many things were crashing in on him at once. His life was moving too fast. He was losing everything that mattered to him.

Jody. JD. His life in Texas.

As he considered the last, he realized that wasn't a loss. Texas meant Jody and without her, that place wasn't anywhere he wanted to be.

Compton Pass was home. It was green mountains, Vicky, his brothers and JD.

A small choked cry escaped before he could call it back. He walked out the front door and sucked in a long, deep breath of fresh Wyoming air. Looking back over his shoulder, he studied the small square office building. Such an innocuous place. It seemed like a place that tore a man away from his father should look more like a prison or a rundown slum or hell on earth.

He cleared his throat and swiped away the wetness on his face. He wasn't going to cry in front of JD or Silas and God knew he had to pull himself together before they faced Vicky. He needed to be strong for her.

His cell phone rang and he rushed to pull it out of his back pocket, praying it was Jody. A quick glance at the screen told him it was Sam. Seth took a second to compose himself before answering.

"Hey, bro," he said, his voice sounding too husky.

"Hey, Seth."

Sam's voice sounded nearly as gruff as Seth's. Of course, the fact that his brother was calling him pretty much guaranteed shit had hit the fan. Either that or Sam had sensed the crushing weight on Seth's heart despite the two thousand miles between them. It wouldn't be the first time one of his brothers had reached out in a moment of need. More often it happened between the twins, but sometimes it happened to them all.

They may have chosen different paths, but in times like this, they stuck together. Sam had achieved his dreams of landing a big city job by working long hours as he climbed to the top. Personally, Seth couldn't understand the appeal of living in a noisy, smelly city like New York, but Sam seemed to thrive in the smog.

"What's wrong?" Seth wished without hope that his brother had called to help instead of piling on more misery.

Sam fell silent for a second. "Who says something's wrong? Where are you? You sound...fucked up. I thought poker night wasn't 'til Wednesday. Are you hungover?"

"No. It's not... Look, I c-can't think right now. Focus on the point. *You* called *me.* Pardon me for saying so, but you don't sound like you're skipping through daisies yourself."

"I'm coming home."

Seth surrendered. He plopped onto the gravelly grass at the edge of the parking lot when his legs refused to hold him. He tried to process his brother's words. The bitterness in his brother's tone made it clear he considered this a curse rather than a blessing, but it couldn't have come at a better time for the family.

"Thank God."

"What the hell?" Seth pictured Sam finger-combing his ultra conservative haircut. "I tell you my cock ruined seven years of hard work for one moronic, not-even-that-great fuck and you say *Thank God*?"

"Yeah." The lump Seth had managed to swallow reformed in his throat. He needed to say the words. He needed to explain how utterly their world had changed even if his brother didn't know it yet. God, if he couldn't tell his brother without falling apart, how could he expect to be worth shit when they told Vicky. "It's JD."

His tone said it all.

"What the fuck? Seth! Don't stop now. Jesus. What's going on back there?"

Seth cleared his throat and forced the ugly truth from his lips despite the fact saying the words made the horror seem more real. "JD has pancreatic cancer, Sam. He's dying."

There was no sound from the other end, and Seth cursed himself for giving his brother news like this over the phone.

"Christ," Sam choked, his voice breaking slightly. "I'll be home tonight."

"When does your flight get in?" Numbness settled in Seth's core. They couldn't fix this, but having Silas and Sam with him would help. "I'll pick you up."

"Six hours from now. Don't worry. I'll find my own way. You have more to worry about than me."

If Sam only knew. Jody's sweet smile flashed through his mind. "Don't be a dumbass. I'll always be there for you. We'll talk on the ride in. I could use an ear myself, okay?"

"Yeah. Okay." Sam mumbled as if to himself. "Pancreatic cancer. There's no hope, is there?"

"Not for JD."

Then Sam said the one name Seth wasn't ready to hear. "Sawyer."

Seth closed his eyes. As hard as it was to tell Sam, Sawyer would be a hundred times worse. While he and Silas and Sam thought JD walked on water, Sawyer was convinced their father created the water. "He doesn't know. Fuck. I'm sitting here outside the doctor's office. Mom doesn't even know yet."

He could hear Sam's heavy sigh through the line, could picture the devastation on his brother's face. "He's out at sea. Got that special assignment he's been gunning for. He left yesterday."

"How long will he be away?"

"Two months. When he gets back, he has two week's leave at which point he told me he was turning off his phone and fucking himself into oblivion."

Seth grinned. That sounded like his kid brother. "Has he decided about re-upping yet?"

"No," Sam said. "I think he was gonna figure out his future while he's at sea."

Seth considered that. "Maybe we should let him make that decision before we tell him about JD."

"Shit," Sam muttered. "He'll kill us."

"Like you said, he's not gonna be able to come home for at least two months. Let him have this time to get his shit together. If things take a turn for the worst, then we'll get him home sooner. Somehow."

"Okay. So you haven't told mom?"

Seth closed his eyes wearily. "No."

"I wanna be there when you do." Sam's voice was regaining its strength.

Seth soaked it in. Let it wash through him. "Okay."

"So I'll see you at the airport."

Seth stood up. "Yeah."

"I'll text you the flight info. Seth?"

"Yeah?"

"We're gonna get through this, right?" Sam's voice took him back. Reminded him of the time his younger brother had broken his leg after falling out of the hayloft. Seth had carried him to the truck, while Sawyer ran to get their folks. Sam had only been ten at the time, and he'd looked at Seth as his savior, asking him if his leg would be okay, if he'd be crippled or walk with a limp.

He said now what he said then. “We’re gonna get through this just fine.”

He hung up the phone, praying his words were true. Seth stiffened his spine and walked toward the truck.

He could do this. All he had to do was put one foot in front of the other.

He could do this.

Chapter Twelve

Seth was surprised by how natural it felt to be back home, sitting around the dinner table with his family. Sam had shown up late last evening. Along with his brothers and JD, they'd broken the news about their father's cancer to their mother.

Seth had wasted countless hours throughout the day worrying about Vicky's reaction, but he should have put the time to better use. His mom was the perfect counterpart to her tough-as-nails husband. She took the news calmly, nodded as they spoke and asked quite a few questions. Luckily Silas had been strong enough to stay put at the doctor's office to get the answers for her.

Afterwards, she simply stood and excused herself. He'd never seen his mother fall apart, never seen a chink in her resolute spirit. JD had followed her out of the room and Seth knew they would comfort each other in private. For her sons, Seth had no doubt Vicky would continue to put on a brave face, offering each of them a comforting shoulder and a sympathetic ear, but he was concerned how she would handle her grief when JD was gone.

Seth looked around the table, studying the composure of his family and he felt humbled by their strength. JD was calmly discussing a problem they were having with one of the ranch hands with Silas and Colby, while Vicky and Lucy laughed about some local gossip regarding the preacher's wife and one of the less devout members of the congregation.

Only Sam was unusually quiet. Seth knew there was a story behind his sudden trip home. Something involving a woman. Something painful. He'd pull him aside tonight with a bottle of Southern Comfort and get to the bottom of it. Maybe Sam could offer him some advice in regards to Jody.

They were just finishing up their meal, when the doorbell rang.

"Damn. Who visits at suppertime?" JD grumbled, rising slowly.

"I'll get it," Sam offered, but JD waved his hand for his brother to sit back down.

"Naw. I'm the closest." JD walked out of the dining room and the conversation continued, as Silas and Colby began filling Seth and Sam in on some of the more recent improvements they'd made to the ranch. Seth had been gone a long time and it would take a while to get up to speed on the way things worked at Compass Ranch.

JD reappeared at the doorway. "Uh, Seth. Maybe you should come out here, son."

Seth felt all eyes at the table looking at him as everyone recognized JD's bewildered tone. The unshakable man was definitely floundering over something out of the ordinary.

"Oookay," he said, drawing out the word and rising slowly.

As he walked to the doorway to the front foyer, he was aware that everyone in the room had risen and was following him. He chuckled softly. Nosy family.

His laughter died when he saw Jody standing just inside the front door to his family's home. She was in her mother's wedding dress.

She looked haughty and irritated.

She'd never looked more beautiful.

Seth studied her silently, trying to find his words while wondering what the devil she was up to. Finally, he said the first thing that came to his mind. "Nice dress."

She ran her hands along the silk skirt. "I wore it for you."

He narrowed his eyes. "For me? Not Paul."

She shook her head. "Paul's still at the ranch."

"What about the will? The marriage of convenience? Your promise?" He stressed the last question, knowing it was that damned promise that was fucking with his future happiness.

She blew out an annoyed breath. "Paul's married. The will's been satisfied."

He was confused. She'd married Paul?

"Why are you in Wyoming if you married *him*?" He wanted to wince at the bitter tone in his voice. The stress of the last few days had worn on him until he thought he'd shatter under the pressure.

She scowled. "I didn't marry him. Chase did."

"Chase?" he asked.

She shrugged and, for the first time, he saw a touch of fear in her eyes hidden behind the anger. Her demeanor didn't make any sense. She was clearly furious, and unless he was misreading her body language, a bit anxious. He'd asked her to choose him and made it clear he would respect her decision. Why was she so mad? So nervous?

"Apparently there was a loophole in the will. It only said Paul had to be married. It didn't specify that the spouse had to be a woman."

Seth heard Silas chuckle softly behind him, but he didn't acknowledge it. He couldn't focus on anything except her.

Jody took a step closer. "Regardless of that, Paul said he wouldn't have held me to the promise. Said he'd started looking for another option the day we showed up at the ranch."

"Why?"

"Because of you." She shook her head. "No, because of me. Because of us. The way—" Her words faltered and again he was struck by the idea that she wasn't sure of his feelings.

Then Seth considered the brief time he'd spent with Paul at

the ranch. Now that Seth was away from the situation, he could see that Paul had been pushing him and Jody together.

Letting Seth take Jody to the barn to see the puppies while he stayed behind with Chase.

Asking Seth to drag her out of the bachelorette party.

Encouraging Jody to sleep with Seth.

Paul knew her, understood her. Paul knew she'd never willingly break a promise, so he broke it for her. "Good friend."

"He thinks so."

Seth gestured at to the white silk. "That still doesn't explain the dress."

"Apparently you and I have a very different opinion of what forever looks like. I thought I'd let you see my version. You left without saying goodbye," she said, her voice equal parts accusation and pain. She glanced around at his family. He got the feeling their presence was holding her back from really tearing into him. What the hell had he done to piss her off?

"I wrote a note. I explained why I had to come home, Jody."

She frowned, angrily. "No. You didn't. There was no note."

Seth was confused, then a light went on and her attitude suddenly made sense. Shit. If she didn't see the note, then she must've thought he'd left her.

Christ. No wonder she hadn't called. Yet here she stood, swallowing her pride and setting herself up for possible rejection. She was one of the bravest women he'd ever met.

"Oh God, Jody. I'm so sorry. I swear to you I left a note on the kitchen counter. At the cabin. I told you my family needed me and that I had to leave. I said the two days were up and the decision was yours to make. I begged you to choose me."

She was silent for several moments. Her face betrayed so many emotions, all tumbling one after another—he couldn't keep up. Anger, confusion, relief, hope.

Then, she smiled. "You begged me?"

Sam laughed and Seth threw his younger brother a dirty

look. “Let’s just say I asked emphatically.”

Jody’s grin grew. “I think I like the sound of begging better.”

JD snorted. “Dear God, son, you need to marry this one.”

Seth chuckled, his father’s words reminding him that his family was probably wondering what the hell was going on. He hadn’t mentioned Jody to anyone, not even Silas. There’d been too much to consider with JD for him to unload his secret fears about losing the love of his life to anyone. “You’re right, JD. I do.”

Jody walked closer and some of the tension drained away from her face. When she was right in front of him, she stopped. There was still something holding her back. “I was afraid when you left without a word that I’d—”

She glanced around at their audience.

Seth didn’t take his eyes off her. “Afraid you’d what?”

She lowered her voice. “Gone too far. When I tied you to the bed.”

“Oh fuck, yeah,” Silas said. “You definitely need to marry her.”

Seth laughed and ignored his brother. He raised his hand and touched her face. He’d been fighting the impulse to drag her into his arms since spotting her in the doorway. “Christ, Jody. I love you. I love your sassy, smartass comments. I love the way you lose your inhibitions when you drink, though I can promise you’ll never do tequila shots with anybody, but me. I love how independent and smart and loyal you are. You’re the only woman in the world for me and if you wanna tie me up every night for the rest of our lives, so be it.”

As he finished speaking, he bent down on one knee as Jody—and his mother —gasped. He took her hand in his as he looked into his beloved’s beautiful face. He quickly spotted a tear in her eye. “I love you, Jody Kirkland, and I wanna marry you. Wanna tie myself to you in the most binding, forever way possible.”

She sucked in a breath that sounded suspiciously like a small sob, and then she nodded. "I wanna tie myself to you too."

He kissed her hand, rising quickly to seal the deal with a stronger sentiment. He claimed her lips, only vaguely aware of the squeals of delight from his mother and Lucy, the loud, joyful laughter of his father and brothers.

"Well, hot damn," JD said. "Looks like we got a wedding to look forward to."

His father's words permeated the lust consuming him and he pulled away, suddenly concerned. Jody blinked in surprise at his quick retreat.

"I wanna get married right away," he said, realizing time wasn't on his father's side. There was no one he wanted at his wedding more than JD. "No long engagement."

Jody laughed and pointed to her dress. "Sweetheart, if there was a minister here, I'd marry you tonight."

"Oh no," Vicky cried out, rushing over to where he and Jody stood. "I want a proper wedding. We can hold it right here at the ranch. Lots of flowers and friends and big-ass party afterward."

Jody turned to Vicky, grinning. "That sounds terrific."

Vicky paused in her planning, realizing she was putting the cart before the horse. "Hell, darlin', here I am organizing your wedding and I haven't even introduced myself. I raised my son to have better manners, but it's clear he's a wee bit too distracted tonight to do the introductions himself. I'm Vicky Compton, Seth's momma."

Jody reached out to shake his mother's hand, but Vicky shook her head, reaching out instead to envelop Jody in a big hug. "Nope. None of that," Vicky said, tightening her grip. "You're gonna be my daughter soon. And given what I've just seen here tonight, I'd say you and I are gonna get along real good."

Seth watched Jody return the embrace and saw the first

tear fall. When they parted, Jody quickly swiped at her damp cheek. "I'm Jody Kirkland."

"Kirkland?" JD asked, coming to stand beside his wife. "Thomas's little girl?"

Jody nodded.

"Well, now, I've had the opportunity to talk to your daddy quite a few times over the years. Great man."

Jody smiled, proudly. "Yes, he is," she agreed, accepting JD's hug.

Seth introduced the rest of his family as they each took turns hugging his bride-to-be, welcoming her to Compass Ranch.

Finally, his parents and brothers returned to the dining room, so that he and Jody could be alone.

They grabbed her suitcase out of the car, and Seth carried it to his bedroom. She studied his childhood room as he shut and locked the door behind them.

"Nice room," she said.

He walked up behind her and wrapped his arms around her waist, his fingers rubbing the soft silk.

She laughed softly. "My father going to have a field day with the *I told you so's*."

He pressed a light kiss on the top of her head. "What do you mean?"

"He said you'd never leave me, that your sudden disappearance would be easily explained and that I'd misunderstood."

He turned her, bending down to kiss her. "I'm so sorry about that damn note. I don't understand—"

She placed her finger against his lips. "It's okay. We're here now. Together."

Her words, though wonderful, reminded him of why they were in Wyoming.

She studied his face, a frown creasing her brow. "What is

it? What's wrong?"

He blinked, amazed at how astute she was. Having her here was the answer to a prayer. He'd felt alone and adrift for days, trying to come to terms with his father's illness. Now that she was with him, the cracks in his composure widened. He swallowed, unable to speak.

"Damn," she whispered, turning quickly. "Take this silly dress off me. It's too bulky. I need to be closer to you."

He unzipped the dress, watching as she pushed it off. Stepping out of the voluminous material, she took his hand in hers. She was wearing only a bra and panties, but even that glorious sight couldn't wipe away his fears, his pain.

"Tell me. Say it fast. It'll be easier. Daddy said you came home because of a family emergency. I thought it was because of Silas, but he looked fine just now."

"My father is dying," he said, the words shattering him.

She didn't say a word. Simply led him to a chair in the corner and pushed him into it. The second he sat down, she climbed onto his lap and gathered him into her embrace. She wrapped her arms about his neck and held him tightly.

"I'm sorry," she whispered.

Her words were his undoing and he let the tears he'd held at bay fall. Men weren't supposed to cry, he'd always heard that, always been able to abide by that unspoken law. This time he couldn't. He was with Jody and she'd never judge him as weak, never think less of him for falling apart. He locked his arms around her waist and let her comfort him as the tears fell.

They were silent for several minutes as Seth soaked up her warmth, let her strength renew his spirit. He wasn't alone anymore. That realization made everything so much easier to bear.

Finally she loosened her hold, leaning back to look at him. With gentle hands, she wiped away the wetness on his face. "I love you." She followed her words with a soft kiss.

She started to pull away, but he followed her lips, not

wanting to let her go. He gripped her face, holding her close as he let himself fall into her kisses. He needed to escape. Needed something pure and good and wonderful to wash away the heavy feelings weighing him down.

"Make me forget, Jody. For a little while, take me away from here. I need you."

She placed her hand against his cheek, nodding once. She leaned forward to place her lips on his—the light touch soothing, comforting.

Then her fingers reached for the buttons on his shirt. He deepened the kiss, pushing his tongue into her mouth. He wanted her, more than he'd ever wanted anyone.

She sensed what he needed as her fingers moved faster along the buttons. By the time she reached the last two, she gave up and pulled the shirt apart roughly, the material tearing.

He rose, lifting her off his lap, but not leaving the sanctuary of her lips. He kicked off his shoes and, together, they hastily worked to free him of his pants. Backing her up slowly, he trapped her legs against his mattress as he stripped off her bra and panties. They were both panting by the time he pushed her onto the bed.

Her legs opened to welcome him, and he didn't waste a second as he accepted all that her body offered. He pushed into her wet heat in one thrust, both of them groaning with relief and arousal. For the first time since returning to Wyoming, he knew he was truly home. With Jody by his side, he could handle whatever life threw his way. She gave him strength and hope.

He pounded into her body, each thrust a promise that he'd always care for her, always be there, always love her.

They came together, a rush of power and joy flowing through him. It wasn't until he pulled out that another realization crashed down on him.

He looked at her face and saw she'd recognized the same thing. She smiled, showing him she wasn't mad.

"Maybe it's a good thing we're planning a quick wedding. Given the fact, I can't seem to remember the damn condom," he said.

He rolled to her side and caressed her cheek as they lay facing each other on the bed.

She put her arm around his waist, her hand drifting up to touch his tattoo. "I hope we did make a baby," she admitted. "I want a family, just like yours. Lots of kids."

He chuckled. "Not exactly like mine. I want a little girl. One who looks just like you."

She kissed him softly. "You might regret that wish one day."

He shook his head. "Never. I want her to have your chestnut hair, your bright blue eyes..."

"My impertinent ways and love of four-letter words?" she added, teasingly.

He laughed, rolling over to tuck her beneath his body. His cock was hard and ready for her again. "Especially those two things."

"I love you, cowboy."

He kissed her as he pressed into her body once more. "I love you too, darlin'. Now how about we try again to make that sassy little girl?"

About the Authors

Jayne Rylon and Mari Carr met at a writing conference in June 2009 and instantly became arch-enemies. Two authors couldn't be more opposite. Mari, when free of her librarian-by-day alter ego, enjoys a drink or two or...more. Jayne, allergic to alcohol, lost huge sections her financial-analyst mind to an epic explosion resulting from Mari gloating about her hatred of math. To top it off, they both had works in progress with similar titles and their heroes shared a name. One of them would have to go.

The battle between them for dominance was a bloody, but short one, when they realized they'd be better off combining their forces for good (or smut). With the ink dry on the peace treaty, they emerged as good friends, who have a remarkable amount in common despite their differences, and their writing partnership has flourished. Except for the time Mari attempted to poison Jayne with a bottle of Patron. Accident or retaliation? You decide.

Jayne and Mari can be found troublemaking on their Yahoo loop at: http://groups.yahoo.com/group/Heat_Wave_Readers.

You can follow their book-loving insanity on Twitter or Facebook or send them a personal note at contact@jaynerylon.com or carmichm1@yahoo.com.

CPSIA information can be obtained at www.ICGtesting.com
Printed in the USA
BVOW031127110713

325696BV00001B/33/P